Uncharted Stars

ALSO BY ANDRE NORTON

Quest Crosstime
Moon of Three Rings
The Zero Stone

Uncharted Stars

ANDRE NORTON

THE VIKING PRESS   NEW YORK

Second printing December 1969

Trade—670–73895–6

VLB—670–73896–4

Printed in U.S.A. by The Book Press

Fic 1. Science fiction

For Patrick Terry
because he has been kind enough
to approve my work

Uncharted Stars

1

It was like any other caravansary at a space port, not providing quarters for a Veep or some off-planet functionary, but not for a belt as sparsely packed with credits as mine was at that moment either. My fingers twitched and I got a cold chill in my middle every time my thoughts strayed to how flat that belt was at present. But there is such a thing as face, or prestige, whatever name you want to give it, and that I must have now or fail completely. And my aching feet, my depressed spirits told me that I was already at the point where one surrendered hope and waited for the inevitable blow to fall. That blow could only fell me in one direction. I would lose what I had played the biggest gamble of my life to win—a ship now sitting on its tail fins in a field I could have sighted from this hotel had I been a Veep and able to afford one of the crown tower rooms with actual windows.

One may be able to buy a ship, but thereafter it sits eating up more and more credits in ground fees, field service—more costs than my innocence would have believed possible a planet month earlier. And one cannot lift off world until he has a qualified pilot at the controls, the which I was not, and the which I had not been able to locate.

It had all sounded so easy in the beginning. My thinking had certainly been clouded when I had plunged into this. No—been plunged! Now I centered my gaze on the door which was the entrance to what I could temporarily call "home," and I had very unkind thoughts, approaching the dire, about the partner waiting me behind it.

The past year had certainly not been one to soothe my nerves, or lead me to believe that providence smiled sweetly at me. It had begun as usual. I, Murdoc Jern, had been going about my business in the way any roving gem buyer's apprentice would. Not that our lives, mine and my master Vondar Ustle's, had been without exciting incident. But on Tanth, in the spin of a diabolical "sacred" arrow, everything had broken apart as if a laser ray had been used to sever me not only from Vondar but from any peace of mind or body.

When the sacrifice arrow of the green-robed priests had swung to a stop between Vondar and me, we had not feared; off-worlders were not meat to satisfy their demonic master. Only we had been jumped by the tavern crowd, probably only too glad to see a choice which had not included one of them. Vondar had died from a knife thrust and I had been hunted down the byways of that dark city, to claim sanctuary in the hold of another of their grisly godlings. From there I had, I thought, paid my way for escape on a Free Trader.

But I had only taken a wide stride from a stinking morass into a bush fire—since my rise into space had started me on a series of adventures so wild that, had another recited them to me, I would have thought them the product of fash-smoke breathing, or something he had heard from a story tape.

Suffice it that I was set adrift in space itself, along with a companion whose entrance into my time and space was as weird as his looks. He was born rightly enough, in the proper manner, out of a ship's cat. Only his father was a black stone, or at least several men trained to observe the unusual would state that. Eet and I had been drawn by the zero stone—the zero stone! One might well term that the seed of all disorder!

I had seen it first in my father's hands—dull, lifeless, set in a great ring meant to be worn over the bulk of a space glove. It had been found on the body of an alien on an unknown asteroid. And how long dead its suited owner was might be anyone's guess—up to and including a million years on the average planet. That it had a secret, my father knew, and its fascination held him. In fact, he died to keep it as a threatening heritage for me.

It was the zero stone on my own gloved hand which had drawn me, and Eet, through empty space to a drifting derelict which might or might not have been the very ship its dead owner had once known. And from that a lifeboat had taken us to a world of forest and ruins, where, to keep our secret and our lives, we had fought both the Thieves' Guild (which my father must have defied, though he had once been a respected member of its upper circles) and the Patrol.

Eet had found one cache of the zero stones. By chance we both stumbled on another. And that one was weird enough to make a man remember it for the rest of his days, for it had been carefully laid up in a temporary tomb shared by the bodies of more than one species of alien, as if intended to pay their passage home to distant and un-known planets of origin. And we knew part of their secret. Zero stones had the power to boost any energy they con-tacted, and they would also home on their fellows, activating such in turn. But that the planet we had landed upon by chance was the source of the stones, Eet denied.

We used the caches for bargaining, not with the Guild, but with the Patrol, and we came out of the deal with credits for a ship of our own, plus—very sourly given—clean records and our freedom to go as we willed.

Our ship was Eet's suggestion. Eet, a creature I could crush in my two hands (sometimes I thought that solution was an excellent one for me), had an invisible presence which towered higher than any Veep I had ever met. In part, his feline mother had shaped him, though I sometimes speculated as to whether his physical appearance did not continue to change subtly. He was furred, though his tail carried only a ridge of that covering down it. But his feet were bare-skinned and his forepaws were small hands which he could use to purposes which proved them more akin to my palms and fingers than a feline's paws. His ears were small and set close to his head, his body elongated and sinuous.

But it was his mind, not the body he informed me had been "made" for him, which counted. Not only was he telepathic, but the knowledge which abode in his memory, and which he gave me in bits and pieces, must have rivaled the lore of the famed Zacathan libraries, which are crammed with centuries of learning.

Who—or what—Eet was he would never say. But that I would ever be free of him again I greatly doubted. I could resent his calm dictatorship, which steered me on occasion, but there was a fascination (I sometimes speculated as to whether this was deliberately used to entangle me, but if it was a trap it had been very skillfully constructed) which kept me his partner. He had told me many times our companionship was needful, that I provided one part, he the other, to make a greater whole.

And I had to admit that it was through him we had come out of our brush with Patrol and Guild as well as we had —with a zero stone still in our possession.

For it was Eet's intention, which I could share at more optimistic times, to search out the source of the stones. Some small things I had noted on the unknown planet of the caches made me sure that Eet knew more about the unknown civilization or confederation which had first used the stones than he had told me. And he was right in that the man who had the secret of their source could name his own price—always providing he could manage to market that secret without winding up knifed, burned, or disintegrated in some messy fashion before he could sell it properly.

We had found a ship in a break-down yard maintained by a Salarik who knew bargaining as even my late master (whom I had heretofore thought unbeatable) did not. I will admit at once that without Eet I would not have lasted ten planet minutes against such skill and would have issued forth owning the most battered junk the alien had sitting lopsidedly on rusting fins. But the Salariki are feline-ancestered, and perhaps Eet's cat mother gave him special insight into the other's mind. The result was we emerged with a useful ship.

It was old, it had been through changes of registry many times, but it was, Eet insisted, sound. And it was small enough for the planet hopping we had in mind. Also, it was, when Eet finished bargaining, within the price we could pay, which in the end included its being serviced for space and moved to the port ready for take-off.

But there it had sat through far too many days, lacking a pilot. Eet might have qualified had he inhabited a body humanoid enough to master the controls. I had never yet come to the end of any branch of knowledge in my companion, who might evade a direct answer to be sure, but whose supreme confidence always led me to believe that he *did* have the correct one.

It was now a simple problem: We had a ship but no pilot. We were piling up rental on the field and we could not lift. And we were very close to the end of that small sum we had left after we paid for the ship. Such gems as remained in my belt were not enough to do more than pay for a couple more days' reckoning at the caravansary, if I could find a buyer. And that was another worry to tug at my mind.

As Vondar's assistant and apprentice, I had met many of the major gem buyers on scores of planets. But it was to Ustle that they opened their doors and gave confidence. When I dealt on my own I might find the prospect bleak, unless I drifted into what was so often the downfall of the ambitious, the fringes of the black market which dealt in stolen gems or those with dubious pasts. And there I would come face to face with the Guild, a prospect which was enough to warn me off even more than a desire to keep my record clean.

I had not found a pilot. Resolutely now I pushed my worries back into the immediate channel. Deal with one thing at a time, and that, the one facing you. We had to have a pilot to lift, and we *had* to lift soon, very soon, or lose the ship before making a single venture into space with her.

None of the reputable hiring agencies had available a man who would be willing—at our wages—to ship out on what would seem a desperate venture, the more so when I could not offer any voyage bond. This left the rejects, men black-listed by major lines, written off agency books for some mistake or crime. And to find such a one I must go down into the Off-port, that part of the city where even the Patrol and local police went on sufferance and in couples, where the Guild ruled. To call attention to myself there was asking for a disagreeable future—kidnaping, mind scanning, all the other illegal ways of gaining my knowledge. The Guild had a long and accurate memory.

There was a third course. I could throw up everything —turn on my heel and walk away from the door I was about to activate by thumb pressure on personal seal, take a position in one of the gem shops (if I could find one), forget Eet's wild dream. Even throw the stone in my belt into the nearest disposal to remove the last temptation. In fact, become as ordinary and law-abiding a citizen as I could.

I was greatly tempted. But I was enough of a Jern not to yield. Instead I set thumb to the door and at the same time beamed a thought before me in greeting. As far as I knew, the seals in any caravansary, once set to individual thumbprints, could not be fooled. But there can always be a first time and the Guild is notorious for buying up or otherwise acquiring new methods of achieving results which even the Patrol does not suspect have been discovered. If we had been traced here, then there just might be a reception committee waiting beyond. So I tried mind-touch with Eet for reassurance.

What I got kept me standing where I was, thumb to doorplate, bewildered, then suspicious. Eet was there. I received enough to be sure of that. We had been mind-coupled long enough for even tenuous linkage to be clear to my poorer human senses. But now Eet was withdrawn, concentrating elsewhere. My fumbling attempts to communicate failed.

Only it was not preoccupation with danger, no warn-off. I pressed my thumb down and watched the door roll back into the wall, intent on what lay beyond.

The room was small, not the cubby of a freeze-class traveler, but certainly not the space of a Veep suite. The various fixtures were wall-folded. And now the room was unusually empty, for apparently Eet had sent every chair, as well as the table, desk, and bed, back into the walls, leaving the carpeted floor bare, a single bracket light going.

A circle of dazzling radiance was cast by that (I noted at once that it had been set on the highest frequency and a small portion of my mind began calculating how many minutes of that overpower would be added to our bill). Then I saw what was set squarely under it and I was really startled.

As was true of all port caravansaries, this one catered to tourists as well as business travelers. In the lobby was a shop—charging astronomical prices—where one could buy a souvenir or at least a present for one's future host or some member of the family. Most of it was, as always, a parade of eye-catching local handicrafts to prove one had been on Theba, with odds and ends of exotic imports from other planets to attract the attention of the less sophisticated traveler.

There were always in such shops replicas of the native fauna, in miniature for the most part. Some were carved as art, others wrought in furs or fabrics to create a very close likeness of the original, often life-size for smaller beasts, birds, or what-is-its.

What sat now in the full beam of the lamp was a stuffed pookha. It was native to Theba. I had lingered by a pet shop (intrigued in spite of my worries) only that morning to watch three live pookhas. And I could well understand their appeal. They were, even in the stuffed state, luxury items of the first class.

This one was not much larger than Eet when he drew his long thin body together in a hunched position, but it was of a far different shape, being chubby and plump and with the instant appeal to my species that all its kind possess. Its plushy fur was a light green-gray with a faint mottling which gave it the appearance of the watered brocade woven on Astrudia. Its forepaws were bluntly rounded pads, unclawed, though it was well provided with teeth, which in live pookhas were used for crushing their food—tich leaves. The head was round with no visible ears, but between the points where ears might normally be, from one side of that skull-ball to the other, there stood erect a broad mane of whisker growth fanning out in fine display. The eyes were very large and green, of a shade several tints darker than its fur. It was life-size and shade several tints darker than its fur. It was life-size and very handsome—also very, very expensive. And how it had come here I did not have the slightest idea. I would have moved forward to examine it more closely but a sharp crack of thought from Eet froze me where I stood. It was not a concrete message but a warning not to interfere.

Interfere in what? I looked from the stuffed pookha to my roommate. Though I had been through much with Eet and had thought I had learned not to be surprised at any action of my alien companion, he now succeeded very well in startling me.

He was, as I had seen, hunched on the floor just beyond the circle of intense light cast by the lamp. And he was staring as intently at the toy as if he had been watching the advance of some enemy.

Only Eet was no longer entirely Eet. His slim, almost reptilian body was not only hunched into a contracted position but actually appeared to have become plumper and shorter, aping most grotesquely the outward contours of the pookha. In addition, his dark fur had lightened, held a greenish sheen.

Totally bewildered, yet fascinated by what was occurring before my unbelieving eyes, I watched him turn into a pookha, altering his limbs, head shape, color, and all the rest. Then he shuffled into the light and squatted by the toy to face me. His thought rang loudly in my head.

"Well?"

"You are that one." I pointed a finger, but I could not be sure. To the last raised whisker of crest, the last tuft of soft greenish fur, Eet was twin to the toy he had copied.

"Close your eyes!" His order came so quickly I obeyed without question.

A little irritated, I immediately opened them again, to confront once more two pookhas. I guessed his intent, that I should again choose between them. But to my closest survey there was no difference between the toy and Eet, who had settled without any visible signs of life into the same posture. I put out my hand at last and lifted the nearest, to discover I had the model. And I felt Eet's satisfaction and amusement.

"Why?" I demanded.

"I am unique." Was there a trace of complacency in that remark? "So I would be recognized, remarked upon. It is necessary that I assume another guise."

"But how did you do this?"

He sat back on his haunches. I had gone down on my knees to see him the closer, once more setting the toy beside him and looking from one to the other for some small difference, though I could see none.

"It is a matter of mind." He seemed impatient. "How little you know. Your species is shut into a shell of your own contriving, and I see little signs of your struggling to break out of it." This did not answer my question very well. I still refused to accept the fact that Eet, in spite of all he had been able to do in the past, could *think* himself into a pookha.

He caught my train of thought easily enough. "Think myself into a hallucination of a pookha," he corrected in that superior manner I found irking.

"Hallucination!" Now *that* I could believe. I had never seen it done with such skill and exactitude, but there were aliens who dealt in such illusions with great effect and I had heard enough factual tales of such to believe that it could be done, and that one receptive to such influences and patterns could be made to see as they willed. Was it because I had so long companied Eet and at times been under his domination that I was so deceived now? Or would the illusion he had spun hold for others also?

"For whom and as long as I wish," he snapped in reply to my unasked question. "Tactile illusion as well—feel!" He thrust forth a furred forelimb, which I touched. Under my fingers it was little different from the toy, except that it had life and was not just fur laid over stuffing.

"Yes." I sat back on my heels, convinced. Eet was right, as so often he was—often enough to irritate a less logical being such as I. In his own form Eet was strange enough to be noticed, even in a space port, where there is always a coming and going of aliens and unusual pets. He could furnish a clue to our stay here. I had never underrated the Guild or their spy system.

But if they had a reading on Eet, then how much more so they must have me imprinted on their search tapes! I had been their quarry long before I met Eet, ever since after my father's murder, when someone must have guessed that I had taken from his plundered office the zero stone their man had not found. They had set up the trap which had caught Vondar Ustle but not me. And they had laid another trap on the Free Trader, one which Eet had foiled, although I did not know of it until later. On the planet of ruins they had actually held me prisoner until Eet again freed me. So they had had innumerable chances of taping me for their hounds—a fact which was frightening to consider.

"You will think yourself a cover." Eet's calm order cut across my uneasiness.

"I cannot! Remember, I am of a limited species—" I struck back with the baffled anger that realization of my plight aroused in me.

"You have only the limits you yourself set," Eet returned unruffled. "Perceive—"

He waddled on his stumpy pookha legs to the opposite side of the room, and as suddenly flowed back into Eet again, stretching his normal body up against the wall at such a lengthening as I would not have believed even his supple muscles and flesh capable of. With one of his paw-hands he managed to touch a button and the wall provided us with a mirror surface. In that I saw myself.

I am not outstanding in any way. My hair is darkish brown, which is true of billions of males of Terran stock. I have a face which is wide across the eyes, narrowing somewhat to the chin, undistinguished for either good looks or downright ugliness. My eyes are green-brown, and my brows, black, as are my lashes. As a merchant who travels space a great deal, I had had my beard permanently eradicated when it first showed. A beard in a space helmet is unpleasant. And for the same reason I wear my hair cropped short. I am of medium height as my race goes, and I have all the right number of limbs and organs for my own species. I could be anyone—except that the identification patterns the Guild might hold on me could go deeper and be far more searching than a glance at a passing stranger.

Eet flowed back across the room with his usual liquid movement, made one of his effortless springs to my shoulder, and settled down in position behind my neck, his head resting on top of mine, his hand-paws flat on either side of my skull just below my ears.

"Now!" he commanded. "Think of another face—anyone's—"

When so ordered I found that I could not—at first. I looked into the mirror and my reflection was all that was there. I could feel Eet's impatience and that made it even more difficult for me to concentrate. Then that impatience faded and I guessed that he was willing it under control.

"Think of another." He was less demanding, more coaxing. "Close your eyes if you must—"

I did, trying to summon up some sort of picture in my mind—a face which was not my own. Why I settled for Faskel I could not say, but somehow my foster brother's unliked countenance swam out of memory and I concentrated upon it.

It was not clear but I persevered, setting up the long narrow outline—the nose as I had last seen it, jutting out over a straggle of lip-grown hair. Faskel Jern had been my father's true son, while I was but one by adoption. Yet it had always seemed that I was Hywel Jern's son in spirit and Faskel the stranger. I put the purplish scar on Faskel's forehead near his hairline, added the petulant twist of lips

21

which had been his usual expression when facing me in later years, and held to the whole mental picture with determination.

"Look!"

Obediently I opened my eyes to the mirror. And for several startled seconds I looked at someone. He was certainly not me—nor was he Faskel as I remembered him, but an odd, almost distorted combination of us both. It was a sight I did not in the least relish. My head was still gripped in the vise maintained by Eet's hold and I could not turn away. But as I watched, the misty Faskel faded and I was myself again.

"You see—it can be done," was Eet's comment as he released me and flowed down my body to the floor.

"*You* did it."

"Only in part. There has been, with my help, a breakthrough. Your species use only a small fraction of your brain. You are content to do so. This wastage should shame you forever. Practice will aid you. And with a new face you will not have to fear going where you can find a pilot."

"If we ever can." I push-buttoned a chair out of the wall and sat down with a sigh. My worries were a heavy burden. "We shall have to take a black-listed man if we get any."

"*Sssss—*" No sound, only an impression of one in my mind. Eet had flashed to the door of the room, was crouched against it, his whole attitude one of strained listening, as if all his body, not just his ear, served him for that purpose.

I could hear nothing, of course. These rooms were completely screened and soundproofed. And I could use a hall-and-wall detect if I wished to prove it so. Space-port caravansaries were the few places where one could be truly certain of not being overlooked, overheard, or otherwise checked upon.

But their guards were not proofed against such talents as Eet's, and I guessed from his attitude not only that he was suspicious of what might be arriving outside but that it was to be feared. Then he turned and I caught his thought. I moved to snap over a small luggage compartment and he folded himself into hiding there in an instant. But his thoughts were not hidden.

"Patrol snoop on his way—coming here," he warned, and it was alert enough to prepare me.

2

As yet, the visitor's light had not flashed above the door. I moved, perhaps not with Eet's speed, but fast enough, to snap the room's furnishings out and in place so that the compartment would look normal even to the searching study of a trained Patrolman. The Patrol, jealous of its authority after long centuries of supremacy as the greatest law-enforcement body in the galaxy, had neither forgotten nor forgiven the fact that Eet and I had been able to prove them wrong in their too-quick declaration of my outlawry (I had indeed been framed by the Guild). That we had dared, actually dared, to strike a bargain and keep them to it, galled them bitterly. We had rescued their man, saved his skin and his ship for him in the very teeth of the Thieves' Guild. But he had fought bitterly against the idea that we did have the power to bargain and that he had to yield on what were practically our terms. Even now the method of that bargaining made me queasy, for Eet had joined us mind to mind with ruthless dispatch. And such an invasion, mutual as it was, left a kind of unhealed wound.

I have heard it stated that the universe is understood

by each species according to the sensory equipment of the creature involved, or rather, the meaning it attaches to the reports of those exploring and testing senses. Therefore, while *our* universe, as we see it, may be akin to that of an animal, a bird, an alien, it still differs. There are barriers set mercifully in place (and I say mercifully after tasting what can happen when such a barrier goes down) to limit one's conception of the universe to what he is prepared to accept. Shared minds between human and human is not one of the sensations we are fitted to endure. The Patrolman and I had learned enough—too much— of each other to know that a bargain could be made and kept. But I think I would face a laser unarmed before I would undergo that again.

Legally the Patrol had nothing against us, except suspicions perhaps and their own dislike for what we had dared. And I think that they were in a measure pleased that if they had to swear truce, the Guild still held us as a target. And it might well be that once we had lifted from the Patrol base we had been regarded as expendable bait for some future trap in which to catch a Veep of the Guild—a thought which heated me more than a little every time it crossed my mind.

I gave a last hurried glance around the room as the warn light flashed on, and then went to thumb the peephole. What confronted my eye was a wrist, around which was locked, past all counterfeiting, the black and silver of a Patrol badge. I opened the door.

"Yes?" I allowed my real exasperation to creep into my voice as I fronted him.

He was not in uniform, wearing rather the ornate, form-fitting tunic of an inner-world tourist. On him, as the Patrol must keep fit, it looked better than it did on most of the flabby, paunchy specimens I had seen in these halls. But that was not saying much, for its extreme of fashion was too gaudy and fantastic to suit my eyes.

"Gentle Homo Jern—" He did not make a question of my name, and his eyes were more intent on the room behind me than on meeting mine.

"The same. You wish?"

"To speak with you—privately." He moved forward and involuntarily I gave a step before I realized that he had no right to enter. It was the prestige of the badge he wore which won him that first slight advantage and he made the most of it. He was in, with the door rolled into place behind him, before I was prepared to resist.

"We are private. Speak." I did not gesture him to a chair, nor make a single hospitable move.

"You are having difficulty in finding a pilot." He looked at me about half the time now, the rest of his attention still given to the room.

"I am." There was no use in denying a truth which was apparent.

Perhaps he did not believe in wasting time either, for he came directly to the point.

"We can deal—"

That really surprised me. Eet and I had left the Patrol base with the impression that the powers there were glee-fully throwing us forth to what they believed certain disaster with the Guild. The only explanation which came to me at the moment was that they had speedily discovered that the information we had given them concerning the zero stones had consisted of the whereabouts of caches only and they suspected the true source was still our secret. In fact, we knew no more than we had told them.

"What deal?" I parried and dared not mind-touch Eet at that moment, much as I wanted his reception to this suggestion. No one knows what secret equipment the Patrol has access to. And it might well be that, knowing Eet was telepathic, they had some ingenious method of monitoring our exchange.

"Sooner or later," he said deliberately, almost as if he savored it, "the Guild is going to close in upon you—"

But I was ready, having thought that out long ago. "So I am bait and you want me for some trap of yours."

He was not in the least disconcerted. "One way of putting it."

"And the right way. What do you want to do, plant one of your men in our ship?"

"As protection for you and, of course, to alert us."

"Very altruistic. But the answer is no." The Patrol's highhanded method of using pawns made me aware that there was something to being their opponent.

"You cannot find a pilot."

"I am beginning to wonder"—and at that moment I was—"how much my present difficulty may be due to the influence of your organization."

He neither affirmed nor denied it. But I believe I was right. Just as a pilot might be black-listed, so had our ship been, before we had even had a chance for a first voyage. No one who wanted to preserve his legal license would sign our log now. So I must turn to the murky outlaw depths if I was to have any luck at all. I would see the ship rust away on its landing fins before I would raise with a Patrol nominee at her controls.

"The Guild can provide you with a man as easily, if you try to hire an off-rolls man, and you will not know it," he remarked, as if he were very sure that I would eventually be forced to accept his offer.

That, too, was true. But not if I took Eet with me on any search. Even if the prospective pilot had been brainwashed and blanked to hide his true affiliation, my companion would be able to read that fact. But that, I hoped, my visitor and those who had sent him did not know. That Eet was telepathic we could not hide—but Eet himself—

"I will make my own mistakes," I allowed myself to snap.

"And die from them," he replied indifferently. He took one last glance at the room and suddenly smiled. "Toys now—I wonder why." With a swoop as quick and sure as that of a harpy hawk he was down and up again, holding the pookha by its whisker mane. "Quite an expensive toy, too, Jern. And you must be running low in funds, unless you have tapped a river running with credits. Now why, I wonder, would you want a stuffed pookha."

I grimaced in return. "Always provide my visitors with a minor mystery. You figure it out. In fact, take it with you—just to make sure it is not a smuggling cover. It might just be, you know. I am a gem buyer—what better way to get some stones off world than in a play pookha's inwards?"

Whether he thought my explanation was as lame as it seemed to me I do not know. But he tossed the toy onto the nearest chair and then, on his way to the door, spoke over his shoulder. "Dial 1–0, Jern, when you have stopped battering your head against a stone wall. And we shall have a man for you, one guaranteed not to sign you over to the Guild."

"No—just to the Patrol," I countered. "When I am ready to be bait, I shall tell you."

He made no formal farewell, just went. I closed the door sharply behind him and was across the room to let Eet out as quickly as I could. My alien companion sat back on his haunches, absent-mindedly smoothing the fur on his stomach.

"They think that they have us." I tried to jolt him—though he must already have picked up everything pertinent from our visitor's mind, unless the latter had worn a shield.

"Which he did," Eet replied to my suspicion. "But not wholly adequate, only what your breed prepares against the mechanical means of detecting thought waves. They are not," he continued complacently, "able to operate against my type of talent. But yes, they believe that they have us sitting on the palm of a hand"—he stretched out his own—"and need only curl their fingers, so—" His clawed digits bent to form a fist. "Such ignorance! However, it will be well, I believe, to move swiftly now that we know the worst."

"Do we?" I asked morosely as I hustled out my flight bag and began to pack. That it was not intelligent to stay where we were with Patrol snoops about, I could well understand. But where we would go next—

"To the Diving Lokworm," Eet replied as if the answer was plain and he was amused that I had not guessed it for myself.

For a moment I was totally adrift. The name he mentioned meant nothing, though it suggested one of those dives which filled the murky shadows of the wrong side of the port, the last place in the world where any sane man would venture with the Guild already sniffing for him.

But at present I was more intent on getting out of this building without being spotted by a Patrol tail. I rolled up my last clean undertunic and counted out three credit disks. In a transit lodging one's daily charges are conspicuous each morning on a small wall plate. And no one can beat the instant force field which locks the room if one does not erase these charges when the scanner below says he is departing. The room might be insured for privacy in other ways, but there are precautions the owners are legally allowed to install.

I dropped the credits into the slot under the charge plate and that winked out. Thus reassured I could get out, I must now figure how. When I turned it was to see that Eet was again a pookha. For a moment I hesitated, not quite sure which of the furry creatures was my companion until he moved out to be picked up.

With Eet in the crook of one arm and my bag in my other hand, I went out into the corridor after a quick look told me it was empty. When I turned toward the down grav shaft Eet spoke:

"Left and back!"

I obeyed. His directions took me where I did not know the territory, bringing me to another grav shaft, that which served the robos who took care of the rooms. There might be scanners here, even though I had paid my bill. This was an exit intended only for machines and one of them rumbled along toward us now.

It was a room-service feeder, a box on wheels, its top studded with call buttons for a choice of meal. I had to squeeze back against the wall to let it by, since this back corridor had never been meant for the human and alien patrons of the caravansary.

"On it!" Eet ordered.

I had no idea what he intended, but I had been brought out of tight corners enough in the past to know that he generally did have some saving plan in mind. So I swung Eet, my bag, and myself to the table top of the feeder, trying to take care that I did not trigger any of the buttons.

My weight apparently was nothing to the machine. It did not pause in its steady roll down the remainder of the corridor. But I was tense and stiff, striving to preserve my balance on this box where there was nothing to grip for safety.

When it moved without pause off the floor and onto the empty air of the grav shaft I could have cried out. But the grav supported its weight and it descended as evenly under me as if it had been a lift platform bringing luggage and passengers out of a liner at the port. A sweeper joined us at the next level, but apparently the machines were equipped with avoid rays, as they did not bump, but kept from scraping against each other. Above and below us, in the dusk of the shaft, I could see other robo-servers descending, as if this was the time when they were through their morning work.

We came down floor by floor, I counting them as we passed, a little more relieved with each one we left behind, knowing that we were that much nearer our goal. But when we reached ground level we faced only blank surface, and my support continued to descend.

The end was some distance below the surface, at least equal, I believed, to three floors above. And the feeder, with us still aboard, rolled out in pitch dark, where the sounds of clanging movement kept me frozen. Nor did Eet suggest any answer to this.

I did gain enough courage to bring out a hand beamer and flash it about us, only to gain disturbing glimpses of machines scuttling hither and thither across a wide expanse of floor. Nor were there any signs of human tenders.

I was now afraid to dismount from my carrier, not knowing whether the avoid rays of the various busy robos would also keep them from running me down. To this hour I had always taken the service department of a caravansary for granted and such an establishment as this I had never imagined.

That the feeder seemed to know just where it was going was apparent, for it rolled purposefully on until we reached a wall with slits in it. The machine locked to one of these and I guessed that the refuse and disposable dishes were being deposited in some sort of refuse system. Not only the feeder was clamped there. Beyond was a sweeper, also dumping its cargo.

A flash of my beamer showed that the wall did not reach the roof, so there might be a passage along its top to take us out of the paths of the roving machines— though such a way might well lead to a dead end.

I stood up cautiously on the feeder, and Eet took the beamer between his stubby pookha paws. The bag was easy to toss to the top of the wall, my furry companion less so, since his new body did not lend itself well to such feats. However, once aloft, he squatted, holding the beamer in his mouth, his teeth gripping more easily than his paws.

With that as my guide I leaped and caught the top of the wall, though I was afraid for a moment my fingers would slip from its slick surface. Then I made an effort which seemed enough to tear my muscles, and drew my whole body up on an unpleasantly narrow surface.

Not only was it narrow but it throbbed and vibrated under me, and I mentally pictured some form of combustion reducing the debris dumped in, or else a conveyer belt running on into a reducer of such refuse.

Above me, near enough to keep me hunched on my hams, was the roof of the place. A careful use of the beamer showed me that the wall on which I crouched ran into a dark opening in another wall met at right angles, as if it were a path leading into a cave.

For want of a better solution I began to edge along, dragging my bag, my destination that hole. Luckily Eet did not need my assistance but balanced on his wide pookha feet behind me.

When I reached that opening I found it large enough to give me standing room in a small cubby. The beam lighted a series of ladder steps bolted to the wall, as though this was an inspection site visited at intervals by a human maintenance man. Blessing my luck, I was ready to try that ladder, for the clanging din of the rushing machines, the whir of their passing rung in my ears, making me dizzy. The sooner I was out of their domain the better.

Eet's paws were not made for climbing, and I wondered if he would loose the disguise for the attempt. I had no desire to carry him; in fact I did not see how I could.

But if he could release the disguise he was not choosing to do so. Thus, in the end, I had to sling the bag on my back by its carrying strap and loosen my tunic to form a sling, with Eet crawling part-way down inside my collar at my shoulders. Both burdens interfered cruelly with my balance as I began to climb. And I had had to put away the beamer, not being conveniently endowed with a third hand.

For the moment all I wanted was to get out of the dark country of the robo-servers, even though I was climbing into the unknown. Perhaps I had come to depend too much on Eet's warnings against approaching dangers. But he had not communicated with me since we had taken transport on the feeder.

"Eet, what is ahead?" I sent that demand urgently as I became aware of just what *might* lie ahead of us.

"Nothing—yet." But his mind-send was faint, as a

voiced whisper might be, or as if most of his mind was occupied with some other pressing problem.

I found, a second or two later, the end of the ladder, as my hand, rising to grope for a new hold, struck painfully instead against a hard surface. I spread my fingers to read what was there. What I traced by touch was a circular depression which must mark a trap door. Having made sure of that, I applied pressure, first gently and then with more force. When there was no reassuring yield I began to be alarmed. If the bolt hole of this door was locked, we would have no recourse but to return to the level of the robos, and I did not want to think of that.

But my final desperate shove must have triggered whatever stiff mechanism held the door and it gave, letting in a weak light. I had wit and control enough left to wait for a very long moment for any warning from Eet.

When he sent nothing I scrambled out into a place where the walls were studded with gauges, levers, and the like, perhaps the nerve center that controlled the robos. Since there was no one there and a very ordinary door in the nearest wall, I breathed a sigh of heart-felt relief and set about making myself more presentable, plucking Eet out of my unsealed tunic and fastening that smoothly. As far as I could tell, examining my clothes with care, I bore no traces of my late venture through the bowels of the caravansary and I should be able to take to the streets without notice. Always providing that the door opposite me would eventually lead me to freedom.

What it did give on was a very small grav lift. I set the indicator for street level and was wafted up to a short corridor with doors at either end. One gave upon a walled court with an entrance for luggage conveyers. And I hop-skipped with what speed I could along one of those, to drop into an alley where a flitter from the port unloaded heavier transport boxes.

"Now!" Eet had been riding on my shoulder, his pookha body less well adapted to that form of transport than his true form. I felt his paws clamp on either side of my head as he had earlier done when showing me how one's face could be altered. "Wait!"

I did not know his purpose, since he did not demand I "think" a face. And though that waiting period spun out, making me uneasy, he did not alter his position. I was sure he was using his own thought power to provide me with a disguise.

"Best—I—can—do—" The paws fell away from my head and I reached up to catch him as he tumbled from his place. He was shaking as if from extreme fatigue and his eyes were closed, while he breathed in short gasps. Once before I had seen him so drained—even rendered unconscious—when he had forced me to share minds with the Patrolman.

Carrying Eet as I might a child, and shouldering my flight bag, I went down the alley. A back look at the building had given me directions. If I had a tail who had not been confused by our exit, he had no place to hide here.

The side way fed into a packed commercial street where the bulk of the freight from the port must pass. There were six heavy-duty transport belts down its middle, flanked on either side by two light-duty, and there remained room for a single man-way, narrow indeed, which scraped along the sides of the buildings it passed. There was enough travel on it to keep me from being unduly conspicuous, mainly people employed at the port to handle the shipments. I dropped my bag between my feet and stood, letting the way carry me along, not adding speed by walking.

Eet had spoken of the Diving Lokworm, which was still a mystery to me, and I had no intention of visiting the Off-port before nightfall. Daytime visitors, save for tourists herded along on a carefully supervised route, were very noticeable there. Thus I would have to hole up somewhere. Another hotel was the best answer. With what I thought a gift of inspiration I chose one directly across from the Seven Planets, from where I had just made my unusual exit.

This was several steps down from the Seven Planets in class, which suited my reduced means. And I was especially pleased that instead of a human desk clerk, who would have added to the prestige, there was a robo—though I knew that my person was now recorded in the files from its scanners. Whether the confusing tactics on my behalf via Eet's efforts would hold here I did not know.

I accepted the thumb lock plate with its incised number, took the grav to the cheapest second-floor corridor, found my room, inserted the lock, and once inside, relaxed. They could force that door now only with super lasers.

Depositing Eet on the bed, I went to the wall mirror to see what he had done to me. What I did sight was not a new face, but a blurring, and I felt a disinclination to look long at my reflection. To watch with any concentration was upsetting, as if I found my present appearance so distasteful that I could not bear to study it.

I sat down on the chair near the mirror. And as I continued to force myself to look at that reflection I was aware that the odd feeling of disorientation was fading, that in the glass my own features were becoming clearer, sharper, visible and ordinary as they had always been.

That Eet could work such a transformation again when the time came to leave here, I doubted. Such a strain might be too much, especially when it was imperative that his esper talents be fully alert. So I might well walk out straight into the sight of those hunting me. But— could I reproduce Eet's effect by my own powers? My trial with Faskel's features had certainly not been any success. And I had had to call upon Eet's help to achieve even that.

But suppose I did not try for so radical a disguise? Eet had supplied me this time, not with a new face, but with merely an overcast of some weird kind which had made me difficult to look at. Suppose one did not try to change a whole face, but only a portion of it? My mind fastened upon that idea, played with it. Eet did not comment, as I thought he might. I looked to the bed. By all outward appearances he was asleep.

If one did not subtract from a face but added to it— in such a startling fashion that the addition claimed the attention, thus overshadowing features. There had been a time in the immediate past when my skin was piebald, due to Eet's counterfeiting of a plague stigma. I could remember only too well those loathsome purple patches. No return to those! I had no wish to be considered again a plague victim. However, a scar—

My mind wandered to the days when my father had kept the hock-lock shop at the space port on my home planet. Many spacers had sought out his inner room to sell finds into whose origin it was best not to inquire too closely. And more than one of those had been scarred or marked unpleasantly.

A scar—yes. Now where—and what? A healed knife

gash, a laser burn, an odd seam set by some unknown wounding? I decided on a laser burn which I had seen and which should fit in well with the Off-port. With it as clear in my mind as I could picture it, I stared into the mirror, striving to pucker and discolor the skin along the left side of my jaw and cheek.

3

It was an exercise against all the logic of my species. Had I not seen it succeed with Eet, seen my partial change under his aid, I would not have believed it possible. Whether I *could* do it without Eet's help was another question, but one I was eager to prove. My dependence upon the mutant, who tended to dominate our relationship, irked me at times.

There is a saying: If you close doors on all errors, truth also remains outside. Thus I began my struggle with errors aplenty, hoping that a small fraction of the truth would come to my aid. I had not, since I had known Eet, been lax in trying to develop any esper talents I might have. Primarily because, I was sure, it was not in my breed to admit that a creature who looked so much an animal could out-think, out-act a man—though in the galaxy the term "man" is, of course, relative, having to do with a certain level of intelligence rather than a humanoid form. In the beginning, this fact was also difficult for my breed, with their many inborn prejudices, to realize. We learned the hard way until the lesson stuck.

I closed the channels of my mind as best I could, tamping down a mental lid on my worries about our lack of a pilot, a shrinking number of credits, and the fact that I might right now be the quarry in a hunt I could sense but not see or hear. The scar—that must be the most important, the *only* thing in my mind. I concentrated on my reflection in the mirror, on what I wanted to see there.

Perhaps Eet was right, as he most always was—we of Terran stock do not use the full powers which might be ours. Since I had been Eet's charge, as it were, I must have stretched, pulled, without even being aware of that fact, in a manner totally unknown to my species heretofore. Now something happened which startled me. It was as if, in that part of me which fought to achieve Eet's ability, a ghostly finger set tip to a lever and pressed it firmly. I could almost feel the answering vibration through my body—and following on that, a flood of certainty that this I could do, a heady confidence which yet another part of me observed in alarm and fear.

But the face in the mirror— Yes! I had that disfiguring seam, not raw and new, which would have been a giveaway to the observant, but puckered and dark, as though it had not been tended quickly enough by plasta restoration, or else such a repair job had been badly botched— as might be true for a crewman down on his luck, or some survivor of a planetary war raid.

So real! Tentatively I raised my hand, not quite daring to touch that rough, ridged skin. Eet's illusion had been— was—tactile as well as visual. Would mine hold as well? I touched. No, I was not Eet's equal as yet, if I could ever be. My fingers traced no scar, as they seemed to do when I looked into the mirror. But visually the scar was there and that was the best protection I could have.

"A beginning, a promising beginning—"

My head jerked as I was startled out of absorption. Eet was sitting up on the bed, his unblinking pookha eyes watching me in return. Then I feared the break in my concentration and looked back to the mirror. But contrary to my fears, the scar was still there. Not only that, but I had chosen rightly—it drew attention, the face behind it blotted out by that line of seamed and darkened skin—as good as a mask.

"How long will it last?" If I ventured out of this room, went delving into the Off-port as I must, I would not be able to find another hole in a hurry into which I could settle safely for the period of intense concentration I would need to renew my disfigurement.

Eet's round head tilted a little to one side, giving the appearance of critical observation of my thought work.

"It is not a large illusion. You were wise to start small," he commented. "With my aid, I think it will hold for tonight. Which is all we need. Though I shall have to change myself—"

"You? Why?"

"Need you parade your incomprehension of danger?" The whisker mane had already winked out of being. "Take a pookha into the Off-port?"

He was right as ever. Pookhas alive were worth more than their weight in credits. To carry one into the Off-port would be to welcome a stun ray, if lucky, a laser burn if not, with Eet popped into a bag and off to some black-market dealer. I was angry with myself for having made such a display of nonthinking, though it was due to the need for concentration on maintaining the scar.

"You must hold it, yes, but not with your whole mind," Eet said. "You have very much to learn."

I held. Under my eyes Eet changed. The pookha dissolved, vanished as though it were an outer husk of plasta

41

meeting the cold of space and so shattering into bits too tiny for the human eye to see. Now he was Eet again, but as unusual to the observer as the pookha had been.

"Just so," he agreed. "But I shall not be observed. I need not change. It will simply be a matter of not allowing the eye to light on me."

"As you did with my face, coming here?"

"Yes. And the dark will aid. We'll head straight for the Diving Lokworm—"

"Why?"

One of my own species might have given an exaggerated sigh of annoyance. The mental sensation which emanated from my companion was not audible but it had the same meaning.

"The Diving Lokworm is a possible meeting place for the type of pilot we must find. And you need not waste time asking me how I know that. It is the truth."

How much Eet could pick out of nearby minds I did not know; I thought that I did not want to know. But his certainty now convinced me that he had some concrete lead. And I could not argue when I had nothing of my own to offer in return.

He made one of his sudden leaps to my shoulder and there arranged himself in his favorite riding position, curled about my neck as if he were an inanimate roll of fur. I gave a last look into the mirror, to reassure myself that my creation was as solid-seeming as ever, and knew a spark of triumph when I saw that it was, even though I might later have to depend upon Eet to maintain it.

So prepared, we went out and took the main crawl walk toward the port, ready to drop off at the first turn which led to the murk of the Off-port. It was dusk, the clouds spreading like smoke across a dark-green sky in which the first of Theba's moons pricked as a single jewel of light.

But the Off-port was awake as we entered it by the side way. Garish signs, not in any one language (though Basic was the main tongue here), formed the symbols, legible to spacemen of many species and races, which advertised the particular wares or strange delights offered within. Many of them were a medley of colors meant to attract nonhuman races, and so, hurtful to our organs of vision. Thus one was better advised not to look above street level. There was also such a blare of noise as was enough to deafen the passerby, and scents to make one long for the protection of a space suit which could be set to shut out the clamor and provide breathable, filtered air.

To come into this maze was to believe one had been decanted on another world, not only dangerous but inhospitable. How I was to find Eet's Diving Lokworm in this pool of confusion was a problem I saw no way of solving. And to wander, deafened and half asphyxiated, through the streets and lanes was to ask for disaster. I had no belted weapon and I was carrying a flight bag, so perhaps ten or more pairs of eyes had already marked me down as possible prey for a portside rolling.

"Right here—" Eet's thought made as clean a cut as a force blade might make through the muddle of my mind.

Right I turned, out of the stridence of the main street, into a small, very small, lessening of the clamor, with a fraction less light, and perhaps one or two breaths now and then of real air. And Eet seemed to know where we were going, if I did not.

We turned right a second time and then left. The spacemen's rests now about were such holes of crime that I feared to poke a nose into any of them. We were fast approaching the last refuge of the desperate, and the stinking hideups of those who preyed upon them, driven from the fatter profits of the main streets.

The Diving Lokworm had, not its name, but a representation of that unwholesome creature set in glow lines about its door. The designer had chosen to arrange it so that one apparently entered through the open mouth— which was perhaps an apt prophecy of what might really await the unwary within. The stench of the outside was here magnified materially by the fumes of several kinds of drink and drug smoke. Two I recognized as lethal indeed to those who settled down to make their consumption the main business of what little life remained to them.

But it was not dark. The outer Lokworm had here its companions, who writhed about the walls in far too lifelike fashion. And though parts of those gleaming runnels of light had darkened through want of replacement, the whole gave enough radiance so one could actually see the customers' faces after a fashion, if not what might be served in the cups, beakers, tubes, and the like placed before them.

Unlike the drinking and eating places in the more civilized (if that was the proper term) part of the port, the Diving Lokworm had no table dials to finger to produce nourishment, no robo-servers whipping about. The trays were carried by humans or aliens, none of whom had a face to be observed long without acute distaste. Some of them were noticeably female, others—well it could be a guess. And frankly, had I been drinking the local poison, it would have stopped a second order to have the first slopped down before me by a lizardoid with two pairs of arms. Unless the drink had been more important than what I saw when I looked about me.

The lizardoid was serving three booths along the wall, and doing it most efficiently; four hands were useful. There was a very drunk party of Regillians in the first. In the second something gray, large, and warty squatted. But in the third slumped a Terran, his head supported on one hand, with the elbow of that arm planted firmly on the table top. He had on the remains of a space officer's uniform which had not been cleaned for a long time. One insignia still clung by a few loose threads to his tunic collar, but there was no house or ship badge on the breast, only a dark splotch there to show he had sometime lost that mark of respectability.

To take a man out of this stew was indeed combing the depths. On the other hand, all we really needed to clear the port was a pilot on board. I did not doubt that Eet and I together could get us out by setting automatic for the first jump. And to accept a black-listed man—always supposing he was not a plant—was our only chance now.

"He is a pilot and a fash-smoker." Eet supplied information, some of which I did not care to hear.

Fash-smoke does not addict, but it does bring about a temporary personality change which is dangerous. And a man who indulges in it is certainly not a pilot to be relied upon. If this derelict was sniffing it now, he was to be my last choice instead of my first. The only bright thought was that fash-smoke is expensive and one who set light to the brazier to inhale it was not likely to patronize the Diving Lokworm.

"Not now," Eet answered. "He is, I believe, drinking veever—"

The cheapest beverage one could buy and enough to make a man as sick as a sudden ripple of color in the tube worm on the wall made this lounger appear. The fact that the light was a sickly green might have had something to do with his queasy expression. But he roused to pull the beaker before him into place and bend his head to catch the suck tube between his lips. And he went on drinking as we came to the side of the booth.

Perhaps he would not have been my first choice. But the stained insignia on his collar was that of a pilot and he was the only one I had sighted here. Also, he was the only humanoid with a face I would halfway trust, and Eet appeared to have singled him out.

He did not look up as I slipped into the bench across from him, but the lizard waiter slithered up and I pointed to the drinker, then raised a finger, ordering a return for my unknown boothmate. The latter glanced at me without dropping the tube from his lip hold. His brows drew together in a scowl and then he spat out his sipper and said in a slurred mumble:

"Blast! Whatever you're offering—I'm not buying."

"You are a pilot," I countered. The lizardoid had made double time to whatever sewer the drinks had been piped from and slammed down another beaker. I flipped a tenth-point credit and one of his second pair of hands clawed it out of the air so fast I never really saw it disappear.

"You're late in your reckoning." He pushed aside his first and now empty beaker, drew the second to him. "I *was* a pilot."

"System or deep-space ticket?" I asked.

He paused, the sipper only a fraction away from his lips. "Deep space. Do you want to see it all plain and proper?" There was a sneer in his growl. "And what's it to you, anyway?"

There is this about fash-smoking—while it makes a man temporarily belligerent during indulgence, it also

46

alters the flow of emotion so that between bouts, where rage might normally flare, one gets only a flash of weak irritation.

"A lot maybe. Want a job?"

He laughed then, seemingly in real amusement. "Again you're too late. I'm planet-rooted now."

"You offered to show your plate. That hasn't been confiscated?" I persisted.

"No. But that's just because no one cares enough to squawk. I haven't lifted for two planet years, and that's the truth. Quite a spiller tonight, aren't I? Maybe they've cooked some babble stuff into this goop." He stared down into his beaker with dim interest, as if he expected to see something floating on its turgid surface.

Then he mouthed the sipper, but with one hand he pulled at the frayed front seam of his tunic and brought out, in a shaking hand, a badly-worn case, which he dropped on the table top, not pushing it toward me, but rather as if he were indifferent to any interest of mine in its contents. I reached for it just as another ripple of light in the wall pattern gave me sight of the plate within that covering.

It had been issued to one Kano Ryzk, certified pilot for galactic service. The date of issuance was some ten years back, and his age was noted as problematical, since he had been space-born. But what did startle me was the small symbol deeply incised below his name—a symbol which certified him as a Free Trader.

From their beginnings as men who were willing to take risks outside the regular lines, which were the monopolies of the big combines, the Free Traders, loners and explorers by temperament, had become, through several centuries of space travel, more and more a race apart.

47

They tended to look upon their ships as their home worlds, knowing no planet for any length of time, ranging out where only First-in Scouts and such explorers dared to go. In the first years they had lived on the short rations of those who snatch at the remnants of the feast the combines grew fat upon.

Not able to bid at the planet auctions when newly discovered worlds were put up for sale to those wanting their trade, they had to explore, take small gains at high risks, and hope for some trick of fate which would render a big profit. And such happened just often enough to keep them in space.

But seeing their ships as the only worlds to which they owed allegiance, they were a clannish lot, marrying among themselves when they wed at all. They had space-hung ports now, asteroids they had converted, on which they established quasi family life. But they did not contact the planet-born save for business. And to find one such as Ryzk adrift in a port—since the Free Traders cared for their own—was so unusual as to be astounding.

"It is true." He did not raise his eyes from the beaker. He must have encountered the same surprise so many times before that he was weary of it. "I didn't roll some star-stepper to get that plate."

That, too, must be true, since such plates were always carried close to a man's body. If any other besides the rightful owner had kept that plate, the information on it would be totally unreadable by now, since it had a self-erase attuned to personal chemistry.

There was no use in asking what brought a Free Trader shipless into the Diving Lokworm. To inquire might turn him so hostile I would not be able to bargain. But the very fact he was a Free Trader was a point in his favor. A broken combine man would be less likely to take to the kind of spacing we planned.

"I have a ship"—I put it bluntly now—"and I need a pilot."

"Try the Register," he mumbled and held out his hand. I closed the case and laid it on his palm. How much was the exact truth going to serve me?

"I want a man off the lists."

That did make him look at me. His pupils were large and very dark. He might not be on fash-smoke, but he was certainly under some type of mind-dampening cloud.

"You aren't," he said after a moment, "a runner."

"No," I replied. Smuggling was a paying game. However, the Guild had it sewed up so well that only someone with addled brains would try it.

"Then what are you?" His scowl was back.

"Someone who needs a pilot—" I was beginning when Eet's thought pricked me.

"We have stayed here too long. Be ready to guide him."

There was silence. I had not finished my sentence. Ryzk stared at me, but his eyes seemed unfocused, as if he did not really see me at all. Then he grunted and pushed aside the still unfinished second beaker.

"Sleepy," he muttered. "Out of here—"

"Yes," I agreed. "Come to my place." I was on his left, helping him to balance on unsteady feet, my hand slipped under his elbow to guide him. Luckily he was still enough in command of his body to walk. I could not have pulled him along, since, though he was several inches shorter than I, his planet days had given him bulk of body which was largely ill-carried lard.

The lizard stepped out as if to bar our way and I felt Eet stir. Whether he planted some warning, as he seemed to have planted the desire to go in Ryzk, I do not know. But the waiter turned abruptly to the next booth, leaving us a free path to the door. And we made it out of the stink of the place without any opposition. Once in the backways of the Off-port, I tried to put on speed, but found that Ryzk, though he did keep on his feet and moving, could not be hurried. And pulling at him seemed to disturb the thought Eet had put in his mind, so I did not dare to put pressure on him. I was haunted by the feeling that we were being followed, or at least watched. Though whether our cover had been detected or we had just been marked down for prey generally by one of the lurking harpies, I did not try to deduce. Either was dangerous.

The floodlights of the port cut out the night, reducing all three moons now progressing at a stately pace over our heads to pallid ghosts of their usual brilliance. To pass the gates and cut across the apron to our ship's berth was the crucial problem. If, as I thought, the Patrol and perhaps the Guild were keeping me under surveillance, there would be a watch on the ship, even if we had lost them in the town. And my scar, if I still wore it, would not stand up in the persona scanner at the final check point. Escape might depend on speed, and Ryzk did not have that.

I lingered no longer at the first check point than it took to snap down my own identity plate and Ryzk's. Somehow he had fumbled it out of hiding as we approached, some part of his bemused brain answering Eet's direction. Then I saw a chance to gain more speed. There was a luggage conveyer parked to one side, a luxury item I with my one flight bag had never seen reason to waste half a credit on. But there was need for it now.

Somehow I pushed and pulled Ryzk to it. There was a

fine for using it as a passenger vehicle, but such minor points of law did not trouble me at that moment. I got him flat on it, pulled a layer of weather covering over his more obvious outlines, and planted my flight bag squarely on top to suggest that it did carry cargo. Then I punched the berth number for our ship, fed in my credit, and let it go. If Ryzk did not try to disembark en route I could be sure he would eventually arrive at the ramp of our ship.

Meanwhile Eet and I had to reach the same point by the least conspicuous and quickest route. I glanced around for some suggestions as to how to accomplish that. A tourist-class inter-system rocket ship was loading, with a mass of passengers waiting below its ramp and more stragglers headed for it. Many of the travelers were being escorted by family parties or boisterous collections of friends. I joined the tail of one such, matching my pace to keep at the end of the procession. Those I walked with were united in commiserating with a couple of men wearing Guard uniforms and apparently about to lift to an extremely disliked post on Memfors, the next planet out in this system, and one which had the reputation of being far from a pleasure spot.

Since most of the crowd were male, and looked like rather hard cases, I did not feel too conspicuous. And it was the best cover I saw. However, I still had to break away when we reached the rocket slot and cross to my own ship. It was during those last few paces I would be clearly seen.

I edged around the fringes of the waiting crowd, putting as many of those between me and the dark as I could, trying to be alert to any attention I might attract. But as far as I could see, I might once more be enveloped in Eet's vision-defying blur.

I wanted to run, or to scuttle along under some protective shell like a pictick crab. But both of those safety devices were denied me. Now I dared not even look around as though I feared any pursuit, for wariness alone could betray me.

Ahead I saw the luggage conveyer crawling purposefully on a course which had been more of a straight line than my own. My bag had not shifted from the top, which meant, I trusted, that Ryzk had not moved. It reached the foot of the ramp well before me and stood waiting for the lifting of its burden to release it.

"Watcher—to the right—Patrol—"

Eet came alive with that warning. I did not glance in the direction he indicated.

"Is he moving in?"

"No. He took a video shot of the carrier. He has no orders to prevent take-off—just make sure you do go."

"So they can know the bait is ready and they need only set their trap. Very neat," I commented. But there was no drawing back now, and I did not fear the Patrol at this moment half as much as the Guild. After all, I had some importance to the Patrol—bait has until the moment for sacrificing it comes. Once we were off planet I had the feeling it was not going to be so easy for them to use me as they so arrogantly planned. I still had what they did not suspect I carried—the zero stone.

So I gave no sign that I knew I was under observation as I hauled Ryzk off the luggage carrier, guided him up the ramp, snapped that in, and sealed ship. I stowed my prize, such as he was, in one of the two lower-level cabins, strapped him down, taking his pilot's plate with me, and climbed with Eet to the control cabin.

There I fed Ryzk's plate into the viewer to satisfy the field law and prepared for take-off, Eet guiding me in the setting of the automatics. But I had no trip tape to feed in, which meant that once in space Ryzk would have to play his part or we would find another port only by the slim margin of chance.

4

Since we lacked a trip tape, we could not go into hyper until Ryzk found us jump co-ordinates. So our initial thrust off world merely set us voyaging within the system itself, an added danger. While a ship in hyper cannot be traced, one system-traveling can readily be picked up. Thus, when I recovered from grav shock, I unstrapped myself and sought out my pilot, Eet making better time, as usual, down the inner stair of the ship.

Our transport, the *Wendwind,* was not as small as a scout, though not as large as a Free Trader of the D class. She might once have been the private yacht of some Veep. If so, all luxury fittings had long since been torn out, though there were painted-over scars to suggest that my guess was correct. Later she had been on system runs as a general carrier. And her final fate had been confiscation by the Patrol for smuggling, after which she had been bought by the Salarik dealer as a speculation.

She had four cabins besides the regular crew quarters. But three of these had been knocked together for a storage hold. And one feature within attracted me, a persona-pressure sealed strongbox, something a dealer in gems could put to use.

At one time the *Wendwind* must have mounted strictly illegal G-lasers, judging by the sealed ports and markings on decks and walls. But now she had no such protection.

Ryzk had been left in the last remaining passenger cabin. As I came in he was struggling against the grav straps, looking about him wildly.

"What—where—"

"You are in space, on a ship as pilot." I gave it to him without long explanation. "We are still in system, ready to go into hyper as soon as you can set course—"

He blinked rapidly, and oddly enough, the slack lines of his face appeared to firm, so that under the blurring of planetside indulgence you could see something of the man he had been. He stretched out his hand and laid it palm flat against the wall, as if he needed the reassurance of touch to help him believe that what I said was true.

"What ship?" His voice had lost the slur, just as his face had changed.

"Mine."

"And who are you?" His eyes narrowed as he stared up at me.

"Murdoc Jern. I am a gem buyer."

Eet made one of his sudden leaps from deck to the end of the bunk, where he squatted on his haunches, his hand-paws resting on what would have been his knees had he possessed a humanoid body.

Ryzk looked from me to Eet and then back again. "All right, all right! I'll wake up sooner or later."

"Not"—I picked up the thought Eet aimed at Ryzk—"until you set us a course—"

The pilot started, then rubbed his hands across his forehead as if he could so rub away what he had heard, not through his ears, but in his mind.

"A course to where?" he asked, as one humoring some image born out of fash-smoke or veever drink.

"To quadrant 7–10–500." At least I had had plenty of time to lay plans such as these during the past weeks when I feared we would never be space-borne. The sooner we began to earn our way the better. And I had Vondar's experience to suggest a good beginning.

"I haven't set a course in—in—" His voice trailed off. Once more he put his hand to the ship's wall. "This is— this is a ship! I'm not dreaming it!"

"It is a ship. Can you get us into hyper now?" I allowed some of my impatience to show.

He pulled himself out of his bunk, moving unsteadily at first. But perhaps the feel of a ship about him was a tonic, for by the time he reached the core ladder to the control cabin he had picked up speed, and he swung up that with ease. Nor did he wait to be shown the pilot's seat, but crossed to sit there, giving quick, practiced looks to the control board.

"Quadrant 7–10–500—" It was not a question but a repetition, as if it were a key to unlock old knowledge. "Fathfar sector—"

Perhaps I had done far better than I had hoped when I had picked up a planeted Free Trader. A pilot for one of the usual lines would not have known the fringes of the travel lanes which must be my hunting trails now.

Ryzk was pushing buttons, first a little slowly, then picking up speed and sureness, until a series of equations flashed on the small map screen to his left. He studied those, made a correction or two with more buttons, and then spoke the usual warning—"Hyper."

Having seen that he did seem to know what he was

doing, I had already retired to the second swing chair in the cabin, Eet curled up tightly against me, ready for that sickening twist which would signal our snap into the hyper space of galactic travel. Though I had been through it before, it had been mostly on passenger flights, where there had been an issue of soothe gas into the cabin to ease one through the wrench.

The ship went silent with a silence that was oppressive as we passed into a dimension which was not ours. Ryzk pushed a little away from the board, flexing his fingers. He looked to me and those firmer underlines of his face were even more in evidence.

"You—I remember you—in the Diving Lokworm." Then his brows drew together in a frown. "You—your face is different."

I had almost forgotten the scar; it must be gone now.

"You on the run?" Ryzk shot at me.

Perhaps he was entitled to more of the truth, since he shared a ship which might prove a target were we unlucky.

"Perhaps—"

But I had no intention of spouting about the past, the secret in my gem belt, and the real reason why we might go questing off into unexplored space, seeking out uncharted stars. However, "perhaps" was certainly not an explanation which would serve me either. I would have to elaborate on it.

"I am bucking the Guild." That gave him the worst, and straight. At least he could not jump ship until we planeted again.

He stared at me. "Like trying to jump the whole nebula, eh? Optimistic, aren't you?" But if he found my admission daunting, it did not appear in any expression or hesitation in his reply. "So we get to the Fathfar sector, and when we set down—on which world by the way?— we may get a warm welcome, crisped right through by lasers!"

"We set down on Lorgal. Do you know it?"

"Lorgal? You picked that heap of sand, rock, and roasting sun for a hide-out? Why? I can give you a nice listing of more attractive places—" It was plain he did know our port. Almost I could suspect he was a plant, except that I had voiced to no one at all my selection for my first essay as a buyer. Lorgal was as grim as his few terse words had said—with hellish windstorms and a few other assorted planetside disasters into the bargain. But its natives could be persuaded to part with zorans. And I knew a place where a selection of zorans, graded as I was competent to do, could give us half a year's supply of credits for cruising expenses.

"I am not hunting a hide-hole. I am after zorans. As I told you, I buy gems."

He shrugged as if he did not believe me but was willing to go along with my story, since it did not matter to him one way or another. But I triggered out the log tape and pushed its recorder to him, setting before him the accompanying pad for his thumbprint to seal the bargain.

Ryzk examined the tape. "A year's contract? And what if I don't sign, if I reserve the right to leave ship at the first port of call? After all, I don't remember any agreement between us before I woke up in this spinner of yours."

"And how long would it take you to find another ship off Lorgal?"

"And how do you know I'll set you down there in the first place? Lorgal is about the worst choice in the Fathfar sector. I can punch out any course I please—"

"Can you?" inquired Eet.

For the second time Ryzk registered startlement. He stared now at the mutant and his gaze was anything but pleasant.

"Telepath!" He spat that out like a curse.

"And more—" I hastened to agree. "Eet has a way of getting things we want done, done."

"You say that you have the Guild after you and you want me to sign on for a year. Your first pick of a landing is a hellhole. And now this—this—"

"Partner of mine," I supplied when he seemed at a loss for the proper term.

"This partner suggests he can make me do as he wishes."

"You had better believe it."

"What do I get out of it? Ship's wages—?"

This was a fair enough protest. I was willing to concede more.

"Take Trade share—"

He stiffened. I saw his hand twitch, his fingers balled into a fist which might have been aimed at me had he not some control over his temper. But I read then his dislike for my knowledge of that fragment of his past. That I had used a Free Trader's term, offering him a Trader deal, was not to his liking at all. But he nodded.

Then he pressed his thumb on the sign pad and recited his license number and name into the recorder, formally accepting duty as pilot for one planet year, to be computed on the scale of the planet from which we had just lifted, which was a matter of four hundred days.

There was little or nothing to do while the ship was in hyper, a matter of concern on the early exploring and trading ships. For idle men caused trouble. It was usually customary for members of a ship's crew to develop hobbies or crafts to keep their minds alert, their hands busy.

But if Ryzk had had such in the past, he did not produce them now.

He did, however, make systematic use of the exercise cabin, as I did also, keeping muscles needed planetside from growing flabby in the reduced gravity of space flight. And as time passed he thinned and fined down until he was a far more presentable man than the one we had steered out of the Off-port drinking den.

My own preoccupation was with the mass of records I had managed, with the reluctant assistance of the Patrol, to regain from several storage points used by Vondar Ustle. With some I was familiar, but other tapes, especially those in code, were harder. Vondar had been a rover as well as a gem merchant. He could have made a fortune had he settled down as a designer and retailer on any inner-system planet. But his nature had been attuned to wandering and he had had the restlessness of a First-in Scout.

His designing was an art beyond me, and of his knowledge of stones I had perhaps a tenth—if I was not grossly overestimating what I had been able to assimilate during the years of our master–apprentice relationship. But the tapes, which I could claim under the law as a legally appointed apprentice, were my inheritance and all I had to build a future upon. All that was reasonably certain, that is. For the quest for the source of the zero stone was a gamble on which we could not embark without a backing of credits.

I watched the viewer as I ran the tapes through, concentrating on that which I had not already absorbed in actual tutelage under Vondar. And my own state of ignorance at times depressed me dismally, leaving me to wonder if Eet had somehow moved me into this action as one moves a star against a comet in that most widely

spread galactic game of chance, named for its pieces—
Stars and Comets.

But I was also sure that if he had, I would never be
really sure of that fact, and it was far better for my peace
of mind not to delve into such speculation. To keep at
my task was the prime need now and I was setting up,
with many revisions, deletions, and additions, a possible
itinerary for us to follow.

Lorgal had been my first choice, because of the simplicity of its primitive type of exchange barter. In my
first solo deal I needed that simplicity. Though I had
cut as close as I could in outfitting the *Wendwind,* I had
had to spend some of our very meager store of credits on
trade goods. These now occupied less than a third of the
improvised storeroom. But the major part of the wares
had been selected for dealing on Lorgal.

As wandering people, traveling from one water hole to
the next across a land which was for the most part volcanic rock (with some still active cones breathing smoke
by day, giving forth a red glow at night), sand, wind to a
punishing degree, and pallid vegetation growing in the
bottom of sharp-cut gullies, the Lorgalians wanted mainly
food for their too often empty bellies, and water, which
for far too many days seemed to have vanished from, or
rather into, their earth's crust.

I had visited there once with Vondar, and he had
achieved instantaneous results with a small solar converter. Into this could be fed the scabrous leaves of the
vegetation, the end product emerging as small blocks
about a finger in length containing a highly nutritious
food which would keep a man going for perhaps five of
their dust- and wind-filled days, one of their plodding
beasts for three. The machine had been simple, if bulky,
and had had no parts so complicated that a nontech-

nically-inclined people could put it out of running order. The only trouble was that it was so large that it had to be slung between two of their beasts for transport—though that had not deterred the chieftain from welcoming it as he might have a supernatural gift from one of his demon gods.

I had found, in my more recent prowlings through supply warehouses where the residue of scout and exploration ships was turned in for resale, a similar machine which was but half the size of that we had offered before. And while I could raise the price of only two of these, I had hopes that they would more than pay for our voyage.

I knew zorans, and I also knew the market for them. They were one of those special gems whose origin was organic rather than mineral. Lorgal must once have had an extremely wet climate which supported a highly varied vegetable growth. This had vanished, perhaps quite suddenly in a series of volcanic outbreaks. Some gas or other had killed certain of those plants, and their substance was then engulfed in earth fissures which closed to apply great pressure. That, combined with the gas the plants had absorbed, wrought the changes to produce zorans.

In their natural state they were often found still in the form of a mat of crushed leaves or a barked limb, sometimes even with a crystalized insect (if you were very lucky indeed) embedded in them. But once polished and cut, they were a deep purple-blue-green through which ran streaked lines of silver or glittering gold. Or else they were a crystalline yellow (probably depending upon some variation in the plant, or in the gas which had slain it) with flecks of glittering bronze.

The chunks or veins of the stuff were regularly mined by the nomads, who, until the arrival of the first off-world traders, used it mainly to tip their spears. It could be sharpened to a needle point which, upon entering flesh, would break off, to fester and eventually kill, even though the initial wound had not been a deep one.

And during the first cutting a zoran had to be handled with gloves, since any break in the outer layer made it poisonous. Once that had been buffed away, the gems could be shaped easily, even more so by the application of heat than by a cutting tool. Then, plunged into deep freeze, they hardened completely and would not yield again to any treatment. Their cutting was thus a complicated process, but their final beauty made them prized, and even in the rough they brought excellent prices.

So it would be zorans, and from Lorgal we could lift next to Rakipur, where zorans could be sold uncut to the priests of Mankspher and the pearls of lonnex crabs bought. From there perhaps to Rohan for caberon sapphires or— But there was no use planning too far ahead. I had learned long ago that all trading was a gamble and that to concentrate on the immediate future was the best way.

Eet wandered in and out while I studied my tapes. Sometimes he sat on the table to follow with a show of interest some particular one, at other times curling up to sleep. At length Ryzk, probably for lack of something to do, also found his way to where I studied, and his casual interest gave way to genuine attention.

"Rohan," he commented when I ran through Vondar's tape on that world. "Thax Thorman had trading rights on Rohan back in 3949. He made a good thing out of it. Not sapphires, though. He was after mossilk. That was before the thrinx plague wiped out the spinners. They never did find out what started the thrinx, though Thorman has his suspicions."

"Those being?" I asked when he did not continue.

"Well, those were the days when the combines tried to make it hard for the Free Men." He gave their own name to the Free Traders. "And there were a lot of tricks pulled. Thorman bid for Rohan in a syndicate of five Free ships, and he was able to overtop the Bendix Combine for it. The Combine had the auction fixed to go their way and then a Survey referee showed up and their bribed auctioneer couldn't set the computer. So their low bid was knocked out and Thorman got his. It was a chance for him. Bendix had a good idea of what was there, and he was just speculating because he knew they were set on it.

"So—he and the other ships had about four planet years of really skimming the good stuff. Then the thrinx finished that. Wiped out three of the other captains. They had been fool enough to give credit for two years running. But Thorman never trusted Bendix and he kind of expected something might blow up. No way, of course, of proving the B people had a hand in it. Nowadays, since the Free Men have had their own confederation, combines can't pull such tricks. I've seen a couple of those sapphires. Tough to find, aren't they?"

"They wouldn't be if anyone could locate the source. What is discovered are the pieces washed down the north rivers in the spring—loose in the gravel. Been plenty of prospectors who tried to get over the Knife Ridge to hunt the blue earth holes which must be there. Most of them were never heard from again. That's taboo country in there."

"Easier to buy 'em than to hunt them, eh?"

"Sometimes. Other times it is just the opposite. We have our dangers, too." I was somewhat irked by what I thought I detected underlying his comment.

But he was already changing the subject. "We come out of hyper on the yellow signal. Where do you want to set down on Lorgal, western or eastern continent?"

"Eastern. As near the Black River line as you can make it. There is no real port, as perhaps you know."

"Been a lot of time spinning by since I was there. Things could be changed, even a port there. Black River region." He looked over my shoulder at the wall of the cabin as if a map had been video-cast there. "We'll fin down in the Big Pot, unless that has boiled over into rough land again."

The Big Pot was noted on Lorgal, a giant crater with a burned-out heart which was relatively smooth and which had been used as an improvised space port. Though we had not landed there on my one visit to Lorgal, I knew enough from what I had heard then to recognize that Ryzk had chosen the best landing the eastern continent could offer.

Though the Big Pot was off the main nomad route along the series of water holes the Black River had shrunk to, we had a one-man flitter in our tail hold. And that could scout out the nearest camp site, saving a trek over the horribly broken land, which could not be traveled on foot by any off-worlder.

I looked to the recorded time dial. It was solidly blue, which meant that the yellow signal was not too far off. Ryzk arose and stretched.

"After we come out of hyper, it will take us four color spans to get into orbit at Lorgal, then maybe one more to set down, if we are lucky. How long do we stay planet-side?"

"I cannot say. Depends upon finding a tribe and setting up a talk fire. Five days, ten, a couple of weeks—"

He grimaced. "On Lorgal that is too long. But you're the owner, it's your ration supply. Only hope you can cut it shorter."

He went out to climb to the control cabin. I packed away the tapes and the viewer. I certainly shared his hope —though I knew that once I entered upon the actual trading, I would find in it the zest which it always held for me. Yet Lorgal was not a world on which one wanted to linger. And now it was for me only a means to an end, the end still lying too far ahead to visualize.

I was not long behind Ryzk in seeking the control cabin and the second seat there. While I could not second his duties, yet I wanted to watch the visa-screen as we came in. This was my first real venture, and success or failure here meant very much. Perhaps Eet was as uncertain as I, for though he curled up in his familiar position against my chest and shoulder, his mind was closed to me.

We snapped out of hyper and it was plain that Ryzk deserved so far the trust I had had to place in him, for the yellow orb was certainly Lorgal. He did not put the ship on automatic, but played with fingers on the controls, setting our course, orbiting us about that golden sphere.

As we cut into atmosphere the contours of the planet cleared. There were the huge scars of old seas, now shrunken into deep pockets in the centers of what had once been their beds, their waters bitterly salt. The continents arose on what were now plateaus, left well above the dried surface of the almost vanished seas. In a short time we could distinguish the broken chains of volcanic mountains, the river valley with lava, country in between.

And then the pockmark of the Big Pot could be seen. But as we rode our deter rockets into that promise of a halfway fair landing, I caught a startling glimpse of something else.

We sat down, waiting that one tense moment to see if it had indeed been a fair three-fin landing. Then, as there came no warning tilt of the cabin, Ryzk triggered the visa-screen, starting its circular sweep of our immediate surroundings. It was only a second before I was able to see that we were indeed not alone in the Big Pot.

There was another ship standing some distance away. It was plainly a trader-for-hire. Which meant dire competition, because Lorgal had only one marketable off-world product—zorans. And the yield in any year from one tribe was not enough to satisfy two gem merchants, not if one had to have a large profit to continue to exist. I could only wonder which one of Vondar's old rivals was now sitting by a talk fire and what he had to offer. The only slim chance which remained to me was the fact that he might not have one of the reduced-in-size converters, and that I could so outbid him.

"Company," Ryzk commented. "Trouble for you?" With that question he disassociated himself from any failure of mine. He was strictly a wage man and would get his pay, from the value of the ship if need be, if I went under.

"We shall see," was the best answer I could make as I unstrapped to go and see to the flitter and make a try at finding a nomad camp.

5

My advantage lay in that I had been to Lorgal before, though then the trade responsibility had lain with Vondar, and I had only been an observer. Our success or failure now depended upon how well I remembered what I had observed. The nomads were humanoid, but not of Terran stock, so dealing with them required X-Tee techniques. Even Terrans, or Terran colonist descendants, could not themselves agree over semantics, customs, or moral standards from planet to planet, and dealing with utterly alien mores added just that much more confusion.

The small converter I selected as my best exhibit could be crowded into the flitter's tail storage section. I strapped on the voca-translator and made sure that a water supply and E-rations were to hand. Eet was already curled up inside waiting for me.

"Good luck." Ryzk stood ready to thumb open the hatch. "Be sure to keep contact beam—"

"That is one thing I will not forget!" I promised. Though we had little in common, save that we shared the same ship and some of the duties of keeping it activated, we were two of the same species on an alien world, a situation which tended to make a strong, if temporary, bond between us now.

Ryzk would monitor me all the time the flitter was away from the ship. And I knew that should disaster strike either of us the other would do what he could to aid. It was a ship law, a planet law—one never put onto actual record tape but one which had existed since the first of our breed shot into space.

My memory of my first visit to Lorgal gave me one possible site for a nomad meeting, a deep pool in the river bed which had been excavated time and time again by the wandering tribes until they were always sure of some moisture at its bottom. I set off in that direction, taking my marking from two volcanic cones.

The churned ground passing under the flitter was a nightmare of broken ridges, knife-sharp pinnacles, and pitted holes. I do not believe that even the nomads could have crossed it—not that they ever wandered far from the faint promise of water along the ancient courses of the river.

While most of the rock about the Big Pot had been of a yellow-red-brown shade, here it was gray, showing a shiny, glassy black in patches. We had planeted about midmorning and now the sun caught those gleaming surfaces to make them fountains of glare. There were more and more of these as the flitter dipped over the Black River, where even the sands were of that somber color.

Here the water pits broke the general dark with their side mounds of reddish under-surface sand, which had been laboriously dug out in the past by the few native animals or the nomads. And on the inner sides of those mounds, ringing what small deposits of moisture there might be, grew the stunted plants which were the nomads only attempts at agriculture.

They saved every seed, carrying them where they went, as another race on a more hospitable world might treasure precious stones or metal, planting them one by one in the newly-dug sides of any hole before they left. When they circled back weeks or months later, they found, if they were fortunate, a meager harvest waiting.

Judging by the height of the scrubby brush around the first two pits I dipped to inspect, the Lorgalians had not yet reached them—which meant I must fly farther east to pick up their camp.

I had seen no sign of life about that other ship as I had taken off. Nor had my course taken me close to it. However, I had noted that its flitter hatch was open and guessed that the trader was already out in the field. Time might already have defeated me.

Then the Black River curved and I saw the splotch of tents dotted about. There was movement there, and as I throttled down the flitter to lowest speed and came in for a set-down I knew I was indeed late. For the cloaked and cowled figures of the tribesmen were moving with rhythmic pacing about the circumference of their camp site, each swinging an arm to crack a long-lashed whip at the nothingness beyond, a nothingness which they believed filled with devils who must be driven away by such precautions before any ceremony or serious business could be transacted.

There was another flitter parked here. It had no distinguishing company markings, so I was not about to buck a combine man. Of course I hardly expected to find one here. The pickings, as far as they were concerned, were too small. No, whoever was ready to deal with the camp was a free lance like myself.

I set down a length from the other transport. Now I could hear the high-pitched, almost squealing chant voiced by the devil-routers. With Eet on my shoulders I plunged into dry, stinging air, and the glare of a sun against which my goggles were only part protection. That air rasped against the skin as if it were filled with invisible but very tangible particles of grit. Feeling it, one did not wonder at the long robes, the cowls, the half-masks the natives wore for protection.

As I approached the ring of devil-lashers two of the whips curled out to crack the air on either side, but I did not flinch, knowing that much of nomad custom. Had I shown any surprise or recoil, I would have labeled myself a demon in disguise and a shower of zoran-pointed spears would have followed that exposure of my true nature.

The tribesmen I passed showed no interest in me; they were concentrating on their duty of protection. I cut between two of the closed tents to a clear space where I could see the assembly the whippers were guarding.

There was a huddle of nomads, all males, of course, and so enwrapped in their robes that only the eye slits suggested that they were not just bales of grimy lakis-wool cloth. The lakises themselves, ungainly beasts with bloated bodies to store the food and water for days when there was need, perched on long, thin legs with great wide, flat feet made for desert travel. These were now folded under them, for they lay to serve as windbreaks behind their masters. Their thick necks rested across each other's bodies if they could find a neighbor to so serve them, and their disproportionately small heads had the eyes closed, as if they were all firmly asleep.

Facing this assembly was the suited and helmeted figure of one of my own race. He stood, some packages about his feet, making the Four Gestures of Greeting, which meant, considering his ease, that he had either visited such a camp before, or else had made a careful study of record tapes.

The chieftain, like everyone else in that muffled crowd, could certainly not be recognized by features, but only by his badge of office, the bloated abdomen which was the result of much prideful padding. That layer upon layer of swaddling was not simply a shield against assassination (chieftainship among the Lorgalians was based upon weapon skill, not birthright); to be fat was a sign of wealth and good fortune here. And he who produced a truely noticeable belly was a man of prestige and standing.

I could not even be sure that this was the tribe with whom Vondar had traded. Only luck might help me in that. But surely, even if it was not, they would have heard of the wonder machine he had introduced and would be the more eager to acquire one of their own.

When I had entered the gathering I had come up behind the trader. And the nomads did not stir as they sighted me. Perhaps they thought me one of the stranger's followers. I do not think he was aware of me until I stepped level with him and began my own gestures of greeting, thus signifying that he was *not* speaking for me, but that I was on my own.

He turned his head and I saw one I knew—Ivor Akki! He had been no match for Vondar Ustle; few were. But he was certainly more than I would have chosen to contend against at the beginning of my independent career. He stared at me intently for a moment and then grinned. And that grin said that in me he saw no threat. We had fronted each other for several hours once at a Salarik bargaining, but there I had been only an onlooker, and he had been easily defeated by Vondar.

He did not pause in his ritual gestures after that one glance to assess his opposition and dismiss it. And I became as unseeing of him. We waved empty hands, pointed north, south, east, and west, to the blazing sun, the cracked, sandy earth under us, outlined symbols of three demons, and that of the lakis, a nomad, and a tent, signifying that by local custom we were devout, honest men, and had come for trade.

By right Akki had the first chance, since he was first on the scene. And I had to wait while he pulled forward several boxes, snapped them open. There was the usual small stuff, mostly plastic—some garish jewelry, some goblets which were fabulous treasure to the eye but all plastic to the touch, and a couple of sun torches. These were all make-gifts—offered to the chief. And seeing their nature I was a little relieved.

For such an array meant this was not a return visit but a first try by Akki. If he was here on spec and had not heard of Vondar's success with the food converter, I could beat him yet. And I had had this much luck, a small flag fluttering by the chieftain's tent told me—this *was* the tribe Vondar had treated with. And I needed only tell them that I had a more easily transported machine to sweep all the zorans they had to offer out of their bags.

But if I felt triumph for a few seconds it was speedily swept away as Akki opened his last box, setting out a very familiar object and one I had not expected to see.

It was a converter, but still more reduced in size and more portable than those I had chanced upon in the warehouse, undoubtedly a later and yet further improved model. I could only hope that he had just the one and that I might halve or quarter his return by offering two.

He proceeded to demonstrate the converter before that silent, never-moving company. Then he waited.

A hairy hand with long dirty nails flipped out from under the bundle of the chieftain's robes, making a sign. And one of his followers hunched forward to unfold a strip of lakis hide on which were many loops. Each loop held a chunk of zoran and only strict control kept me standing, seemingly indifferent, where I was. Four of those unworked stones were of the crystalline type and each held an insect. It was a better display than I had ever heard of. Vondar had once taken two such stones and the realization of their value off world had seemed fabulous to me. Four—with those I would not have to worry about a year's running of the ship. I would not even have to trade at all. We could be off after the zero stone after a single sale.

Only Akki was the one to whom they were offered, and I knew very well that none of them was ever going to come to me.

He deliberated, of course—that was custom again. Then he made his choice, sweeping up the insect pieces, as well as three of the blue-green-purple stones of size large enough to cut well. What was left after his choices had been fingered seemed refuse.

Then he raised his head to grin at me again as he slipped his hoard into a travel case, clapped his hand twice on the converter, and touched the rest of the goods he had spread out, releasing them all formally.

"Tough luck," he said in Basic. "But you've been having that all along, haven't you, Jern? To expect to fill Ustle's boots—" He shook his head.

"Good fortune," I said, when I would rather have voiced disappointment and frustration. "Good fortune, smooth lifting, with a sale at the end." I gave him a trader's formal farewell.

But he made no move to leave. Instead he added the insulting wave of hand signifying among the Lorgalians a master's introduction of a follower. And that, too, I had to accept for the present, since any dispute between us must be conducted outside the camp. A flare of temper would be swift indication that a devil had entered and all trading would be under ban, lest that unchancy spirit enter into some piece of the trade goods. I was almost tempted to do just that, in order to see Akki's offerings ritually pounded into splinters, the zorans treated the same way. But though such temptation was hot in me for an instant, I withstood it. He had won by the rules, and I would be the smaller were I to defeat him so, to say nothing of destroying all thought of future trade with Lorgal not only for the two of us, but for all other off-worlders.

I could take a chance and try to find another tribe somewhere out in the stark wilderness of the continent. But to withdraw from this camp now without dealing would be a delicate matter and one I did not know quite how to handle. I might offend some local custom past mending. No, like it or not, I would have to take Akki's leavings.

They were waiting and perhaps growing impatient. My hands spun into the sign language, aided by the throaty rasping my translator made as it spoke words in their own sparse tongue.

"This"—I indicated the converter—"I have also—but larger—in the belly of my sky lakis."

Now that I had made that offer there was no turning back. In order to retain the good will of the nomads I would have to trade, or lose face. And inwardly I was aware of my own inaptitude in the whole encounter. I had made my mistake in ever entering the camp after I had seen Akki's flitter already here. The intelligent move would have been then to prospect for another clan. But I had rushed, believing my wares to be unduplicated, and so lost.

Again that hairy hand waved and two of the bundled warriors arose to tail me to the flitter, cracking their whips above us as we crossed the line kept by the lashing guards. I pulled the heavy case from where I had so hopefully wedged it. And with their aid, one protecting us from the devils, the other helping me to carry it, I brought it back to the camp.

We set it before the chieftain. Either by accident or design, it landed next to Akki's, and the difference in bulk was marked. I went through the process of proving it was indeed a food converter and then awaited the chieftain's decision.

He gestured and one of my assistants booted a lakis to its feet, the creature bubbling and complaining bitterly with guttural grunts. It came up with a splayfooted shuffle which, awkward as it looked, would take it at an unvarying pace day after day across this tormented land.

A kick on one foreknee brought it kneeling again and the two converters were set beside it. Then proceeded a demonstration to prove the inferiority of my offering. Akki's machine might be put in a luggage sling on one side of the beast, a load of other equipment on the other —while if it bore the one I had brought, it could carry nothing else.

The chieftain wriggled his fingers and a second roll of lakis hide was produced. I tensed. I had thought I would be offered Akki's leavings, but it would seem I was too pessimistic. My elation lasted, however, only until the roll was opened.

What lay within its loops were zorans right enough. But nothing to compare with those shown to Akki. Nor was I even allowed to choose from his rejects. I had to take what was offered—or else return to the ship empty-handed, with a profitless set-down to my credit, or rather discredit. So I made the best of a very bad bargain and chose. There were, naturally, no insect pieces, and only two of the more attractive yellow ones. The blues had faults and I had to examine each for flaws, taking what I could, though in the end I was certain I had hardly made expenses.

I still had the second converter, and I might just be able to contact another tribe. With that small hope, I concluded the bargain and picked up what still seemed trash compared with Akki's magnificent haul.

He was grinning again as I wrapped the pieces of my choice into a packet and stood to make the farewell gestures. All this time Eet had been as inert as if he were indeed a fur piece about my shoulders. And it was not until I had to walk away from the camp, badly defeated, that I wondered why he had not taken some part in the affair. Or had I come to lean so heavily on him that I was not able to take care of myself? As that thought hit me I was startled and alarmed. Once I had leaned upon my father, feeling secure in his wisdom and experience. Then there had been Vondar, whose knowledge had so far exceeded my own that I had been content to accept his arrangement of both our lives. Soon after disaster had broken that tie, Eet had taken over. And it would seem that I was only half a man, needing the guidance of a stronger will and mind.

I could accept that, become Eet's puppet. Or I could be willing to make my own mistakes, learn by them, hold Eet to a partnership rather than a master-servant relationship. It was up to me, and perhaps Eet wanted me to make such a choice, having deliberately left me to my own bungling today as a test, or even an object lesson as to how helpless I was when I tried to deal on my own.

"Good fortune, smooth lifting—" That was Akki mockingly echoing my farewell of minutes earlier. "Crab pearls next, Jern? Want to wager I will take the best there, too?"

He laughed, not waiting for my answer. It was as if he knew that any defiance on my part would be in the nature of a hollow boast. Instead, he tramped off to his flitter, letting me settle into mine.

I did not take off at once to follow him back to his ship. If he also expected to hunt another camp, I did not want him to follow my path—though he might put a scanner on me.

Triggering the com, I called Ryzk. "Coming in." I would not add to that. The channels of all flitter coms were the same and Akki could pick up anything I now said.

Nor did I try to contact Eet, stubbornly resolved I would leave him in mental retirement as I tried to solve my own problems.

Those problems were not going to become any lighter, I saw as I took off. There was an odd greenish-yellow cast to the sky. And the surface of the ground, wherever there was a deposit of sand, threw up whirling shapes of grit. Seconds later the very sky about us seemed to explode and the flitter was caught in a gust which even her power could not fight.

For a space we were caught in that whirlwind and I knew fear. The flitter was never meant for high altitudes, and skimming the surface beneath the worst of the wind carried with it the danger of being smashed against some escarpment. But I had little choice. And I fought grimly to hold the craft steady.

We were driven south and west, out over the dead sea bottom. And I knew bleakly that even if I did get back to the *Wendwind* my chances of finding another tribe were finished. Such a storm as this drove them to shelter and I could spend fruitless weeks hunting them. But I was able bit by bit to fight back to the Big Pot. And when I finally entered the hatch I was so weak I slumped forward over the controls and was not really aware of anything more until Ryzk forced a mug of caff into my hands and I knew I was in the mess cabin.

"This pest hole has gone crazy!" He was drumming with his fingers on the edge of the table. "According to our instruments we are sitting over a blowhole now. We up ship, or we are blown out!"

I did not quite realize what he meant and it was not until we had spaced that he explained tersely; the readings of planet stability under the Big Pot had suddenly flared into the danger zone, and he had feared I would not get back before he would be forced to lift. That I had squeezed in by what he considered a very narrow margin he thought luck of a fabulous kind.

But that danger was not real to me, since I had not been aware of it until afterward. The realization of my trade failure was worse. I must lay better plans or lose out as badly as I would have, had we never raised from Theba.

Akki had mentioned crab pearls—which might or might not mean that his itinerary had been planned along the same course as mine. I laid out the poor results of my zoran dealing and considered them fretfully. Akki might have done two things: he might have boastfully warned me off the planet where he was going to trade (his ship had lifted, Ryzk informed me, at once upon his return), or he might just have said that out of malice to make me change my own plans.

I wondered. Eet could tell me. But straightaway I rebelled. I was not going to depend on Eet!

Where was my next-best market? I tried to recall Vondar's listings. There was—Sororis! And it was not from Ustle's notes that memory came, but from my father. Sororis had been an "exit" planet for years, that is, a very far out station in which outlaws could, if they were at the end of their resources and very desperate indeed, find refuge. It had no regular service of either passenger or trade ships, though tramps of very dubious registry would put in there now and then. The refuse of the galaxy's criminal element conjoined around the half-forgotten port and maintained themselves as best they could, or died. They were too useless for even the Guild to recruit.

However, and this was the important fact, there was a native race on Sororis, settled in the north where the off-worlders found the land too inhospitable. And they were supposed to have some formidable weapons of their own to protect themselves against raiders from the port.

The main thing was that they had a well-defined religion and god-gifts were an important part of it. To present their god with an outstanding gift was the only real means of winning status among them. Such presentations gave the donor the freedom of their city for a certain number of days.

My father had been given to telling stories, always supposedly about men he knew during his years as a Guild appraiser. I believed, however, that some concerned his own exploits as a youth. He had told of an adventure on Sororis in detail, and now I could draw upon that for a way to retrieve the Lorgal fiasco.

To the inhabitants of Sororis these chunks of zoran

would be rare and strange, since they would not have seen them before. Suppose I presented the largest at the temple, then offered the rest to men who wished to make similar gifts and thus enhance their standing among their fellows? What Sororisan products might be taken in exchange I did not know. But the hero of my father's story had come away with a greenstone unheard of elsewhere. For there was this about the Sororisans—they traded fairly.

It was so wild a chance that no one but a desperate man would think of it. But the combination of my defeat by Akki and the need for asserting my independence of Eet made me consider it. And after I had finished the caff I went to the computer in the control cabin and punched the code for Sororis, wagering with myself that if I received no answer I would accept that as meaning there was no chance of carrying through such a wild gamble.

Ryzk watched me speculatively as I waited for the computer's answer. And when, in spite of my half-hopes, a series of numbers did appear on the small screen, he read them aloud:

"Sector 5, VI—Norroute 11— Where in the name of Asta-Ivista is that? Or what?"

I was committed now. "That is where we are going." I wondered if he had heard of it. "Sororis."

6

"Where are your beam lasers and protect screens?" Ryzk asked in the voice, I decided, one used for addressing someone whose mental balance was in doubt. He even glanced at the control board, as if expecting to see such armaments represented there. And so convincing was his question that I found myself echoing that glance—which might not have been so fruitless had the ship still carried what scars proclaimed she once had.

"If you don't have those," he continued, his logic an irritation, "you might just as well blow her tubes and end us all right here without wasting the energy to take us to Sororis—if you do know what awaits any ship crazy enough to planet there. It's a rock prison and those dumped on it will storm any ship for a way to lift off again. To set down at whatever port they do have is simply inviting take-over."

"We are not going in—that is, the ship is not." At least I had planned that far ahead, drawing on my father's very detailed account of how his "friend" had made that single visit to the planet's surface. "There is the LB. It can be fitted with a return mechanism if only one is to use it."

Ryzk looked at me. For a very long moment he did not answer, and when he did, it was obliquely.

"Even a parking orbit there would be risky. They may have a converted flitter able to try a ship raid. And who is going down and why?"

"I am—to Sornuff—" I gave the native city the best pronunciation I could, though its real twist of consonants and vowels was beyond the powers of the human tongue and larynx to produce. The Sororisans were humanoid, but they were not of Terran colony stock, not even mutated colony stock.

"The temple treasures!" His instant realization of what I had in mind told me that his Free Trader's knowledge of the planet's people was more than just surface.

"It has been done," I told him, though I was aware that I was depending perhaps too much on my father's story.

"An orbit park for Sornuff," Ryzk continued, almost as if thinking aloud, "could be polar, and so leave us well away from the entrance route for anything setting down at the real port. As for the LB, yes, there can be lift-off modifications. Only"—he shrugged—"that's a job you don't often tackle in space."

"You can do it?" I demanded. I would admit frankly that I was no mech-tech and such adjustments were beyond either my knowledge or my skill. If Ryzk could not provide the knowledge, then we would have to risk some other and far more dangerous way to gain Sornuff.

"I'll take a look—" He was almost grudging.

But that was all I wanted for now. Free Traders by the very nature of their lives were adept in more fields than the usual spacer. While the fleet men were almost rigorously compartmented as to their skills, the men of the irregular ships had to be able to take over some other's duties when need arose.

The LB must have been periodically overhauled or it would not have had the certification seal on its lock. But it still dated to the original fitting of the ship, and so must have been intended to carry at least five passengers. Thus we were favored in so much room. And Ryzk, dismantling the control board with the ease of one well used to such problems, grunted that it was in better shape for conversion than he had supposed.

It suddenly occurred to me that, as on Lorgal, Eet had made no suggestions or comments. And that started a small nagging worry in my mind, gave me a twinge of foreboding. Had Eet read in my mind my decision for independence? If so, had he some measure of foreknowledge? For never yet had I been able to discover the limit of his esper powers. Whenever I thought I knew, he produced something new, as he had on Theba. So, possessing foreknowledge, was he now preparing to allow me to run into difficulty from which he alone could extricate us, thus proving for once and for all that our association was less a partnership than one of master and servant, with Eet very much in the master's seat? He had closed his mind, offering no comments or suggestions. Nor did he now ever accompany us to the lock where Ryzk and I— I as the unhandy assistant—worked to give us possible entry to a hostile world where I had a thin chance of winning a gamble. I began to suspect he was playing a devious game, which made me more stubborn-set than ever to prove I could plan and carry through a coup which did not depend upon his powers.

On the other hand, I was willing enough to use what I had learned from Eet, even though it now irked me to admit I owed it to him. The hallucinatory disguise was so apt a tool that I systematically worked at the exercise of mind and will which produced the temporary changes. I found that by regular effort I could hold a minor alteration such as the scar I had worked so hard to produce as long as I pleased. But complete change, a totally new face for instance, came less easily. And I must labor doggedly even to produce the slurring of line which would pass me through a crowd unnoticed for a short space. It was Eet's added force which had held that before, and I despaired of ever having enough power to do it myself.

Practice, Eet had said, was the base of any advance I could make, and practice I had time for, in the privacy of my own cabin, with a mirror set up on a shelf to be my guide in success or failure.

At the back of my mind was always the hope that so disguised I might slip through Guild watch at any civilized port. Sororis might be free of their men, but if I won out with a precious cargo, I would have to reach one of the inner planets and there sell my spoil. Stones of unknown value were only offered at auction before the big merchants. Peddled elsewhere, they were suspect and could be confiscated after any informer (who got a percentage of the final sale) turned in a tip. It did not matter if they had been honestly enough acquired on some heretofore unmarked world; auction tax had not been paid on them and that made them contraband.

So I spent our voyage time both acting as an extra pair of inept hands for Ryzk and staring into a mirror trying to reflect there a face which was not that I had seen all my life.

We came out of hyper in the Sororis system with promptitude, which again testified to Ryzk's ability, leading me to wonder what had grounded him in the scum of the Off-port. There were three planets, two, dead worlds, balls of cracked rock with no atmosphere, close enough to the sun to fuse any ship finning down on them like a pot to fry its crew.

On the other hand, Sororis was a frozen world, or largely so, with only a belt of livable land, by the standards of my species, about its middle. It was covered by glaciers north and south of that, save where there were narrow fingers of open land running into that ice cover. In one of these Sornuff was supposed to exist, well away from the outcast settlement about the port.

Ryzk, whom I left at the controls, set up his hold orbit to the north while I packed into the LB what I judged I would need for my visit to the ice-bound city. Co-ordinates would be fed to the director, and that, too, was Ryzk's concern. On such automatic devices would depend my safe arrival not too far from Sornuff and my eventual return to the ship, the latter being even less sure than the former.

If Ryzk's fears were realized and a high-altitude conditioned flitter from the port raised with a pilot skillful or reckless enough to attempt a take-over of the *Wendwind,* it might be that the ship would be forced out of orbit in some evasive maneuvering during my absence. If so, I had a warning which would keep me planetside until the ship was back on a course the LB was programed to intercept.

I checked all my gear with double care, as if I had not already checked it at least a dozen times while we were in hyper. I had a small pack containing special rations, if the local food was not to be assimilated, a translator, a mike call Ryzk would pick up if he were safely in orbit, and, of course, the stones from Lorgal. There was no weapon, not even a stunner. I could not have smuggled one on board at Theba. I could only depend upon my knowledge of personal defense until I was able to outfit myself with whatever local weapons were available.

Ryzk's voice rasped over the cabin com to say that all was clear and I picked up the pack. Eet was stretched on the bunk, apparently asleep as he had been every time I had come in recently. Was he sulking, or simply indifferent to my actions now? That small germ of worry his unexpected reaction to my bid for independence had planted in me was fast growing into a full-sized doubt of myself—one I dared not allow if I were to face the tests of my resourcefulness below.

Yet I hesitated just to walk out and leave him. Our growing rift hurt in an obscure way, and I had to hold stubbornly to my purpose to keep from surrender. Now I weakened to the degree that I aimed a thought at him.

"I am going—" That was weakly obvious and I was ashamed I had done it.

Eet opened his eyes calmly. "Good fortune." He stretched out his head as if savoring a comfort he was not in the least desirous of leaving. "Use your hind eyes as well as the fore." He closed his own and snapped our linkage.

"Hind eyes as well as fore" made little sense, but I chewed angrily upon it as I went to the LB, setting the door seals behind me. As I lay down in the hammock I gave the eject signal to Ryzk, and nearly blacked out when the force of my partition from the ship hit.

Since I was set on automatics, using in part the LB's built-in function to seek the nearest planet when disaster struck the ship, I had nothing to do but lie and try to plan for all eventualities. There was an oddly naked feel to traveling without Eet, we had been in company for so long. And I found that my rebellion did not quite blank out that sense of loss.

Still, there was an exultation born of my reckless throwing over of all prudent warnings, trying a wholly new and dangerous venture on my own. This, too, part of me warned against. But I was not to have very long to think about anything. For the cushioning for landing came on and I knew I had made the jump to planetside and was about to be faced by situations which would demand every bit of my attention.

The LB had set down, I discovered, in the narrow end of one of those claw-shaped valleys which cut into the ice. Perhaps the glacial covering of Sororis was now receding and these were the first signs of thaw. There was water running swiftly and steadily from the very point of the earth claw, forming a good-sized stream by the time it passed the LB. But the air was so chill that its freezing breath was a blow against the few exposed portions of my face. I snapped down the visor of my helmet as I set the LB hatch on persona lock and, taking up my pack, crunched the ice-packed sand under my space boots.

If Ryzk's reckoning had been successful I had only to go down this valley to where it joined a hand-shaped wedge from which other narrow valleys stretched away to the north and I would be in sighting distance of the walls of Sornuff. When I reached that point I must depend upon my father's tale for guidance. And now I realized he had gone into exhaustive detail in describing the country, almost as if he were trying to impress it upon my memory for some reason—though at the time it had not seemed so. But then I had listened eagerly to all his stories, while my foster brother and sister had apparently been bored and restless.

Between me and the city wall was a shrine of the ice spirit Zeeta. While she was not the principal deity of the Sororisans, she had a sizable following, and she had acted for the hero of my father's story as an intermediary with the priests of the major temple in the city. I say "she" for there was a living woman—or priestess—in that icy fane who was deemed to be the earth-bound part of the ice spirit, and was treated as a supernatural being, even differing in body from her followers.

I came to the join of "claw" and "hand" and saw indeed the walls of the city—and not too far away, the shrine of Zeeta.

My landing had been made just a little after dawn, and only now were thin beams of the hardly warm sun reaching to raise glints from the menace of the tall ice wall at my back. There was no sign of any life about the shrine and I wondered, with apprehension, if Zeeta had been, during the years since that other visitor was here, withdrawn, forsaken by those who had petitioned her here.

My worries as to that were quickly over as I came closer to the building of stone, glazed over with glistening ice. It was in the form of a cone, the tip of which had been sliced off, and it was perhaps the size of the *Wendwind*. Outside, a series of tables which were merely slabs of hewn ice as thick as my arm mounted on sturdy pillars of the same frozen substance encircled the whole truncated tower. On each of these were embedded the offerings of Zeeta's worshipers, some of them now so encased in layers of ice that they were only dark shadows, others lying on the surface with but a very thin coat of moisture solidifying over them.

Food, furs, some stalks of vegetable stuff black-blasted by frost lay there. It would seem that Zeeta never took from these supplies, only left them to become part of the growing ice blocks on which they rested.

I walked between two of these chill tables to approach the single break in the rounded wall of the shrine, a door open to the wind and cold. But I was heartened to see further proof of my father's story, a gong suspended by that portal. And I boldly raised my fist to strike it with the back of my gloved hand as lightly as I could—though the booming note which answered my tap seemed to me to reach and echo through the glacier behind.

My translator was fastened to my throat and I had rehearsed what I would say—though the story had not supplied me with any ceremonial greeting and I would have to improvise.

The echoes of the gong continued past the time I thought they would die. And when no one came to answer, I hesitated, uncertain. The fairly fresh offerings spelled occupancy of the shrine, but perhaps that was not so, and Zeeta, or her chosen counterpart, was not in residence.

I had almost made up my mind to go on when there was a flicker of movement within the dark oblong of the door. That movement became a shape which faced me.

It was as muffled as a Lorgalian. But they had appeared to have humanoid bodies covered by ordinary robes. This was as if a creature completely and tightly wound in strips or bandages which reduced it to the likeness of a larva balanced there to confront me.

The coverings, if they were strips of fabric, were crystaled with patterns of ice which had the glory of individual snowflakes and were diamond-bright when the rising sun touched them. But the body beneath was only dimly visible, having at least two lower limbs (were there any arms they were bound fast to the trunk and completely hidden), a torso, and above, a round ball for a head. On the fore of that the crystal encrustations took the form of two great faceted eyes—at least they were ovals and set where eyes would be had the thing been truly humanoid. There were no other discernible features.

I made what I hoped would be accepted as a gesture of reverence or respect, bowing my head and holding up my hands empty and palm out. And though the thing had no visible ears, I put my plea into speech which emerged from my translator as a rising and falling series of trills, weirdly akin in some strange fashion to the gong note.

"Hail to Zeeta of the clear ice, the ice which holds forever! I seek the favor of Zeeta of the ice lands."

There was a trilling in return, though I could see that the head had no mouth to utter it.

"You are not of the blood, the bones, the flesh of those who seek Zeeta. Why do you trouble me, strange one?"

"I seek Zeeta as one who comes not empty-handed, as one who knows the honor of the Ice Maiden—" I put out my right hand now, laying on the edge of the nearest table the gift I had prepared with some thought—a thin chain of silver on which were threaded rounded lumps of rock crystal. On one of the inner worlds it had no value, but worth is relative to the surroundings and here it flashed bravely in the sunlight as if it were a string of the crystals such as adorned Zeeta's wrappings.

"You are not of the blood, the kind of my people," came her trilling in reply. She made no move to inspect my offering, nor even, as far as I could deduce, to turn her eyes to view it. "But your gift is well given. What ask you of Zeeta? Swift passage across ice and snow? Good thoughts to light your dreams?"

"I ask the word of Zeeta spoken into the ear of mighty Torg, that I may have a daughter's fair will in approaching the father."

"Torg also does not deal with men of your race,

stranger. He is the Guardian and Maker of Good for those who are not of your kind."

"But if one brings gifts, is it not meet that the gift-giver be able to approach the Maker of Good to pay him homage?"

"It is our custom, but you are a stranger. Torg may not find it well to swallow what is not of his own people."

"Let Zeeta but give the foreword to those who serve Torg and then let him be the judge of my motives and needs."

"A small thing, and reasonable," was her comment. "So shall it be done."

She did turn her head then so those blazing crystal eyes were looking to the gong. And though she raised nothing to strike its surface, it suddenly trembled and the sound which boomed from it was enough to summon an army to attack.

"It is done, stranger."

Before I could give her any thanks she was gone, as suddenly as if her whole crystal-encrusted body had been a flame and some rise of wind had extinguished it. But though she vanished from my sight, I still lifted my hand in salute and spoke my thanks, lest I be thought lacking in gratitude.

As before, the gong note continued to rumble through the air about me, seemingly not wholly sound but a kind of vibration. So heralded, I began to walk to the city.

The way was not quite so far as it seemed and I came to the gates before I was too tired of trudging over the ice-hardened ground. There were people there and they, too, were strangely enough clad to rivet the attention.

Fur garments are known to many worlds where the temperature is such that the inhabitants must add to their natural covering to survive. Such as these, though, I had not seen. Judging by their appearance, animals as large as a man standing at his full height had been slain to obtain skins of shaggy, golden fur. These had not been cut and remade into conventional garb but had retained their original shape, so that the men of Sornuff displayed humanoid faces looking out of hoods designed from the animal heads and still in one piece with the rest of the hide; the paws, still firm on the limbs, they used as cover for hands and feet. Save for the showing of their faces they might well be beasts lumbering about on their hind legs.

Their faces were many shades darker than the golden fur framing them, and their eyes narrow and slitted, as if after generations of holding them so in protection against the glare of sun on snow and ice this had become a normal characteristic.

They appeared to keep no guard at their gate, but three of them, who must have been summoned by the gong, gestured to me with short crystal rods. Whether these were weapons or badges of office I did not know, but I obediently went with them, down the central street. Sornuff had been built in circular form, and its center hub was another cone temple, much larger than Zeeta's shrine.

The door into it was relatively narrow and oddly fashioned to resemble an open mouth, though above it were no other carvings to indicate the rest of a face. This was Torg's place and the test of my plan now lay before me.

I could sense no change in warmth in the large circular room into which we came. If there was any form of heating in Sornuff it was not used in Torg's temple. But the chill did not in any way seem to bother my guides or the waiting priests. Behind them was the representation of Torg, again a widely open mouth, in the wall facing the door.

"I bring a gift for Torg," I began boldly.

"You are not of the people of Torg." It was not quite a protest, but it carried a faint shadow of warning and it came from one of the priests. Over his fur he wore a collar of red metal from which hung several flat plaques, each set with a different color stone and so massively engraved in an interwined pattern that it could not be followed.

"Yet I bring a gift for the pleasures of Torg, such as perhaps not even his children of the blood have seen." I brought out the best of the zorans, a blue-green roughly oval stone which nearly filled the hollow of my hand when I had unrolled its wrappings and held it forth to the priest.

He bent his head as if he sniffed the stone, and then he shot out a pale tongue, touching its tip to the hard surface. Having to pass it through some strange test, he plucked it out of my hold and turned to face the great mouth in the wall. The zoran he gripped between the thumb and forefinger of each hand, holding it in the air at eye level.

"Behold the food of Torg, and it is good food, a welcome gift," he intoned. I heard a stir and mutter from behind me as if I had been followed into the temple by others.

"It is a welcome gift!" the other priests echoed.

Then he snapped his fingers, or appeared to do so, in an odd way. The zoran spun out and away, falling through the exact center of the waiting mouth, to vanish from sight. The ceremony over, the priest turned once more to face me.

"Stranger you are, but for one sun, one night, two suns,

two nights, three suns, three nights, you have the freedom of the city of Torg and may go about such business as is yours within the gates which are under the Guardianship of Torg."

"Thanks be to Torg," I answered and bowed my head. But when I in turn faced around I found that my gift giving had indeed had an audience. There were a dozen at least of the furred people staring intently at me. And though they opened a passage, giving me a free way to the street without, one on the fringe stepped forward and laid a paw-gloved hand on my arm.

"Stranger Who Has Given to Torg." He made a title of address out of that statement. "There is one who would speak with you."

"One is welcome," I replied. "But I am indeed a stranger within your gates and have no house roof under which to speak."

"There is a house roof and it is this way." He trilled that hurriedly, glancing over his shoulder as if he feared interruption. And as it did seem that several others now coming forth from the temple were minded to join us, he kept his grasp on my arm and drew me a step or two away.

Since time was a factor in any trading I would do here, I was willing enough to go with him.

7

He guided me down one of the side streets to a house which was a miniature copy of shrine and temple, save that the cone tip, though it had been cut away, was mounted with a single lump of stone carved with one of the intricate designs, one which it somehow bothered the eyes to study too closely.

There was no door, not even a curtain, closing the portal, but inside we faced a screen, and had to go between it and the wall for a space to enter the room beyond. Along its walls poles jutted forth to support curtains of fur which divided the outer rim of the single chamber into small nooks of privacy. Most of these were fully drawn. I could hear movement behind them but saw no one. My guide drew me to one, jerked aside the curtain, and motioned me before him into that tent.

From the wall protruded a ledge on which were more furs, as if it might serve as a bed. He waved me to a seat there, then sat, himself, at the other end, leaving a goodly expanse between us as was apparently demanded by courtesy. He came directly to the point.

"To Torg you gave a great gift, stranger."

"That is true," I said when he paused as though expecting some answer. And then I dared my trader's advance. "It is from beyond the skies."

"You come from the place of strangers?"

I thought I could detect suspicion in his voice. And I had no wish to be associated with the derelicts of the off-world settlement.

"No. I had heard of Torg from my father, many sun times ago, and it was told to me beyond the stars. My father had respect for Torg and I came with a gift as my father said must be done."

He plucked absent-mindedly at some wisps of the long fur making a ruff below his chin.

"It is said that there was another stranger who came bringing Torg a gift from the stars. And he was a generous man."

"To Torg?" I prompted when he hesitated for the second time.

"To Torg—and others." He seemed to find it difficult to put into words what he wanted very much to say. "All men want to please Torg with fine gifts. But for some men such fortune never comes."

"You are, perhaps, one of those men?" I dared again to speak plainly, though by such speech I might defeat my own ends. To my mind he wanted encouragement to state the core of the matter and I knew no other way to supply it.

"Perhaps—" he hedged. "The tale of other days is that the stranger who came carried with him not one from-beyond-the-stars wonders but several, and gave these freely to those who asked."

"Now the tale which I heard from my father was not

quite akin to that," I replied. "For by my father's words the stranger gave wonders from beyond, yes. But he accepted certain things in return."

The Sororisan blinked. "Oh, aye, there was that. But what he took was token payment only, things which were not worth Torg's noting and of no meaning. Which made him one of generous spirit."

I nodded slowly. "That is surely true. And these things which were of no meaning—of what nature were they?"

"Like unto these." He slipped off the ledge to kneel on the floor, pressing at the front panel of the ledge base immediately below where he had been sitting. That swung open and he brought out a hide bag from which he shook four pieces of rough rock. I forced myself to sit quietly, making no comment. But, though I had never seen greenstone, I had seen recorder tri-dees enough to know that these were uncut, unpolished gems of that nature. I longed to handle them, to make sure they were unflawed and worth a trade.

"And what are those?" I asked as if I had very little interest in the display.

"Rocks which come from the foot of the great ice wall when it grows the less because the water runs from it. I have them only because—because I, too, had a tale from my father, that once there came a stranger who would give a great treasure for these."

"And no one else in Sornuff has such?"

"Perhaps—but they are of no worth. Why should a man bring them into his house for safekeeping? They have made laughter at me many times when I was a youngling because I believed in old tales and took these."

"May I see these rocks from the old story?"

"Of a surety!" He grabbed up the two largest, pushed

them eagerly, with almost bruising force, into my hands. "Look! Did your tale speak also of such?"

The larger piece had a center flaw, but it could be split, I believed, to gain one medium-sized good stone and maybe two small ones. However, the second was a very good one which would need only a little cutting. And he had two other pieces, both good-sized. With such at auction I had my profit, and a bigger, more certain one than I had planned in my complicated series of tradings beginning with the zorans.

Perhaps I could do even better somewhere else in Sornuff. I remembered those other men who had moved to contact me outside the temple before my present host had hurried me off. On the other hand, if I made this sure trade I would be quicker off world. And somehow I had had an eerie sensation ever since I had left the LB that this was a planet it was better to visit as briefly as possible. There were no indications that the outlaws of the port came this far north, but I could not be sure that they did not. And should I be discovered and the LB found— No, a quick trade and a speedy retreat was as much as I dared now.

I took out my pouch and displayed the two small and inferior zorans I had brought.

"Torg might well look with favor on him who offered these."

The Sororisan lunged forward, his fur-backed hands reaching with the fingers crooked as if to snatch that treasure from me. But that I did not fear. Since I had fed Torg well this morning, I could not be touched for three days or the wrath of Torg would speedily strike down anyone trying such a blasphemous act.

"To gift Torg," the Sororisan said breathlessly. "He who did so—all fortune would be his!"

"We have shared an old tale, you and I, and have believed in it when others made laughter concerning that belief. Is this not so?"

"Stranger, it is so!"

"Then let us prove their laughter naught and bring truth to the tale. Take you these and give me your stones from the cold wall, and it shall be even as the tale said it was in the days of our fathers!"

"Yes—and yes!" He thrust at me the bag with the stones he had not yet given me, seized upon the zorans I had laid down.

"And as was true in the old tale," I added, my uneasiness flooding in now that I had achieved my purpose, "I go again into beyond-the-sky."

He hardly looked up from the stones lying on the fur.

"Yes, let it be so."

When he made no move to see me forth from his house, I stowed the bag of greenstones into the front of my weather suit and went on my own. I could not breathe freely again until I was back in the ship, and the sooner I gained that safety the better.

There was a crowd of Sororisans in the street outside, but oddly enough none of them approached me. Instead they looked to the house from which I had come, almost as if it had been told them what trade had been transacted there. Nor did any of them bar my way or try to prevent my leaving. Since I did not know how far the protection of Torg extended, I kept a wary eye to right and left as I walked (not ran as I wished) to the outer gate.

Across the fields which had been so vacant at my coming a party was advancing. Part of them wore the fur suits of the natives. But among them were two who had on a queer mixture of shabby, patched, off-world weather clothing. And I could only think they must have connection with the port. Yet I could not retreat now; I was sure I had already been sighted. My only hope was to get back to the LB with speed and raise off world.

The suited men halted as they sighted me. They were too far away for me to distinguish features within their helmets, and I was sure they could not see mine. They would only mark my off-world clothing. But that was new, in good condition, which would hint to them that I was not of the port company.

I expected them to break from their traveling companions, to cut me off, and I only hoped they were unarmed. I had been schooled by my father's orders in unarmed combat which combined the lore of more than one planet where man made a science of defending himself using only the weapons with which nature had endowed him. And I thought that if the whole party did not come at me at once I had a thin chance.

But if such an attack was in the mind of the off-worlders, they were not given a chance to put it to the test. For the furred natives closed about them and hustled them on toward the gate of the city. I thought that they might even be prisoners. Judging by the tales I had heard of the port, an inhabitant there might well give reason for retaliation by the natives.

My fast walk had become a trot by the time I passed the shrine of Zeeta and I made the best speed I could back to the LB, panting as I broke the seal and scrambled in. I snapped switches, empowering the boat to rise and latch on to the homing beam to the *Wendwind,* and threw myself into a hammock for a take-off so ungentle that I blacked out as if a great hand had squeezed half the life out of me.

When I came groggily to my senses again, memory returned and I knew triumph. I had proved my belief in the old story right. Under the breast of my suit was what would make us independent of worry—at least for a while —once we could get it to auction.

I rendezvoused with the ship, thus proving my last worry wrong, and stripped off the weather suit and helmet, to climb to the control cabin. But before I could burst out with my news of success, I saw that Ryzk was frowning.

"They spy-beamed us—"

"What!" From a normal port such a happening might not have been too irregular. After all, a strange ship which did not set down openly but cruised in a tight orbit well away from any entrance lane would have invited a spy beam as a matter of regulation. But by all accounts Sororis had no such equipment. Its port was not defended, needed no defense.

"The port?" I demanded, still unable to believe that.

"On the contrary." For the first time in what seemed to me days, Eet made answer. "It came from the direction of the port, yes, but it was from a ship."

This startled me even more. To my knowledge only a Patroler would mount a spy beam, and that would be a Patroler of the second class, not a roving scout. The Guild, too, of course, had the reputation of having such equipment. But then again, a Guild ship carrying such would be the property of a Veep. And what would any Veep be doing on Sororis? It was a place of exile for the dregs of the criminal world.

"How long?"

"Not long enough to learn anything," Eet returned. "I saw to that. But the very fact that they did not learn will make them question. We had better get into hyper—"

"What course?" Ryzk asked.

"Lylestane."

Not only did the auction there give me a chance to sell the greenstones as quickly as possible, but Lylestane was one of the inner planets, long settled, even overcivilized, if you wish. Of course the Guild would have some connections there; they had with every world on which there was a profit to be made. But it was a well-policed world, one where law had the upper hand. And no Guild ship would dare to follow us boldly into Lylestane skies. So long as we were clear of any taint of illegality, we were, according to our past bargain with the Patrol, free to go as we would.

Ryzk punched a course with flying fingers, and then signaled a hyper entrance, as if he feared that at any moment we might feel the drag of a traction beam holding us fast. His concern was so apparent it banished most of my elation.

But that returned as I brought out the greenstones, examined them for flaws, weighed, measured, set down my minimum bids. Had I had more training, I might have attempted cutting the two smaller. But it was better to take less than to spoil the stones, and I distrusted my skill. I had cut gems, but only inferior stones, suitable for practice.

The largest piece would cut into three, and the next make one flawless one. The other two might provide four stones. Not of the first class. But, because greenstone was so rare, even second- and third-quality stones would find eager bidders.

I had been to auctions on Baltis and Amon with Vondar, though I had never visited the more famous one of Lylestane. Only two planet years ago one of Vondar's friends, whom I knew, had accepted the position of appraiser there, and I did not doubt that he would remember me and be prepared to steer me through the local legalities to offer my stones. He might even suggest a private buyer or two to be warned that such were up for sale. I dreamed my dreams and spun my fantasies, turning the stones around in my fingers and thinking I had redeemed my stupidity on Lorgal.

But when we had set down on Lylestane, being relegated to a far corner of the teeming port, I suddenly realized that coming to such as a spectator, with Vondar responsible for sales and myself merely acting as a combination recording clerk and bodyguard, was far different from this. Alone— For the first time I was almost willing to ask Eet's advice again. Only the need to reassure myself that I could if I wished deal for and by my lone kept me from that plea. But as I put on the best of my limited wardrobe—inner-planet men are apt to dress by station and judge a man by the covering on his back—the mutant sought me out.

"I go with you—" Eet sat on my bunk. But when I turned to face him I saw him become indistinct, hazy, and when the outlines of his person again sharpened I did not see Eet, but rather a pookha. On this world such a pet would indeed be a status symbol.

Nor was I ready to say no. I needed that extra feeling of confidence Eet would supply by just riding on my shoulder. I went out, to meet Ryzk in the corridor.

"Going planetside?" I asked.

He shook his head. "Not here. The Off-port is too rich for anyone less than a combine mate. This air's too thick for me. I'll stay ramp-up. How long will you be?"

"I shall see Kafu, set up the auction entry, if he will do it, then come straight back."

"I'll seal ship. Give me the tone call." I wondered a little at his answer. To seal ship meant expectation of trouble. Yet of all the worlds we might have visited we had the least to fear from violence here.

There were hire flitters in the lanes down-field and I climbed into the nearest, dropping in one of my now very few credit pieces and so engaging it for the rest of the day. At Kafu's name it took off, flying one of the low lanes toward the heart of the city.

Lylestane was so long a settled world that for the most part its four continents were great cities. But for some reason the inhabitants had no liking for building very high into the air. None of the structures stood more than a dozen stories high—though underground each went down level by level deep under the surface.

The robo-flitter set down without a jar on a rooftop and then flipped out an occupied sign and trundled off to a waiting zone. I crossed, to repeat Kafu's name into the disk beside the grav shaft, and received a voiced direction in return:

"Fourth level, second crossing, sixth door."

The grav float was well occupied, mostly by men in the foppish inner-planet dress, wherein even those of lower rank went with laced, puffed, tagged tunics. To my frontier-trained eyes they seemed more ridiculous than in fashion. And my own plain tunic and cropped hair attracted sideways eyeing until I began to wish I had applied some of the hallucinatory arts at least to cloud my appearance.

Fourth level down beneath the ground gave Kafu's standing as one of reasonably high rank. Not that of a Veep, who would have a windowed room or series of rooms above surface, but not down to the two- and three-mile depth of an underling.

I found the second crossing and stopped at the sixth door. There was an announce com screwed in its surface, a pick-up visa-plate above it—a one-way visa-plate which would allow the inhabitant to see me but not reveal himself in return.

I fingered the com to on, saw the visa-plate come to life.

"Murdoc Jern," I said, "assistant to Vondar Ustle."

The wait before any answer came was so long I began to wonder if perhaps Kafu was out. Then there did come a muffled response from the com.

"Leave to enter." The barrier rolled back to let me into a room in vivid contrast to the stone-walled Sororisan house where I had done my last trading.

Though men went in gaudy and colorful wear, this room was in subdued and muted tones. My space boots trod springy summead moss, a living carpet of pale yellow. And along the walls it had raised longer stalks with dangling green berries which had been carefully twined and massed together to form patterns.

There were easirests, the kind which yielded to one's weight and size upon bodily contact, all covered in earth-brown. And the light diffused from the ceiling was that of the gentle sun of spring. Directly ahead of me as I came in, one of the easirests had been set by the wall where the berry stalks had been trained to frame an open space. One might have been looking out of a window, viewing miles upon miles of landscape. And this was not static but flowed after holding for a time into yet another view, and with such changes in vegetation one could well believe that the views were meant to show not just one planet but many.

In the easirest by this "window" sat Kafu. He was a Thothian by birth, below what was considered to be the norm in height for Terran stock. His very brown skin was pulled so tightly over his fragile bones that it would seem he was the victim of starvation, hardly still alive. But from the deep sockets of his prominent skull, his eyes watched me alertly.

Instead of the fripperies of Lylestane he wore the robe of his home world, somewhat primly, and it covered him from throat, a stiffened collar standing up in a frame behind his skull, to ankles, with wide sleeves coming down over his hands to the knucklebones.

Across the easirest a table level had been swung, and set out on that were flashing stones which he was not so much examining as arranging in patterns. They might be counters in some exotic game.

But he swept these together as if he intended to clear the board for business, and they disappeared into a sleeve pocket. He touched his fingers to forehead in the salute of his people.

"I see you, Murdoc Jern."

"And I, you, Kafu." The Thothians accepted no address of honor, making a virtue of an apparent humbleness which was really a very great sense of their own superiority.

"It has been many years—"

"Five." Just as I had been suddenly restless on Sororis, so this room, half alive with its carefully tended growth, affected me with a desire to be done with my business and out of it.

Eet shifted weight on my shoulder and I saw, I thought, a flicker of interest in Kafu's eyes.

"You have a new companion, Murdoc Jern."

"A pookha," I returned, tamping down impatience.

"So? Very interesting. But you are thinking now that you did not come to discuss alien life forms or the passage of years. What have you to say to me?"

I was truly startled then. Kafu had thrown aside custom

in coming so quickly to the point. Nor had he offered me a seat or refreshment, or gone through any of the forms always used. I did not know whether I faced veiled hostility, or something else. But that I was not received with any desire to please I did know.

And I decided that such an approach might be met by me with its equal in curtness.

"I have gems for auction."

Kafu's hands came up in a gesture which served his race for that repudiation mine signified by a shake of the head.

"You have nothing to sell, Murdoc Jern."

"No? What of these?" I did not advance to spill the greenstones onto his lap table as I might have done had his attitude been welcoming, but held the best on the palm of my hand in the full light of the room. And I saw that that light had special properties—no false, doctored, or flawed stone could reveal aught but its imperfections in that glow. That my greenstones would pass this first test I did not doubt.

"You have nothing to sell, Murdoc Jern. Here or with any of the legally established auctions or merchants."

"Why?" His calmness carried conviction. It was not in such a man as Kafu to use a lie to influence a sale. If he said no sale, that was true and I was going to find every legitimate market closed to me. But the magnitude of such a blow had not yet sunk in, and as yet I only wanted an answer.

"You have been listed as unreliable by the authorities," he told me then.

"The lister?" I clung desperately to that one way of possible clearance. Had my detractor a name, I could legally demand a public hearing, always supposing I could raise the fees to cover it.

"From off world. The name is Vondar Ustle."

"But—he is dead! He was my master and he is dead!"

"Just so," Kafu agreed. "It was done in his name, under his estate seal."

This meant I had no way of fighting it. At least not now, and maybe never, unless I raised the astronomical fees of those legal experts who would be able to fight through perhaps more than one planet's courts.

Listed, I had no hope of dealing with any reputable merchant. And Kafu said I had been listed in the name of a dead man. By whom, and for what purpose? The Patrol, still wishing to use me in some game for the source of the zero stones? Or the Guild? The zero stone—I had not really thought of it for days; I had been too intent on trying my trade again. But perhaps it was like a poison seeping in to disrupt my whole life.

"It is a pity. They look like fine stones—" Kafu continued.

I slapped the gems back in their bag, stowing it inside my tunic. Then I bowed with what outward impassiveness I could summon.

"I beg the Gentle Homo's pardon for troubling him with this matter."

Kafu made another small gesture. "You have some powerful enemy, Murdoc Jern. It would be best for you to walk very softly and look into the shadows."

"If I go walking at all," I muttered and bowed again, somehow getting myself out of that room where all my triumph had been crushed into nothingness.

This was bottom. I would lose the ship now, since I could not pay field fees and it would be attached by the port authorities. I had a small fortune in gems I could not legally sell.

Legally—

"This may be what they wish." Eet followed my thoughts.

"Yes, but when there is only one road left, that is the one you walk," I told him grimly.

8

On some worlds I might have moved into the shadowy places with greater ease than I could on Lylestane. I did not know any contacts here. Yet it seemed to me when I had a moment to think that there had been something in Kafu's talk with me—perhaps a small hint—

What had he said? "You have nothing to sell with any of the legally established merchants or auctions—" Had he or had he not stressed that word "legally"? And was he so trying to bait me into an illegal act which would bring him an informer's cut of what I now carried? With a lesser man than Kafu my suspicions might be true. But I believed that the Thothian would not lend his name and reputation to any such murky game. Vondar had considered Kafu one of those he could trust and I knew there had been an old and deep friendship between my late master and the little brown man. Did some small feeling of friendliness born of that lap over to me, so that he had been subtly trying to give me a lead? Or was I now fishing so desperately for anything which might save me that I was letting my imagination rule my common sense?

"Not so—" For the second time Eet interrupted my

train of thought. "You are right in supposing he had friendly feelings for you. But there was such in that room that he could not express them—"

"A spy snoop?"

"A pick-up of some sort," Eet returned. "I am not as well attuned to such when they are born of machines rather than the mind. But while this Kafu spoke for more than your ears alone, his thoughts followed different paths, and they were thoughts of regret that he must do this thing. What does the name Tacktile mean to you?"

"Tacktile?" I repeated, speculating now as to why Kafu had been under observation and who had set the spy snoop. My only solution was that the Patrol was not done with me and were bringing pressure to bear so that I would agree to the scheme their man had outlined when he offered me a pilot of their choosing.

"Yes—yes!" Eet was impatient now. "But the past does not matter at this moment—it is the future. Who is Tacktile?"

"I do not know. Why?"

"The name was foremost in this Kafu's mind when he hinted of an illegal sale. And there was a dim picture there also of a building with a sharply pointed roof. But of that I could see little and it was gone in an instant. Kafu has rudimentary esper powers and he felt the mind-touch. Luckily he believed it some refinement of the spy snoop and did not suspect us."

Us? Was Eet trying to flatter me?

"He had a crude shield," the mutant continued. "Enough of a one to muddle reception when I did not have time to work on him. But this Tacktile, I believe, would be of benefit to you now."

"If he is an IGB—a buyer of illegal gems—he might just be the bait in someone's trap."

"No, I think not. For Kafu saw in him a solution for you but no way to make that clear. And he is on this planet."

"Which is helpful," I returned bitterly, "since I lack the years it could take to run him down on name alone. This is one of the most densely populated worlds in the inner systems."

"True. But if a man such as Kafu saw this Tacktile as your aid, then he would be known to other gem dealers also, would he not? And I would suggest—"

But this time I was ahead of him. "I make the rounds, not accepting Kafu's word that I am listed. While you try to mind-pick those I meet."

It might just work, though I must depend upon Eet's gifts and not my own this time. However, there was also the thin chance that some one of the minor merchants might take a chance at an undercounter sale when they saw the quality of the stones I had to offer. And I decided to begin with these smaller men.

Evening was close when I had finished that round of disappointing refusals. Disappointing, that is, on the surface. For though some of those I had visited looked with greed on what I had to offer, all of them repeated the formula that I was listed and there was no deal. Only Eet had done his picking of minds, and as I sat in the ship's cabin again, very tired, I was not quite so discouraged as I might have been, for we knew now who Tacktile was and that he was right here in the Off-port.

As my father had done, so did Tacktile here—he operated a hock-lock for spacers wherein those who had tasted too deeply of the pleasures of the Off-port parted with small portable treasures in return for enough either to hit the gaming tables unsuccessfully again or to eat until they shipped out.

Being a hock-lock, he undoubtedly had dealings with the Guild, no matter how well policed his establishment might be. But, and this was both strange and significant, he was an alien from Warlock, a male Wyvern, which was queer. Having for some reason fled that matriarchy and reached Lylestane, he kept his own planet's citizenship and had some contact with it still which the Patrol did not challenge. Thus his holding was almost a quasi consulate for the world of his birth. His relationship with the female rulers of Warlock no one understood, but he was able to handle some off-world matters for them and was given a semidiplomatic status here which allowed him the privilege of breaking minor laws.

Tacktile was not his right name, but a human approximation of the sounds of his clacking speech—for audible speech was used by the males of Warlock while the females were telepathic.

"Well"—Ryzk faced me—"what luck?"

There was no reason to keep the worst from him. And I did not think he would jump ship here in a port where he had already decided he could not even afford to visit the spacer's resorts.

"Bad. I am listed. No merchant will buy."

"So? Do we move out now or in the morning?" He leaned back against the wall of the cabin. "I don't have anything to be attached. And I can always try the labor exchange." His tone was dry and what lay behind it was the dull despair of any planet-bound spacer.

"We do nothing—until I make one more visit—tonight." Time, as it had been since the start of our venture, was our enemy. We must raise our port fees in a twenty-four hour period or we would have the ship base-locked and confiscated.

"But not," I continued, "as Murdoc Jern." For I had

this one small thread of hope left. If I were listed and suspect, then this ship and its crew of two—for Eet might well be overlooked as a factor in our company—would be watched and known. I would have to go in disguise. And already I was working out how that might be done.

"Dark first, then the port passenger section—" I thought out loud. Ryzk shook his head.

"You'll never make it. Even a Guild runner could be picked up here. That entrance is the focus of every scanner in the place. They screen out all the undesirables when they are funneled through at landing."

"I shall chance it." But I did not tell him how. My attempts at Eet's art were still my secret. And all the advantages of any secret lie in the fact that it is not shared.

We ate and Ryzk went back to his own cabin—I think to consider gloomily what appeared to be a black future. That he had any faith in me was now improbable. And I could not be sure he was not right.

But I set up the mirror in my cabin and sat before it. Nothing as simple as a scar now. I must somehow put on another face. I had already altered my clothing, taking off my good tunic and donning instead the worn coveralls of an undercrew man on a tramp freighter.

Now I concentrated on my reflection. What I had set up as a model was a small tri-dee picture. I could not hope to make my copy perfect, but if I could only create a partial illusion—

It required every bit of my energy, and I was shaking with sheer fatigue when I could see the new face. I had the slightly greenish skin of a Zorastian, plus the large eyes, the show of fanged side teeth under tight-stretched, very thin, and near colorless lips. If I could hold this, no watcher could identify me as Murdoc Jern.

"Not perfect." I was shaken out of my survey of my

new self by Eet's comment. "The usual beginner's reach for the outré. But in this case, possible, yes, entirely possible, since this is an inner planet with a big mingling of ship types."

Eet—I had turned to look—was no longer a pookha. Nor was he Eet. Instead there lay on my bunk a serpent shape with a narrow, arrow-shaped head. The kind of a life form it was I could not put name to.

There was no question that Eet was going to accompany me. I could not depend now on my limited human senses alone, and what rested on my visit to Tacktile was more important than my pride.

The reptile wound about my arm, coiled there as a massive and repulsive bracelet, its head a little upraised to view. And we were ready to go, but not openly down the ramp.

Instead I descended through the core of the ship to a hatch above the fins, and in the dark felt for the notches set on one of those supports for the convenience of repair techs. So that we hit ground in the ship's shadow.

I had Ryzk's ident disk, but hoped I would not have to show it. And luckily there was a liberty party from one of the big intersolar ships straggling across the field. As I had done when disembarking from our first port, I tailed this and we tramped in a group through the gate. Any reading on me would be reported as my own and I had the liberty of the port. But the scanners, being robos, would not report that my identity did not match my present outward appearance. Or so I hoped as I continued to tag along behind the spacers, who steered straight for the Off-port.

This was not as garish and strident as that in which I had found Ryzk—at least on the main street. I had a very short distance to go, since the sharply peaked roof of

Tacktile's shop could be seen plainly from the gate. He appeared to depend upon the strange shape of his roof rather than a sign for advertisement.

That roof was so sharply slanted that it formed a very narrow angle at the top and the eaves well overhung the sides. There was an entrance door so tall it seemed narrower than it was, but no windows. The door gave easily under my touch.

Hock-locks were no mystery to me. Two counters on either side made a narrow aisle before me. Behind each were shelves along the wall, crowded with hock items, protected by a thin haze of force field. It would seem Tacktile conducted a thriving business, for there were four clerks in attendance, two on either side. One was of Terran blood, and there was a Trystian, his feathered head apparently in molt, as the fronds had a ragged appearance. The gray-skinned, warty-hided clerk nearest me I did not recognize, but beyond him was another whose very presence there was a jarring note.

In the galaxy there is an elder race, of great dignity and learning—the Zacathans, of lizard descent. These are historians, archaeologists, teachers, scholars, and never had I seen one in a mercantile following before. But there was no mistaking the race of the alien, who stood in a negligent pose against the wall, fitting the strip of reader tape in his clawed hands into a recorder.

The gray creature blinked sleepily at me, the Trystian seemed remote in some personal misery, and the Terran grinned ingratiatingly and leaned forward.

"Greetings, Gentle Homo. Your pleasure is our delight." He mouthed the customary welcome of his business. "Credits promptly to hand, no hard bargaining—we please at once!"

I wanted to deal directly with Tacktile and that was going to be a matter of some difficulty—unless the Wyvern had Guild affiliations. If that were so, I could use the knowledge of the correct codes gained from my father to make contact. But I was going to have to walk a very narrow line between discovery and complete disaster. If Tacktile was honest, or wanted to protect a standing with the Patrol, the mere showing of what I carried would lead to denunciation. If he was Guild, the source of my gems would be of interest. Either way I was ripe for betrayal and must make my deal quickly. Yet I knew well the value of what I held and was going to lose no more of the profit than I was forced to.

I gave the Terran what I hoped was a meaningful stare and out of the past I recalled what I hoped would work— unless the code had been changed.

"By the six arms and four stomachs of Saput," I mumbled, "it is pleasing I need now."

The clerk did not show any interest. He was either well schooled or wary.

"You invoke Saput, friend. Are you then late from Jangour?"

"Not so late that I am forgetful enough to wish to return. Her tears make a man remember—too much." I had now given three of the Guild code phrases which in the old days had signified an unusual haul, for the attention of the master of the shop only. They had been well drilled into me when I had stood behind just such a counter in my father's establishment.

"Yes, Saput is none too kind to off-worlders. You will find better treatment here, friend." He had placed one hand palm-down on the counter. With the other he pushed out a dish of candied bic plums, as if I must be wooed as a buyer in one of the Veep shops uptown.

I picked up the top plum, laying the smallest of the greenstones in its place. A quick flicker of eyes told him what I had done. He withdrew the dish, putting it under the counter, where I knew a small visa-com would pick up the sight for Tacktile.

"You have, friend?" he continued smoothly. I laid down one of the lesser zorans from my unhappy Lorgal trade.

"It is flawed." He gave it a quick professional examination. "But as it is the first zoran we have taken in in some time, well, we shall do our best for you. Hock or sale?"

"Sale."

"Ah, we can hock but not buy. For sale you must deal with the master. And sometimes he is not in the mood. You would do better at hock, friend. Three credits—"

I shook my head as might a stupid crewman set for a higher price. "Four credits—outright sale."

"Very well, I shall ask the master. If he says no, it will not even be hock, friend, and you will have lost all." He allowed his finger to hover over the call button set in the counter as if awaiting some change in my mind. I shook my head and with a commiserating shrug he pressed the button.

Why the elaborate byplay I did not know. Except for me there was no one else in the shop, and surely the other clerks were equally well versed in the code. The only answer must be that they feared some type of snoop ray, at least in the public portion of the shop.

A brief spark of light flashed by the button and the clerk motioned me toward the back of the shop. "Don't say you weren't warned, friend. Your stone is not enough to interest the master, and you shall lose all the way."

"I will see." I passed the other clerks, neither of whom looked at me. As I came to the end of the aisle a section of wall swung in and I was in Tacktile's office.

It did not surprise me to see the dish of sticky plums on his desk, the greenstone already laid out conspicuously in a pool of light. He raised his gargoyle head, his deep-set eyes searching me, and I was glad that he lacked that other sense given Wyvern females and could not read my thoughts.

"You have more of these?" He came directly to the point.

"Yes, and better."

"They are listed stones, with a criminal history?"

"No, received in fair trade."

He rapped his blunted talons on the desk top, almost uneasily. "What is the deal?"

"Four thousand credits, on acceptance of value."

"You are one bereft of wits, stranger. These on the open market—"

"At auction they would bring five times that amount." He did not offer me a seat, but I took the stool on the other side of the desk.

"If you want your twenty thousand, let them go at auction," he returned. "If they are indeed clean stones, there is no reason not to."

"There is a reason." I moved two fingers in a sign.

"So that is the way of it." He paused. "Four thousand— well, they can go off world. You want cash?"

I gave an inward sigh of relief. My biggest gamble had paid off—he had accepted me as a Guild runner. Now I shook my head. "Deposit at the port."

"Well, very well." Eet's words were in my mind: "He is too afraid not to be honest with us."

Tacktile pulled a recorder to him. "What name?"

"Eet," I told him. "Port credit, four thousand, to one Eet. To be delivered on a voice order repeating," and I gave him code numerals.

I had come to Lylestane with high hopes. I was getting away with a modest return of port fees and supplies, and the danger of making a contact which could alert my enemies.

Now I produced the greenstones, and the Wyvern rapidly separated them. I could tell by his examination that he had some knowledge of gems. Then he nodded and gave the final signal to the recorder.

I retraced my path through the shop and now none of the clerks noticed me. The word had been passed I was to be invisible. When I reached the outside Eet spoke.

"It might be well to drink to your good fortune at the Purple Star." And so out of the ordinary was that suggestion that I was startled into breaking stride. It would be far wiser and better to get back to the ship, to prepare for take-off and rise off world before we got into any more difficulty. Yet Eet's suggestions were, as I well knew from the past, never to be disregarded.

"Why?" I asked and kept on my way, the port lights directly ahead.

"That Zacathan has been planted in Tacktile's," Eet returned as smoothly as if he were reading it all from a tape. "He is hunting for information. Tacktile has it. The Wyvern is to meet someone at the Purple Star within the hour and it is of vast importance."

"Not to us," I denied. The last thing to do was to become involved in some murky deal, especially one with the Guild—

"Not Guild!" Eet cut into my train of thought. "Tacktile is not of the Guild, though he deals with them. This is something else again. Piracy—or Jack raiding—"

"Not for us!"

"You are listed. If the Patrol has done this, you can perhaps buy your way out with pertinent information."

"As we did before? I do not think we can play that game twice. It would have to be information worth a lot—"

"Tacktile was excited, tempted. He visualized a fortune," Eet continued. "Take me into the Purple Star and I can discover what excites him. If you are listed, what kind of future voyages can you expect? Let us buy our freedom. We are still far from seeking the zero stones."

The source of the zero stones had receded from my mind to a half-remembered dream, smothered by the ever-present need to provide us with a living. All my instincts told me that Eet proposed running us headlong into a meteor storm, but the gamble might go two ways. Supposing he could mind-read a meeting between the Wyvern and some mysterious second party—the affair must be important if the Zacathans had seen fit to plant an agent in the shop. And having a drink in a spacers' bar would add to my disguise as an alien crewman who had made a successful deal at the hock-lock.

"Back four buildings," Eet dictated. And when I turned I saw the purple five-pointed light.

It was one of the better-class drinking places and the door attendant eyed me questioningly as I entered with all the boldness I could muster. I thought he was going to bar me, but if that was so he changed his mind and stepped aside.

"Take the booth to the right under the mask of Iuta," Eet ordered. There was another beyond that but the curtain had been dropped to give its occupants privacy. I settled in and punched the robo-server on the table for the least expensive drink in the house—it was all I could afford and I did not intend to drink it anyway. The lights were dim and the occupants very mixed, but more were of Terran descent than alien. I had no sight of Tacktile. Eet moved on my arm so that his arrow head now pointed to the wall between me and the curtained booth.

"Tacktile has arrived," he announced. "Through a sliding wall panel. And his contact is already there. They are scribo-writing."

I could hear the murmur of voices and guessed that those behind me were discussing some ordinary matter while their fingers were busy with the scribos, which could communicate impervious to any snoop ray. But if their thoughts were intent upon their real business, that dodge would not hide their secrets from Eet.

"It is a Jack operation," my companion reported. "But Tacktile is turning it down. He is too wary—rightly so —the victims are Zacathans."

"Some archaeological find, then—"

"True. One of great value apparently. And this is not the first one to be so jacked. Tacktile says the risk is too great, but the other one says it has been set up with much care. There is no Patrol ship within light-years, it will be easy. The Wyvern is holding fast, telling the other to try elsewhere. He is going now."

I raised my glass but did not sip the brew it contained.

"Where and when is the raid?"

"Co-ordinates for the where—he thought of them while talking. No when."

"No concrete proof then for the Patrol," I said sourly, and spilled most of my glass's contents on the floor.

"No," Eet agreed with me. "But we do have the co-ordinates and a warning to the intended victims—"

"Too risky. They might already have been raided and then what? We are caught suspiciously near a Jack raid."

"They are Zacathans," Eet reminded me. "The truth cannot be hid from them, not with one telepath contacting another."

"But you do not know when—it might be now!"

"I do not believe so. They have failed with Tacktile. They must now hunt another buyer, or they may feel they can eventually persuade him. You took a gamble on Sororis. Perhaps this is another for you, with a bigger reward at the end. Get Zacathan backing and your listing will be forgotten."

I got up and went out on the noisy street, the port my goal. In spite of my intentions it would seem that Eet could mold my future, for reason and logic were on his side. Listed, I no longer had a trade. But suppose I did manage to warn some Zacathan expedition of a Jack raid. Not only would it mean that I would gain some very powerful patrons, but the Zacathans dealt only in antiquities and the very great treasure the stranger had used to tempt Tacktile might well be zero stones!

"Just so." There was smug satisfaction in Eet's thought. "And now I would advise a speedy rise from this far from hospitable planet."

I jogged back to the ship, wondering how Ryzk would accept this latest development. To go up against a Jack raid was no one's idea of an easy life. More often it was quick death. Only, with Zacathans involved, the odds were the least small fraction inclined to our side.

9

Below us the ball of the planet was a sphere of Sirenean amber, not the honey-amber or the butter-amber of Terra, but ocher very lightly tinged with green. The green areas grew, assumed the markings of seas. There were no very large land masses but rather sprays of islands and archipelagoes, with only two providing possible landing sites.

Ryzk was excited. He had protested the co-ordinates we had brought back from the Purple Star, saying they were in a sector completely off any known map. Now I think all his Free Trader instincts awoke when he realized that we had homed in on an uncharted world.

We orbited with caution, but there was no trace of any city, no sign that this was anything but an empty world. However, we decided at last that the same tactics used at Sororis would be best here—that Eet and I should leave the ship in orbit and make an exploratory trip in the converted LB. And since it seemed logical that the two largest land masses were the most probable sites for any archaeological dig, I made a choice of the northern.

Dawn was the time we descended. Ryzk, having experimented with the LB, had added some refinements to his original adaptations, making it possible to switch from automatics to hand controls. He had run through the drill patiently with me until he thought I could master the craft. Though I did not have the training of a spacer pilot, I had used flitters since I was a child and the techniques of the LB were not too far from that skill.

Eet, once more in his own form, curled up on the second hammock, allowing me to navigate unhindered as we went in. As the landscape became more distinct on the view-plate I saw that its ocher color was due to trees, or rather giant, lacy growths, waving fronds with delicate trunks hardly thicker than my two fists together. They were perhaps twenty or thirty feet tall and swayed and tossed as if they were constantly swept by wind. In color they shaded from a bright rust-brown to a pale green-yellow with brighter tints of reddish tan between. And they seemed to grow uniformly across the ground, with no sign of any clearing where the LB might set down. I had no desire to crash into the growth, which might be far tougher than it looked, and I went on hand controls to cruise above it, searching vainly for some break. So untouched was that willowy expanse that I had about decided my choice of island had been wrong and that we must head south to investigate the other.

Now the fronds gave way from tall to shorter. Then there was a stretch of red sand in which the sunlight awoke points of sharp glitter. This was washed by the green waves of the sea, and such green I had only seen in the flawless surface of a fine Terran emerald.

At this point the beach was wide and in the middle of it was my first signpost, a broad blot of glassified sand blasted by deter rockets, a ship's landing place. I guided the LB past that a little along the fringe of the growth, bringing it down under the overhang of vegetation with a care of which I was rightfully proud. Unless that mark had been left by a scout, I should be able to find traces of the archaeological camp not too far away, or so I hoped.

The atmosphere was breathable without a helmet. But I took with me something Ryzk had put together. We might not be allowed lasers or stunners, but the former Free Trader had patiently created a weapon of his own, a spring gun which shot needle darts. And those darts were tipped with my contribution, made from zorans too flawed to use, cut with a jeweler's tool, and deadly.

I have used a laser and a stunner, but this, at close range, was to my mind an even deadlier weapon, and only the thought that I might have to front a Jack crew prepared me to carry it. Those in space learned long ago that the first instinct of our species, to attack that which is strange as being also dangerous, could not be allowed to influence us. And in consequence, mind blocks were set on the first explorers. Such precautions continued until those who were explorers and colonizers became inhibited against instant hostility. But there were times when we still needed arms, mainly against our own species.

The stunner with its temporary effect on the opponent was the approved weapon. The laser was strictly a war choice and outlawed for most travelers. But as a former Patrol suspect, I could not have my permit to carry either renewed for a year. I was a "pardoned" man, pardoned for an offense I never committed—something they conveniently forgot. And I had not wish to demand a permit and give them some form of control over me again.

Now that I dropped out of the LB, Eet riding on my shoulder, I was very glad Ryzk had found such an arm. Not that this seemed a hostile world. The sun was bright and warm but not burning hot. And the breeze which kept the fronds ever in play was gentle, carrying with it a scent which would have made a Salarik swoon in delight. From ground level I could see that the trunks of those fronds had smaller branches and those bent under the weight of brilliant scarlet flowers rimmed with gold and bronze. Insects buzzed thickly about these.

The soil was a mixture of red sand and a darker brown earth where the beach gave way to forested land. But I kept to the edge between sand and wood, angling along until I was opposite that patch of glass formed by the heat of the rockets at some ship's fin-down.

There I discovered what had not been visible from above, covered by the trees and vegetation—a path back into the interior of the forest. I am no scout, but elementary caution suggested that I not walk that road openly. However, I soon found that forcing a passage along parallel to the route was difficult. The clusters of flowers beat against my head and shoulders, loosing an overpowering scent, which, pleasant as it was, became a cloying, choking fog when close to the nose. That and a shower of floury, rust-yellow pollen which made the skin itch where it settled finally forced me into the path.

Though fronds had been cut down to open that way, yet the press of the thick growth had spread out overhead to again roof in the channel, providing a dusky, cooling shade. On some of the trees the clusters of flowers were gone and pods hung there, pulling the trunks well out of line with their weight.

The path ran straight, and in the ground underfoot were the marks of robo-carriers. But if the camp had been so well established, why had I not been able to sight it from the air as the LB had passed overhead? Certainly they must have cut down enough fronds to make a clearing for their bubble tents.

Suddenly the trail dipped, leaving rising banks on either side. They had not had to cut a path here, for the earth had been scraped away by their carriers to show a pavement, while the fronds growing on the bank spread to cover the cut completely.

I knelt to examine the pavement, sure that it had been set of a purpose a long time ago, that it was no fortuitous rock shelf. Thus the banks on either hand might well be walls long covered by earth.

The passage continued to deepen and narrow, growing darker and more chill as it went. I slowed my advance to a creep, trying to listen, though the constant sighing of the wind through the fronds might cover any sound.

"Eet?" Finally, out of a need for more than my own five senses, I appealed to my companion.

"Nothing—" His head was raised, swaying slowly from side to side. "This is an old place, very old. There have been men here—" Then he stopped short and I could feel his small body tense against mine.

"What is it?"

"Death smell—there is death ahead."

I had my weapon ready. "Danger for us?"

"No, not now. But death here—"

The cut had now led underground, the earth lips closing the slit above, and what lay ahead was totally dark. I had a belt beamer, but to use it might bring on us the very attention which would be danger.

"Is there anyone here?" I demanded of Eet as I halted, unwilling to enter that pocket of utter black.

"Gone," Eet told me. "But not long ago. And—no—there is a trace of life, very faint. I think someone still lives—a little—"

Eet's answer was obscure, and I did not know whether we dared go on.

"No danger to us," he flashed. "I read pain—no thoughts of anger or of waiting our coming—"

I dared then to trigger the beamer, which flashed on stone walls. The blocks had been so set together that only the faintest of lines marked their joining, with no trace of mortar at all, only a sheen on their surface, as if their natural roughness had been either polished away or given a slick coating. They were a dull red in hue, a shade unpleasantly reminiscent of blood.

As we advanced the space widened, the walls almost abruptly expanding on either side to give one the feeling of being on the verge of some vast underground chamber. But my beamer had picked up something else, a tangle of wrecked gear which had been thrown about, burned by lasers. It was as if a battle had been fought in this space.

And there were bodies—

The too-sweet scent of the flowers was gone, lost in the stomach-twisting stench of seared flesh and blood—until I wanted to reel out of that hole into the clean open.

Then I heard it, not so much a moan as a kind of hissing plaint, with that in it which I could not refuse to answer. I detoured around the worst of the shambles to a place near the wall where something had crawled, leaving a ghastly trail of splotches on the floor that glistened evilly in the beam ray.

It was a Zacathan and he had not been burned down in a surprise attack as had the others I had caught glimpses of amid the chaos of the camp. No, this was such treatment as only the most sadistic and barbaric tribe of some backward planet might have dealt a battle slave.

That he still lived was indicative of the strong bodies of

his species. That he would continue to live I greatly doubted. But I would do all I could for him.

I summoned up determination enough to search through the welter of the camp until I found their medical supplies. Even these had been smashed about. In fact, the whole mess suggested either a wild hunt for something hidden or else destruction for the mere sake of wanton pillage.

One who roves space must learn a little of first aid and what I knew I applied now to the wounded Zacathan, though I had no idea of how one treated alien ills. But I did my best and left him in what small comfort I could before I went to look about the chamber. To take him back to the LB I needed some form of transportation and the camp trail had the marks of robo-carriers. I had not seen any such machines among the wreckage, which might mean they were somewhere in the dark.

I found one at last, its nose smashed against the wall at the far end of that space as if it had been allowed to run on its own until the stone barrier halted it. But beside it was something else, a dark opening where stones had been taken out of the wall, piled carefully to one side.

Curiosity was strong and I pushed in through that slit and flashed the beamer. There was no mistaking the purpose of the crypt. It had been a tomb. Against the wall facing me was a projecting stone outline, still walled up. Instead of being set horizontally as might be expected of a tomb, it was vertical, so that what lay buried there must stand erect.

There were shelves, but all of them were now bare. And I could imagine that what had stood there once had been taken to the camp and was now Jack loot. I had been too late. Perhaps he who had dealt with Tacktile had not known that the raid was already a fact, or had chosen to suppress that knowledge.

I returned to the carrier. In spite of the force with which it had rammed the wall it was still operative, and I put it in low gear, so that it crawled, with a squeal of protesting metal, back to the Zacathan. Since he was both taller and heavier than I, it was an effort to load his inert body on the top of the machine. But fortunately he did not regain consciousness and I thought one of the balms Eet had suggested I employ had acted as an anesthetic.

There was no use searching the wreckage. It was very plain that the raiders had found what they came for. But the wanton smashing was something I did not understand —unless Jacks were a different breed of thief from the calmly efficient Guild.

"Can you run the carrier?" I asked Eet. It obeyed a simple set of buttons, usable, I believed, by his hand-paws. And if he could run it I would be free to act as guard. Though I thought the Jacks had taken off, there was no sense in not being on the alert.

"Easy enough." He leaped to squat behind the controls, starting the machine, though it still complained noisily.

We reached the LB without picking up any sign that the raiders had lingered here or that there were any other survivors of the archaeological party. Getting the Zacathan into the hammock of the craft was an exhausting job. But I did it at last and flipped the automatic return which would take us to the *Wendwind*.

With Ryzk's help I carried the wounded survivor to one of the lower cabins. The pilot surveyed my improvised treatment closely and at last nodded.

"Best we can do for him. These boys are tough. They

walk away from crashes that would pulp one of us. What happened down there?"

I described what I had found—the opened tomb, the wreckage of the camp.

"They must have made a real find. Now there's something worth more than all your gem hunting, even if you made a major strike! Forerunner stuff—must have been," Ryzk said eagerly.

The Zacathans are the historians of the galaxy. Being exceptionally long-lived by our accounting of planet years, they have a bent for the keeping of records, the searching out of the source of legends and the archaeological support for such legends. They knew of several star-wide empires which had risen and fallen again before they themselves had come into space. But there were others about whom even the Zacathans knew very little, for the dust of time had buried deep all but the faintest hints.

When we Terrans first came into the star lanes we were young compared to many worlds. We found ruins, degenerate races close to extinction, traces over and over again of those who had proceeded us, risen to heights we had not yet dreamed of seeking, then crashed suddenly or withered slowly away. The Forerunners, the first explorers had called them. But there were many Forerunners, not just of one empire or species, and those Forerunners had Forerunners until the very thought of such lost ages could make a man's head whirl.

But Forerunner artifacts were indeed finds to make a man wealthy beyond everyday reckoning. My father had shown me a few pieces, bracelets of dark metal meant to fit arms which were not of human shape, odds and ends. He had treasured these, speculated about them, until all such interest had centered upon the zero stone. Zero stone—I had seen the ruins with the caches of these stones. Had there been any in this tomb which the Zacathans had explored? Or was this merely another branch of limitless history, having no connection with the Forerunner who had used the stones as sources of fantastic energy?

"The Jacks have it all now anyway," I observed. We had rescued a Zacathan who might well die before we could get him to any outpost of galactic civilization, that was all.

"We did not miss them by too much," Ryzk said. "A ship just took off from the south island—caught it on radar as it cut atmosphere."

So they might have set down there and used a flitter to carry out the raid—which meant they had either scouted the camp carefully or had a straight tip about it. Then what Ryzk had said reached my inner alarms.

"You picked them up—could they have picked us up in return?"

"If they were looking. Maybe they thought we were a supply ship and that's why they cut out so fast. In any case, they will not be coming back if they have what they wanted."

No, they would be too anxious to get their loot into safe hiding. Zacathans, armed with telepathic powers, did not make good enemies, and I thought that the Jacks who had pulled this raid must be very sure of a safe hiding place at some point far from any port or they would not have attempted it at all.

"Makes you think of Waystar," commented Ryzk. "Sort of job those pirates would pull."

A year earlier I would have thought Ryzk subscribing to a legend, one of the tall tales of space. But my own experience, when Eet had informed me that the Free Traders who had taken me off Tanth, apparently to save my life after Vondar's murder, had intended to deliver me at Waystar, had given credibility to the story. At least the crew of that Free Trader had believed in the port to which I had been secretly consigned.

But Ryzk's casual mention of it suddenly awoke my suspicions. I had had that near-fatal brush with one Free Trader crew who had operated on the shady fringe of the Guild. Could I now have taken on board a pilot who was also too knowing of the hidden criminal base? And was Ryzk—had he been planted?

It was Eet who saved me from speculation and suspicion which might have been crippling then.

"No. He is not what you fear. He knows of Waystar through report only."

"He"—I indicated the unconscious Zacathan—"might just as well write off his find then."

My try at re-establishing our credit had failed, unless the Zacathan lived long enough for us to get him to some port. Then perhaps the gratitude of his House might work in my favor. Perhaps a cold-blooded measuring of assistance to a fellow intelligent being. Only I was so ridden by my ever-present burden of worry that it was very much a part of my thinking—though I would not have deserted any living thing found in that plundered camp.

I appealed to Ryzk for the co-ordinates to the nearest port. But, though he searched through the computer for any clue as to where we were, he finally could only suggest return to Lylestane. We were off any chart he knew of and to try an unreckoned jump through hyper was a chance no one took, except a First-in Scout as part of his usual duty.

But we did not decide the matter, for as we were arguing it out Eet broke into our dispute to say that our passenger had regained consciousness.

"Leave it up to him," I said. "The Zacathans must have co-ordinates from some world to reach here. And if he can remember those, we can return him to his home base. Best all around—"

However, I was not at all sure that the alien, as badly wounded as he was, could guide us. Yet a return to Lylestane was for me a retracing of a way which might well lead to more and more trouble. If he died and we turned up with only his body on board, who would believe our story of the Jacked camp? It could be said that we had been responsible for the raid. My thinking was becoming more and more torturous the deeper I went into the muddle. It seemed that nothing had really gone right for me since I had taken the zero stone from its hiding place in my father's room, that each move I made, always hoping for the best, simply pushed me deeper into trouble.

Eet flashed down the ladder at a greater speed than we could make. And we found him settled by the head of the bed we had improvised for the wounded alien. The latter had his bandaged head turned a little, was watching the mutant with his one good eye. That they were conversing telepathically was clear. But their mental wave length was not mine, and when I tried to listen in, the sensation was like that of hearing a muttering of voices at the far side of a room, a low sound which did not split into meaning.

As I came from behind Eet the Zacathan looked up, his eye meeting mine.

"Zilwrich thanks you, Murdoc Jern." His thoughts had a sonorous dignity. "The little one tells me that you have the mind-touch. How is it that you came before the last flutters of my life were done?"

I answered him aloud so Ryzk could also understand, telling in as few words as possible about our overhearing of the Jack plot, and why and how we had come to the amber world.

"It is well for me that you did so, but ill for my comrades that it was not sooner." He, too, spoke Basic now. "You are right that it was a raid for the treasures we found within a tomb. It is a very rich find and a remainder of a civilization not heretofore charted. So it is worth far more than just the value of the pieces—it is worth knowledge!" And he provided that last word with such emphasis as I might accord a flawless gem. "They will sell the treasure to those collectors who value things enough to hide them for just their own delight. And the knowledge will be lost!"

"You know where they take it?" Eet asked.

"To Waystar. So it would seem that that is not a legend after all. They have one there who will buy it from them, as has been done twice lately with such loot. We have tried to find who has betrayed our work to these stit beetles, but as yet we have no knowledge. Where do you take me now?" He changed the subject with an abrupt demand.

"We have no co-ordinates from here except those for return to Lylestane. We can take you there."

"Not so!" His denial was sharp. "To do that would be to lose important time. I am hurt in body, that is true, but the body mends when the will is bent to its aid. I must not lose this trail—"

"They blasted into hyper. We cannot track them." Ryzk shook his head. "And the site of Waystar is the best-guarded secret in the galaxy."

"A mind may be blocked where there is fear of losing such a secret. But a blocked mind is also locked against needful use," returned Zilwrich. "There was one among those eaters of dung who came at the last to look about, see that nothing of value was left. His mind held what we must know—the path to Waystar."

"Oh, no!" I read enough of the thought behind his words to deny what he suggested at once. "Maybe the Fleet could blast their way in there. We cannot."

"We need not blast," corrected Zilwrich. "And the time spent on the way will be used to make our plans."

I stood up. "Give us the co-ordinates of your base world. We will set you down there and you can contact the Patrol. This is an operation for them."

"It is anything but a Patrol operation," he countered. "They would make it a Fleet matter, blast to bits any opposition. And how much would then be left of the treasure? One man, two, three, four"—he could not move his head far but somehow it was as if he had pointed to each of us in turn—"can go with more skill than an army. I shall give you only those co-ordinates."

I had opened my mouth for a firm refusal when Eet's command rang in my head. "Agree! There is an excellent reason."

And, in spite of myself, in spite of knowing that no excellent reason for such stupidity could exist, I found myself agreeing.

10

It was so wild a scheme that I suspected the Zacathan of exerting some mental influence to achieve his ends—though such an act was totally foreign to all I had ever heard of his species. And since we were committed to this folly, we would have to make plans within the framework of it. We dared not go blindly into the unknown.

To my astonishment, Ryzk appeared to accept our destination with equanimity, as if our dash into a dragon's mouth was the most natural thing in the world. But I held a session in which we pooled what we knew of Waystar. Since most was only legend and space tales, it would be of little value, a statement I made gloomily.

But Zilwrich differed. "We Zacathans are sifters of legends, and we have discovered many times that there are rich kernels of truth hidden at their cores. The tale of Waystar has existed for generations of your time, Murdoc Jern, and for two generations of ours—"

"That—that means it antedates our coming into space!" Ryzk interrupted. "But—"

"Why not?" asked the Zacathan. "There have always been those outside the law. Do you think your species alone invented raiding, crime, piracy? Do not congratulate or shame yourselves that this is so. Star empires in plenty have risen and fallen and always they had those who set their own wills and desires, lusts and envies, against the common good. It is perfectly possible that Waystar has long been a hide-out for such, and was rediscovered by some of your kind fleeing the law, who thereafter put it to the same use. Do you know those co-ordinates?" he asked Ryzk.

The pilot shook his head. "They are off any trade lane. In a 'dead' sector."

"And what better place—in a sector where only dead worlds spin about burned-out suns? A place which is avoided, since there is no life to attract it, no trade, no worlds on which living things can move without cumbersome protection which makes life a burden."

"One of those worlds could be Waystar?" I hazarded.

"No. The legend is too plain. Waystar is space-borne. Perhaps it was even once a space station, set up eons ago when the dead worlds lived and bore men who reached for the stars. If so, it has been in existence longer than our records, for those worlds have always been dead to us."

He had given us a conception of time so vast we could not measure it. Ryzk frowned.

"No station could go on functioning, even on atomics—"

"Do not be too sure even of that," Zilwrich told him. "Some of the Forerunners had machines beyond our comprehension. You have certainly heard of the Caverns of Arzor and of that Sargasso planet of Limbo where a device intended for war and left running continued to pull ships to crash on its surface for thousands of years. It is not beyond all reckoning that a space station devised by such aliens would continue to function. But also it could have been converted, by desperate men. And those criminals would thus have a possession of great value, if they could continue to hold it—something worth selling—"

"Safety!" I cut in. Though Waystar was not entirely Guild, yet surely the Guild had some ties there.

"Just so," agreed Eet. "Safety. And if they believe they have utter safety there we may be sure of two things. One, that they do have some defenses which would hold perhaps even against Fleet action, for they cannot think that the situation of their hole would never be discovered. Second, that having been so long in the state of safety, they might relax strict vigilance."

But before Eet had finished, Ryzk shook his head. "We had better believe the former. If anyone not of their kind had gotten in and out again, we would know it. A story like that would sweep the lanes. They have defenses which really work."

I called on imagination. Persona detectors, perhaps locked, not to any one personality, but rather to a state of mind, so that any invader could pass only if he were a criminal or there on business. The Guild was rumored to buy or otherwise acquire inventions which the general public did not know existed. Then they either suppressed them or exploited them with care. No, such a persona detector might be possible.

"But such could be 'jammed,'" was Eet's answer.

Ryzk, who could follow Eet's mental broadcast but not mine (which was good for us both, as I well knew), looked puzzled. I explained. And then he asked Eet:

"How could you jam it? You can't tamper with a persona beam."

"No one ever tried telepathically," returned the mutant. "If disguise can deceive the eye, and careful manipulation of sound waves, the ear, a change in mental channels can do the same for a persona detector of the type Murdoc envisioned."

"That is so," Zilwrich agreed. I must accept the verdict of the two of our company who best knew what was possible with a sixth sense so few of my own species had.

Ryzk leaned back in his seat. "Since we two do not have the right mental equipment, that lets us out. And you, and you"—he nodded to Eet and Zilwrich—"are not able to try it alone."

"Unfortunately your statement is correct," said the alien. "Limited as I now am by my body, I would be a greater hindrance than help—in person—to any such penetration. And if we wait until I am healed"—he could not move enough to shrug—"then we are already lost. For they will have disposed of what they have taken. We were under Patrol watch back there—"

I stiffened. So we had been lucky indeed in our quick descent and exit from the island world. Had we come during a Patrol visit—

"When the expedition's broadcast signal failed they must have been alerted. And since the personnel of our expedition are all listed, they will be aware of my absence. But also they have evidence of the raid. The Jacks must have foreseen this, since they have been acting on a reliable source of information. And so they will be quick to dispose of their loot."

I thought I saw one fallacy in his reasoning. "But if they have taken the loot to Waystar, and they need not fear pursuit there, then they may believe they have plenty of time to wait for a high bid on it and not be so quick to sell."

"They will sell it, probably to some resident buyer. No

Jack ship will have the patience to sit on a good haul." Surprisingly Ryzk took up the argument. "They may even have a backer. Some Veep who wants the stuff for a private deal."

"Quite true," said Zilwrich. "But we must get there before the collection is dispersed, or even, Zludda forbid, broken up for the metal and gems! There was that among it—yes, I will tell you so you may know the prime importance of what we seek. There was among the pieces a star map!"

And even I who was sunk in foreboding at that moment knew a thrill at that. A star map—a chart which would give those who could decode it a chance to trace some ancient route, even the boundaries of one of the fabled empires. Such a find had never been made before. It was utterly priceless and yet its worth might not be understood by those who had stolen it.

Not be recognized for what it was—my thoughts clung to that. From it sprang a wilder idea. My father had had fame throughout the Guild for appraising finds, especially antiquities. He had had no ambition to climb to Veep status with always the fear of death from some equally ambitious rival grinning behind his shoulder. He had indeed bought out and presumedly retired when his immediate employer in the system had been eliminated. But he was so widely known that he had become an authority, borrowed at times from his Veep to assist in appraising elsewhere. And he had been noted for dealing with Forerunner treasure.

Who would be the appraiser on Waystar? He would have to be competent, trusted, undoubtedly with Guild affiliations. But supposing that a man of vast reputation turned up at Waystar fleeing the Patrol, which was a very common occupational hazard. He might make his way quietly at first, but then that very reputation would spread to the Veep who had the treasure and he might be asked for an independent report. All a series of if's, and's, but's, but still holding together with a faint logic. The only trouble was that the man who could do this was dead.

I was so intent upon my thoughts that I was only dimly aware that Ryzk had begun to say something and had been silenced by a gesture from Eet. They were all staring at me, the two who were able to follow my thoughts seemingly bemused. My father was dead, and that appeared to put a very definite end to what might have been accomplished had he been alive. It was a useless speculation to follow, yet I continued to think about the advantage my father would have had. Suppose an appraiser in good standing with the Guild when he retired, one with special knowledge of Forerunner artifacts, were to show up at Waystar, settle down without any overt approach to the Veep who had the treasure. It would very logically follow that he would be asked to inspect the loot and then— But at that point my speculation stopped short. I could not foresee action leading to the retaking of the treasure—that could only be planned after the setup on Waystar had been reconnoitered.

Must be planned! I was completely moon-dazed to build on something impossible. Hywel Jern was dead for near to three planet years now. And his death, which had undoubtedly been ordered by the Guild, would be common knowledge. His reputation, in spite of his years of retirement, was too widespread for it to be otherwise. He was *dead!*

"Reports have been wrong before." That suggestion

slid easily into my thoughts before I knew Eet had fed it.

"Not in the case of executions carried out by the Guild," I retorted, aroused from my preoccupation with a plan which might have been useful had I only stood in my father's boots.

My father's boots—had that been a sly manipulation of Eet's? No, I was sensitive enough now to his insinuations to be sure that it had been born inside my own mind. When I was a child I had looked forward to being a copy of Hywel Jern. He had filled my life nearly to the exclusion of all else. I did not know until years later that my luke-warm feeling for his wife, son, and daughter must have come from the fact that I was a "duty" child, one of those babies sent from another planet for adoption by a colony family in order to vary what might become too inborn a strain. I had felt myself Jern's son, and I continued to feel that even when my foster mother disclosed the true facts after Jern's death, jealously pointing out that my "brother" Faskel was the rightful heir to Jern's shop and estate.

Hywel Jern had done as well by me as he could. I had been apprenticed to a gem buyer, a man of infinite resources and experience, and I had been given the zero stone, as well as all I could absorb of my father's teachings. He had considered me, I was fully convinced, the son of his spirit, if not of his body.

There might be some record somewhere of my true parentage; I had never cared to pursue the matter. But I thought that the same strain of aloof curiosity and restlessness which had marked Hywel Jern must also have been born into me. Given other circumstances I might well have followed him into the Guild.

So—I had wanted to be like Hywel Jern. Would it be

possible for me to *be* Jern for a period of time? The risk such an imposture would entail would be enormous. But with Eet and his esper powers—"

"I wondered," the mutant thought dryly, "when you would begin to see clearly."

"What's this all about?" Ryzk demanded with some heat. "You"—he looked almost accusingly at me—"you have some plan to get into Waystar?"

But I was answering Eet, though I did so aloud, as if to deny the very help which might be the key to the whole plan. "It is too wild. Jern is dead, they would be sure of that!"

"Who is Jern and what has his death got to do with it?" Ryzk wanted to know.

"Hywel Jern was the top appraiser for one sector Veep of the Guild, and my father." I stated the facts bleakly. "They murdered him—"

"On contract?" asked Ryzk. "If he's dead, how is he of any use to us now? Sure, I can see how an appraiser with Guild rank might get into Waystar. But—" He paused and scowled. "You got some idea of pretending to be your father? But they would know—if there was a contract on him, they'd know."

Only now I was not quite so sure of that. My father had been in retirement. True enough, he had been visited from time to time by Guild men. I had had my proof of that when I had recognized as one of those visitors the captain of the Guild ship who had ordered my questioning on the unknown world of the zero-stone caches. Jern must have been killed by Guild orders for the possession of the zero stone, which his slayers did not find. But supposing they had left a body in which they thought life extinct and my father had revived? There had been a funeral service carried out by his family. But that, too, was an old cover for a man's escape from vengeance. And on the sparsely settled frontier planet he had chosen for his home, they could not have investigated too much for fear of detection.

So, we had Hywel Jern resurrected, smuggled off world perhaps— There were many radical medical techniques —plastic surgery which could alter a man. No, that was wrong. It must be an unmistakable Hywel Jern to enter Waystar. I tried again to dismiss the plan busy fitting itself together piece by piece in my mind—utter folly, logic told me it was. But I could not. I must look like Hywel Jern. And my appearance would be baffling, for who would believe that someone would assume the appearance of a dead man, and one who had been killed by Guild orders? Such a circumstance might give me even quicker access to the Veeps on Waystar. If past rumor spoke true, there was a rivalry between the Veeps of Waystar and the center core of the Guild. The former might well receive a fugitive, one they could use, even if he were now Guild-proscribed. After all, once at their station, he would be largely a prisoner they could control utterly.

Thus—Hywel Jern, running from the Patrol. After all, I *had* been a quarry of both sides for a while because I had the zero stone. The zero stone. My thoughts circled back to that. I had not put to any use the one I carried next to my body—not experimented to step up the *Wendwind*'s power as Eet and I had discovered it could do. I had not even looked at it in weeks, merely felt in my belt at intervals to know I still carried it.

To dare even hint that I carried such would make me an instant target for the Guild, break the uneasy truce, if that still held, between the Patrol (who might suspect but could not be sure) and me. No, that I could not use to enter the pirate station. Back to Hywel Jern. He had never been on Waystar. Of that I was reasonably certain. So he would not have to display familiarity with any part of it. And with Eet to pick out of minds what I *should* know—

But could I be Hywel Jern for the length of time it would—might well—take for the locating of the loot? I had held my scar-faced disguise for only hours, the alien countenance I had devised for the Lylestane venture even less. And I would have to be Hywel Jern perhaps for days, keeping up that façade at all times lest I be snooped or surprised.

"It cannot be done, not by me," I told Eet, since I knew that he, of the three facing me, was the one waiting for my decision, preparing arguments to counter it.

"You could not hold it either," I continued, "not for so long."

"There you speak the truth," he agreed.

"Then it is impossible."

"I have discovered"—Eet assumed that pontifical air which I found most irksome, which acted on me as a spur even when I was determined not to be ridden by him in any direction—"that few things, very few things, are impossible when one has all the facts and examines them carefully. You did well with the scar—for one of your limited ability—your native ability. You did even better with your alien space man. There is no reason why you cannot—"

"I cannot hold it—not for the necessary length of time!" I shot back at him, determined to find, for once and all, an answer which would satisfy my own thoughts as well as the subtle compulsion I sensed coming from both telepaths.

"That, too, can be considered," Eet returned evasively. "But now, rest is needed for our friend."

148

And I awoke to the fact that the Zacathan had indeed slumped on his bed. His eye was near closed and he appeared to be completely exhausted. Together with Ryzk I worked to make him as comfortable as possible and then I went to my own cabin.

I threw myself on my bunk. But I found that I could not shut off my thoughts, bent as they were, in spite of my desires, on the solving of what seemed to be the first of the insurmountable problems. So I lay staring up at the ceiling of the cabin, trying to break my problem down logically. Hywel Jern might get into Waystar. Possibly I could use Eet's form of disguise to become Hywel Jern. But the exertion of holding that would be a drain which could exhaust both of us and might not leave my mind clear enough to be as alert as I must be to cope with the dangers awaiting us in the heart of the enemies' territory.

If there was only some way to increase my power to hold the illusion without draining myself and Eet. For Eet must have freedom for the mind reading which would be the additional protection we had to have. Increase the power—just as we were able to increase the power of the Patrol scout with the zero stone. The zero stone!

My fingers sought that very small bulge in my belt. I sat up and swung my feet to the cabin floor. For the first time in weeks I unsealed that pocket and brought out the colorless, unattractive lump which was the zero stone in its unawakened phase.

Zero stone—energy, extra energy for machines, for stepping up their power. But when I strove to create the illusions, I used energy of another kind. Still it was energy. But my race had for so long been used to the idea of energy only in connection with machines that this was a new thought. I closed both my hands over the gem, so that its rough edges pressed tightly, painfully, into my flesh.

The zero stone plus a machine already alive with energy meant a heightened flow, an output which had been almost too much for the engine in the scout ship to handle. Zero stones had apparently powered the drifting derelict we had found in space, Eet and I. And it had been their energy broadcast that had activated the stone I then carried, causing it to draw us to the derelict in the first place. Just as on the unnamed planet a similar broadcast had guided us to the long-forsaken ruins where the stones' owners had left their caches.

Energy— But the idea which was in my mind was no wilder than others that had visited me lately. There was a very simple trial. Not on myself, not yet. I was wary of experimentation I might not be able to control. I looked about me hurriedly, seeing Eet curled, apparently asleep, on the foot of my bunk. For a moment I hesitated—Eet? There was humor in that, and something else—the desire to see Eet for once startled out of his usual competent control over the situation.

I stared at Eet. I held the zero stone, and I thought—

The cold gem between my hands began to warm, grew hotter. And the lines of Eet's body began to dim. I dared not allow one small spark of triumph to break my concentration. The stone was afire almost past the point where I could continue to hold it. And Eet—Eet was gone! What lay on the foot of my bunk now was what his mother had been, a ship's cat.

I had to drop the stone. The pain was too intense for me to continue to hold it. Eet came to his feet in one of those quick feline movements, stretched his neck to right and left, to look along his body, and then faced me, his cat's ears flattened to his skull, his mouth open in an angry hiss.

"You see!" I was exultant.

But there was no answer to my mind-touch—nothing at all. It was not that I met the barrier which Eet used to cut off communication when he desired to retire into his own thoughts. Rather it seemed that Eet was not!

I sank down on the pull seat to stare back at the angry cat now crouched snarling, as if to spring for my throat. Could it be true that I had done more than create an illusion? It was as if Eet *was* now a cat and not himself at all! I had indeed stepped up energy and to what disastrous point? Frantically I took the stone tightly into my seared hands, grasped it between my painful palms, and set about undoing what I had done.

No cat, I thought furiously, but Eet—Eet in his mutation from the enraged bundle of fur now facing me with anger enough, had it been larger, to tear out my life. Eet, my thoughts commanded as I fought panic and tried only to concentrate on what I *must* do—get Eet back again.

Again the stone warmed, burned, but I held it in spite of the torment to my flesh. The furry contours of the cat dimmed, changed. Eet crouched there now, his rage even somehow heightened by the change into his rightful body. But was it truly Eet?

"Fool!" That single word, hurled at me as a laser beam might be aimed, made me relax. This was Eet.

He leaped to the table between us, stalked back and forth, lashing his ridged tail; in his fury, very feline.

"Child playing with fire," he hissed.

I began to laugh then. There had been little to amuse one in the weeks immediately behind us, but the relief of having pulled off this impossibility successfully, plus the pleasure of having at last surprised and bested Eet in his own field, made me continue to laugh helplessly, until I leaned weakly back against the wall of the cabin, unwitting of the pain in my hands.

Eet stopped his angry pacing, sat down in a feline posture (it seemed to me his cat ancestry was more notable than before) with his tail curled about him so that its tip rested on his paws. He had closed his mind tightly, but I was neither alarmed nor abashed by his attitude. I was very sure that Eet's startled reaction to transformation was only momentary and that his alert intelligence would speedily be bent to consider the possibilities of what we had learned.

I stowed the stone carefully in my belt and treated my burned hands with a soothing paste. The mutant continued to sit statue-still and I made no further attempts at mind-touch, waiting for him to make the first move.

That I had made a momentous discovery exhilarated me. At that moment nothing seemed outside my grasp. It was not only machine energy which the zero stone furthered; it could also be mental. As a cat, Eet had been silenced and, I was sure, unable by himself to break the image I had thought on him, even for his own defense. This must mean that any illusion created with the aid of the stone would have no time limit, remaining so until one thought it away.

"Entirely right." Eet came out of his sulk—or perhaps it was a deep study. His rage also seemed to have vanished. "But you were indeed playing with a fire which might have consumed us both!" And I knew that he did not mean the burns on my hands. Even so, I was not going to say that I was sorry the experiment had worked. We needed it. Hywel Jern could indeed go to Waystar and it would require no expenditure of energy to keep the illusion intact as long as he carried the zero stone.

"To take that in," remarked Eet, "is a great hazard." And his reluctance puzzled me.

"You suspect"—I thought I guessed what bothered him—"they might have one, able to pick up emanations from ours?"

"We do not know what the Guild had as their original guide to the stones. And Waystar would be an excellent stronghold for the keeping of such. But I agree that we cannot be choosers. We must take such a chance."

11

"It must be here." Ryzk had brought us out of hyper in a very old system where the sun was an almost-dead red dwarf, the planets orbiting around it black and burned-out cinders. He indicated a small asteroid. "There is a defense shield up there. And I don't see how you are going to break through that. They must have an entrance code and anything not answering that and getting within range—" He snapped his fingers in a significant gesture of instantaneous extinction.

Zilwrich studied what showed on the small relay visa-screen we had set up in his cabin. He leaned against the back rest we had improvised, his inert head frill crumpled about his neck. But though he appeared very weak, his eye was bright, and I think that the interest in the un-usual which motivated his race made him forget his wounds now.

"If I only had my equipment!" He spoke Basic with the hissing intonation of his species. "Somehow I do not believe that is a true asteroid."

"It may be a Forerunner space station. But knowing that is not going to get us in undetected," rasped Ryzk.

"We cannot all go in," I said. "We play the same game over. Eet and I shall take in the LB."

"Blasting through screens?" scoffed Ryzk. "I tell you, our detect picked up emanations as strong as any on a defensive Patrol outpost. You'd be lasered out of existence quicker than one could pinch out an angk bug!"

"Suppose one dogged in a ship which did have the pass code," I suggested. "The LB is small enough not to enlarge the warn beep of such a one—"

"And when are you going to pick up a ship to dog in?" Ryzk wanted to know. "We might hang here for days—"

"I think not," Eet cut in. "If this is truly Waystar, then there will be traffic, enough to cut down days of waiting. You are the pilot. Tell us if this could be done —could the LB ride in behind another ship in that way?"

It secretly surprised me that there were some things Eet did *not* know. Ryzk scowled, his usual prelude to concentrated thought.

"I could rig a distort combined with a weak traction beam. Cut off the power when that connected with another ship. You'd have this in your favor—those defenses may only be set for big stuff. They'd expect the Fleet to burn them out, not a one-man operation. Or they might detect and let you through. Then you'd find a welcome-guard waiting, which would probably be worse than being lasered out at first contact."

He seemed determined to paint the future as black as possible. I had only what I had learned of the zero stone to support me against the very unpleasant possibilities ahead. Yet the confidence my experiment had bred in me wavered only in the slightest degree.

In the end, Ryzk turned his Free Trader's ingenuity to more work on the LB, giving it what defenses he could devise. We could not fight, but we were now provided with distorters which would permit us to approach the blot our ship's radar told us was Waystar, and then wait for the slim chance of making a run into the enemies' most securely guarded fortress.

Meanwhile, the *Wendwind* set down on the moon of the nearest dead planet, a ball of creviced rock so bleak and black that it should afford a good hiding place. And the co-ordinates of that temporary landing site were fed into the computer of the LB to home us if and when we left the pirate station—though Ryzk was certain we would never be back and said so frankly, demanding at last that I make a ship recording releasing him from contract and responsibility after an agreed-upon length of time. This I did, Zilwrich acting as witness.

All this did not tend to make me set about the next part of our venture with a great belief in success. I kept feeling the lump of the zero stone as a kind of talisman against all that could go wrong, too long a list of possible disasters to count.

Eet made a firm statement as we prepared our disguise.

"I choose my own form!" he said in a manner I dared not question.

We were in my cabin, for I had no wish to share the secret of the zero stone with either Ryzk or the Zacathan —though what they might think of our disguises I could not tell.

But Eet's demand was fair enough. I took the dull, apparently lifeless gem and laid it on the table between us. My own change was already thought out. But in case I needed a reminder on some details, I had something else, a vividly clear tri-dee of my father. He had never willingly allowed such to be taken, but this had belonged to my foster mother and had been the one thing I had taken, besides the zero stone, from my home when his death closed its doors to me. Why I had done so I could not have said—unless there was buried deep inside me a fragment of true esper talent, that of precognition. I had not looked at the tri-dee since the day I had lifted from that planet. Now, studying it carefully, I was very glad I had it. The face I remembered had, as usual, been hazed by time, and I found memory differed from this more exact record.

Warned by the fury of heat in the stone when I had used it on Eet, I touched it now with some care, my attention centering on the tri-dee, concentrating on the face appearing therein. I was only dimly aware that Eet crouched on the table, a clawed hand-paw joining mine in touching the jewel.

I could not be sure of the change in my outward appearance. I felt no different. But after an interval I glanced at the mirror ready for the necessary check, and indeed saw a strange face there. It was my father, yes, but in a subtle way younger than I remembered him last. But then I was using as my guide a picture taken planet years before I knew him, when he had first wed my foster mother.

There could certainly be no mistaking his sharp, almost harsh features by anyone who had ever known him. And I hoped that Eet could help me carry out the rest of the deception by mind reading and supplying me with the memories necessary to make me a passable counterfeit of a man known in Guild circles.

Eet—what had been his choice of disguise? I fully expected something such as the pookha or the reptilian form he had taken on Lylestane. But this I did not foresee. For it was no animal sitting cross-legged on the table, but a humanoid perhaps as large as a human child of five or six years.

The skin was not smooth, but covered with a short plushy fur, much like that of the pookha. On the top of the head this grew longer, into a pointed crest. Only the palms of the hands were bare of the fur, which in color was an inky black, and the skin bared there was red, as were the eyes, large and bulging a little from their sockets, the red broken only by vertical pupils. The nose had a narrow ridge of fur up and down it, giving a greater prominence to that feature. But the mouth showed only very narrow slits of lips and those as black as the fur about them.

To my knowledge I had neither seen nor heard described such a creature, and why Eet had chosen to assume this form first intrigued and then bothered me. Space-rovers were addicted to pets and one met with many oddities accompanying their masters. But this was no pet, unusual as it looked. It had the aura of an intelligent life form, one which could be termed "man."

"Just so." Eet gave his old form of agreement. "But I think you will discover that this pirate hold will have varied life forms aboard. And also this body has possibilities which may be an aid in future difficulties."

"What are you?" curiosity made me ask.

"You have no name for me," Eet returned. "This is a life form which I believe long gone from space."

He ran his red-palmed hands over his furred sides, absent-mindedly scratching his slightly protrudent middle. "You, yourselves, admit you are late-comers to the stars. Let it suffice that this is an adequate body for my present need."

I hoped Eet was right, as there was no use in arguing with him. Now I saw something else. That hand not occupied with methodical hide-scratching hovered near the zero stone—though if Eet was preparing to snatch that treasure I did not see where, in his present un-clothed state, he would stow it. However, my fingers closed promptly on the gem and sealed it back in my belt. Eet was apparently not concerned, for his straying hand dropped back on his knee.

We bade good-by to Ryzk and the Zacathan. And I did not miss that Zilwrich watched Eet with an attention which might have been rooted in puzzlement but which grew into a subdued excitement, as if he recognized in that black-furred body something he knew.

Ryzk stared at us. "How long can you keep that on?" It was plain that he thought our appearances the result of some plasta change. But how he could have believed we carried such elaborate equipment with us I did not know.

"As long as necessary," I assured him and we went to board the greatly altered LB.

As we took off, forceably ejected from the parent ship by the original escape method, we aimed in the general direction of the pirate station. But Ryzk's modifications allowed us to hover in space, waiting a guide. And it was Eet in his new form who took over the controls.

How long we would have to patrol was the question. Waiting in any form is far more wearisome than any ac-tion. We spent the slowly dragging time in silence. I was trying to recall every small scrap of what my father had said about his days with the Guild. And what lay in Eet's mind I would not have tried to guess. In fact, I was far too occupied with the thought that my father had been remarkably reticent about his Guild activities and that there might be as many pitfalls ahead as those pocking the dead moon, with only hair-thick bridges spanning them.

But our silence was broken at last by a clatter from the

control board and I knew our radar had picked up a moving object. The tiny visa-screen gave us a ship heading purposefully for the station. Eet glanced over his shoulder and I thought he was looking at me for orders. The mutant was not accustomed, once a matter had been decided, to wait for permission or agreement. I found myself nodding my head, and his fingers made the necessary adjustments to bring us behind that other ship, a little under its bulk where we might apply that weak traction beam without being sighted, or so we hoped.

The size of the newcomer was in our favor. I had expected something such as a scout ship, or certainly not larger than the smallest Free Trader. But this was a bulk-cargo vessel, of the smallest class, to be sure, but still of a size to be considered only a wallowing second-rate transfer ship.

Our traction beam centered and held, drawing us under the belly of the bigger vessel, which overhung us, if anyone had been out in space to see, as a covering shadow. We waited tensely for some sign that those in the other ship might be alarmed. But as long moments slipped by we breathed more freely, reassured by so much, though it was very little.

However, on the visa-screen what we picked up now was not the ship, but what lay ahead. For additional safety Eet had snapped on the distort beam and through that we could see just a little of the amazing port we neared.

Whatever formed its original core—an asteroid, a moon, an ancient space station—could not be distinguished now. What remained was a mass of ships, derelicts declared so by their broken sides, their general decrepit appearances. They were massed, jammed tightly together into an irregular ovoid except in one place directly before us, where there was a dark gap, into which the ship controlling our path was now headed.

"Looted ships—" I hazarded, ready to believe now in every wild story of Waystar. Pirates had dragged in victim ships to help form their hiding place—though why any such labor was necessary I could not guess. Then I saw—and felt—the faint vibration of a defense screen. The LB shuddered but it did not break linkage with the ship. Then we were through without any attack.

As the wall of those crumpled and broken ships funneled about us, I foresaw a new danger, that we might be scraped or caught by the wreckage, for that space down which we were being towed narrowed the farther we advanced.

Also, though the ships had seemed tightly massed at first sight, this proved not to be so upon closer inspection. There were evidences that they had been intended as an enveloping cover for whatever core lay at the heart. There were girders and patches of skin welded together, anchoring one wreck to another. But it was a loose unity and there were spaces in between, some large enough to hold the LB.

Seeing those, and calculating that we might come to grief ahead were the passage to narrow to the point where only the cargo ship might wedge through, I decided one gamble was better than another.

"Wedge in here"—I made this more a suggestion than an order—"then suit up and go through?"

"Perhaps that is best," Eet answered. However, I suddenly remembered that though I might suit up, there was no protective covering on board which would take Eet's smaller body.

"The disaster bag," Eet reminded me as his hands moved to loose our tie with the bulk of ship overhead.

Of course, the baglike covering intended to serve a seriously injured escapee using the LB, one whose hurt body could not be suited up if the emergency landing had been made on a planet with a hostile atmosphere and it was necessary to leave the boat. I unstrapped, and opened the cupboard where the suit lay at full length. The disaster bag was in tight folds beside its booted feet. Passage in that would leave Eet helpless, wholly dependent on me, but there was hope it would not be for long.

He was busy at the controls, turning the nose of the LB to the left, pointing it into one of those hollows in the mass of wreckage. The impetus left us by the pull of the ship sufficed to give us forward movement, and two girders welded just above the hole we had chosen held the pieces of wreckage forming its walls steady. There was a bump as we scraped in, and another, moments later, as the nose of the LB rammed against some obstacle. We could only hope that the crevice had swallowed us entirely and that our tail was not sticking betrayingly into the ship passage.

I suited up as fast as I could, wanting to make sure of that fact—though what we could do to remedy matters if that had happened I did not have the slightest idea. Then I hauled out the disaster bag and Eet climbed in so that I could make the various sealings tight and inflate its air supply. Since it was made for a man he had ample room, in fact moved about in it in the manner of one swimming in a very limited pool, for there was no gravity in this place and we were in free fall.

Activating the exit port, I crawled out with great care, fearing more than I wanted to admit some raw edge which could pierce the protecting fabric of the suit or Eet's bag. But there was space enough to wriggle down the length of the LB, mostly by feel, for I dared not flash a beamer here.

Fortune had served us so far. The tail of the LB was well within the hole. And I had to hitch and pull, the weight of Eet dragging me back, by grasping one piece of wreckage and then the next for several lengths until I was in the main passage.

There was a weak light here, though I could not see its source, enough to take me from one handhold to the next, boring into the unknown. I made that journey with what speed I could, always haunted by the fear that another ship might be coming in or going out and I would be caught and ground against the wreckage.

The band of murdered ships ended suddenly in a clear space, a space which held other ships—three I could see. One was the cargo ship which had brought us in, another was one of those needle-nosed, deadly raiders I had seen used by the Guild, and the third was plainly a yacht. They were in orbit around what was the core of this whole amazing world in space. And it was a station, oval in shape like the protecting mass of wreckage, with landing stages at either end. Its covering was opaque, but with a crystalline look to the outer surface, which was pitted and pocked and had obviously been mended time and time again with substances that did not match the original material.

The cargo ship had opened a hatch and swung out a robo-carrier, heavily laden. I held on to my last anchorage and watched the robo spurt into a landing on a stage. The top half carrying the cargo dropped off and moved into an open hatch of the station while the robo took off for another load. There was no suited overseer to be seen, just robos. And I thought I saw a chance to make use of them to reach the station, just as we had used the robos to leave the caravansary.

Only I was not to have an opportunity to try. Out of nowhere came a beam, the force of which plastered me as tightly to the wreckage at my back as if my suit had indeed been welded in eternal bondage.

There was no breaking that hold. And my captors were very tardy about coming to collect me, finally spurting from the hatch of the yacht on a mini air sled. They lashed me into a tangle cord and used it as a drag to pull me behind them, not back to the ship from which they had issued, but to the landing stage where the robo had set down. Then, dismounting from their narrow craft, they tugged us both through a lock and into the interior of the station, where a weak gravity brought my boots and Eet's relaxed body to the floor.

Those who had taken me prisoner were humanoid, perhaps even of Terran breed, for they had that look. They snapped up their helmets and one did the same for me, letting in breathable air, though it had that peculiar faint odor of reprocessed oxygen. Leaving the tangle about my arms, they loosed me enough to walk, pointing with a laser to enforce my going. One of them took the bag from me and towed Eet, turning now and then to study the mutant narrowly.

So it was as prisoners that we came to the legendary Waystar, and it was an amazing place. The center was open, a diffused light filling it, a greenish light which gave an unpleasant sheen to most of the faces passing. By some unknown means there was a light gravity giving a true up and down to the corridors and balconies opening on that center. I caught sight of what could be labs, passed other doors tightly shut. There was population enough to equal that of a village on an ordinary planet—

though, as I guessed, those who used the station as home base were often in space and the permanent dwellers were limited in number.

It was one of the latter I was taken before. He was an Orbsleon, his barrel bulk immersed in a bowl chair with the pink fluid he needed for constant nourishment washing about his wrinkled shoulders, his boneless upper tentacles floating just beneath its surface. His head was very broad in the lower part, dwindling toward a top in which two eyes were set far apart, well to the sides. His far-off ancestor of the squid clan was still recognizable in this descendant. But that alien body housed a very shrewd and keen intelligence. A Veep in Waystar would be a Veep indeed, no matter what form of body held him.

A tentacle tip flashed from the bowl chair to trigger keys on a Basic talker, for the Orbsleon was a tactile communicator.

"You are who?"

"Hywel Jern." I gave him an answer as terse as his question.

Whether that name meant anything to him I had no way of knowing. And I received no aid from Eet. For the first time I doubted that the mutant could carry some of the burden of my impersonation. It might well be that the alien thought process would prove, in some cases, beyond his reading. Then I would be in danger. Was this such a time?

"You came—how?" The tentacle tip played out that question.

"On a one-man ship. I crashed on a moon—took an LB—" I had my story ready. I could only hope it sounded plausible.

"How through?" There was of course no readable expression on the alien's face.

"I saw a cargo ship coming in, hung under it. The LB played out halfway through the passage. Had to suit up and come along—"

"Why come?"

"I am a hunted man. I was Veep Estampha's value expert, I thought to buy out, live in peace. But the Patrol were after me. They sent a man on contract when they could not take me legally. He left me for dead. I have been on the run ever since." So thin a tale it might hold only if I were recognized as Hywel Jern. Now that I was well into this I realized more and more my utter folly.

Suddenly Eet spoke to me. "They have sent for one who knew Jern. Also they did not register 'dead' when you gave your name."

"What do here?" my questioner went on.

"I am an appraiser. There is perhaps need for one here. Also—this is the one place the Patrol is not likely to take me." I kept as bold a front as I could.

A man came in at the slow and rather stately pace the low gravity required. To my knowledge I had not seen him before. He was one of the mutants of Terran stock having the colorless white hair and goggle protected eyes of a Faltharian. Those goggles made his expression hard to read. But Eet was ready.

"He did not know your father well, but had seen him several times in Veep Estampha's quarters. Once he brought him a Forerunner piece, a plaque of irridium set with bes rock. Your father quoted him a price of three hundred credits but he did not want to sell."

"I know you," I said swiftly as Eet's mind read that for me. "You had a piece of Forerunner loot—irridium with bes setting—"

"That is the truth." He spoke Basic with a faint lisp. "I sold it to you."

"Not so! I offered three hundred, you thought you could do better. Did you?"

He did not answer me. Rather his goggled head swung toward the Orbsleon. "He looks like Hywel Jern, he knows what Jern would know."

"Something—you do not like?" queried the tentacles on the keys.

"He is younger—"

I managed what I hoped would register as a superior smile. "A man on the run may not have time or credits enough for a plasta face change, but he can take rejub tablets."

The Faltharian did not reply at once. I wished I could see the whole of his face without those masking goggles. Then, almost reluctantly, he did answer.

"It could be so."

During all those moments the Orbsleon's gaze had held on me. I did not see his small eyes blink; perhaps they did not. Then he played the keys of the talker again.

"You appraiser, maybe use. Stay."

With that, not sure whether I was a prisoner or perhaps now an employee, I was marched out of the room and led to a cubby on a lower level, where Eet and I, having been searched for weapons and had the suit and bag taken from us, were left alone. I tried the door and was not surprised to find it sealed. We were prisoners, but to what degree I could not be sure.

12

What I needed most at that moment was sleep. Life in space is always lived to an artificial timetable which has little relationship to sun or moon, night or day, in the measured time of planets. In hyper, when there is little to do for the smooth running of the ship, one simply sleeps when tired, eats when hungry, so that regular measurement of time does not apply. I did not know really how long it had been since I had had a meal or slept. But now sleep and hunger warred in me.

The room in which we had been so summarily stowed was a very small one, having little in the way of furnishings. And what there was resembled that planned for the economy of space, such as is found in a ship. There was a pull-down bunk, snapped up into a fold in the wall when not in use, a fresher, into which I would have to pack myself, when needful, with some care, and a food slot. On the off chance that it might be running, I whirled the single dial above it (there seemed to be no choice of menu). And somewhat to my surprise, the warn lights in the panel snapped on and the front flipped open to display a covered ration dish and a sealed container of liquid.

It would appear that the inhabitants of Waystar were on tight rations, or else they believed that uninvited guests were entitled only to the bare minimum of sustenance. For what I uncovered were truly space rations, nutritious and sustaining, to be sure, but practically tasteless—intended to keep a man alive, not in any way to please his taste buds.

Eet and I shared that bounty, as well as the somewhat sickening vita drink in the container. I did have a fleeting suspicion that perhaps some foreign substance had been introduced into either, one of those drugs which will either make a man tell all he knows or eradicate his will, so that for a time thereafter he becomes merely the tool of whoever exerts mastery over him. But that suspicion did not keep me from eating.

As I dumped the empty containers down the disposal unit I knew that just as I had had to eat, so I must now sleep. But it seemed that Eet did not agree, or not as far as he himself was concerned.

"The stone!" He made a command of those two words.

I did not have to ask what stone. My hand was already at the small pocket in my belt.

"Why?"

"Do you expect me to go exploring in the body of a phwat?"

Go exploring? How? I had already tried the cabin door and found it sealed. Nor did I doubt that they had guards outside, perhaps in the very walls about us—scan rays—

"Not here." Eet appeared very sure of that. "As to how —through there." He indicated a narrow duct near the ceiling, an opening which, if the grill over it were removed, might offer a very small exit.

I sat on the bunk and glanced from the hairy man-thing Eet now was to that opening. When we had first tried this kind of change I had believed it all illusion, though tactile as well as visual. But now, had Eet really altered in bulk so that what I saw before me was actually many times the size of my alien companion? If so—how had that been done? And (in me a sharp fear stabbed) if one did not have the stone, would changes remain permanent?

"The stone!" Eet demanded. He did not answer any of my thoughts. It was as if he were suddenly pressed for time and must be off on some important errand from which I detained him.

I knew I was not going to get any answers from Eet until he was ready to give them. But his ability to read minds was perhaps our best key to this venture and if he now saw the necessity for crawling through ventilation ducts, then I must aid him.

I kept my hand cupped about the stone. Though Eet had said there were no snoop rays on us, yet I would not uncover that treasure in Waystar. I stared at Eet where he hunkered on the floor and forced myself to see with the mind's eye, not a furred humanoid, but rather a mutant feline, until just that crouched at my feet.

It was easy to screw out the mesh covering of the duct. And then Eet, using me as a ladder, was up into it with speed. Nor did he leave me with any assurance as to when he would return, or where his journey would lead, though perhaps he did not know himself.

I wanted to keep awake, hoping that Eet might report via mind-touch, but my body needed sleep and I finally collapsed on the bunk into such slumber as might indeed have come from being drugged.

From that I awoke reluctantly, opening eyes which seemed glued shut. The first thing I saw was Eet, back in his hairy disguise, rolled in a ball. I sat up dazedly, trying to win out over the stupor of fatigue.

Eet was back, not only in this cell but in his other body. How had he managed the latter? Fear sharpened my senses and sent my hand to my belt again, but I felt with relief the shape of the stone in the pocket.

Even as I watched bleerily, he unwound, sat up blinking, and stretched his arms, as if aroused from a sleep as deep as mine had been.

"Visitors coming." He might give the outward seeming of one only half awake, but his thought was clear.

I shambled to the fresher. Best not let any arrival know I had warning. I used the equipment therein and emerged feeling far more alert. Even as I looked to the food server, the door opened and one of the Orbsleon's followers looked in.

"Veep wants you."

"I have not eaten." I thought it well to show some independence at the suggestion that I was now the Orbsleon's creature.

"All right. Eat now." If he made that concession (and the very fact that he did was a matter of both surprise and returning confidence for me) he was not going to enlarge upon it. For he stood in the doorway watching me dial the unappetizing food and share it with Eet.

"You—" The guard stared at the mutant. "What do you do?"

"No good talking to him," I improvised hurriedly. "You would need a sonic. He is—was—my pilot. Only fourth part intelligence, but good as a tech."

"So. What is he anyway?" Whether he spoke out of idle curiosity or was following an order to learn more, I did not know. But I had made a reasonable start on providing Eet with a background and I enlarged upon it a little with the name he had given himself.

"He is a phwat, from Formalh—" I added to my inventions. With so many planets supporting intelligent or quasi-intelligent life in the galaxy, no one could be expected to know even a thousandth of them.

"He stays here—" As I prepared to leave, the guard stepped in front of Eet.

I shook my head. "He is empathic-oriented. Without me he will will himself to death." Now I referred to something I had always thought a legend—that two species could be so emotionally intertied. But since I had believed, until last year, that the place in which I now stood was also a legend, there might be truth in other strange tales. At least the guard seemed inclined to accept what I said as a fact; he allowed Eet to shamble along behind me.

We did not return to the room in which the Orbsleon had interviewed me, but rather to one which might be a small edition of the hock-locks I well knew. There was a long table with various specto-devices clamped on it. In fact, it was a lab which many an appraiser on a planet might have envied. And on the walls were outlines of "safe" cupboards, each one with the locking thumb hole conspicuous in the center, where only the thumb of one authorized to open it would register to release its contents.

"Snooper ray on us," Eet informed me. But I had already guessed that, knowing why I had been brought here. They were going to prove my claim of being an appraiser, which meant tricky business. I would have to call on all I had learned from the man I seemed to be, all that I had picked up since I had left his tutelage, in order to survive such a test.

The things to be valued were spread on the table, under a protective ull web. I went straight to it, for in that moment my lifetime preoccupation took command.

There were four pieces in all, gemmed and set in metal —their glitter sparking life clear across the room. The first was a necklace—koro stones, those prized gems from out of the Sargolian seas which the Salariki doubly value because of their ability to give forth perfume when warmed by the body heat of the wearer.

I held it up to the light, weighed each of the jewels in my hand, sniffed at each stone. Then I let it slide carelessly from my grasp to the bare surface of the table.

"Synthetic. Probably the work of Ramper of Norstead —or of one of his apprentices—about fifty planet years old. They used marquee scent on it—five, maybe six steepings." I gave my verdict and turned to the next piece, knowing I did not have to impress the guard, or the two other men in the room, but rather those who held the snooper ray on me.

The second piece was set in a very simple mounting. And its dark rich fire held me for a moment or two. Then I put it in the cup below the infrascope and took two readings.

"This purports to be a Terran ruby of the first class. It is unflawed, true enough. But it has been subjected to two forms of treatment. One I can identify, the other is new to me. This has resulted in a color shift. I think it was originally a much lighter shade. It will pass, save for quality lab testing. But any expert gemologist would be uneasy about it."

The third on that table was an arm band of metal which

was reddish but carried a golden overcast that shifted across the surface when the ornament was handled. The maker had taken advantage of that overcast in working out the pattern on it, which was of flowers and vine, so that the gold appeared to line some of the leaves at all times. There was no mistaking it and my mind jumped back to the day my father had shown me such work, but then as a small pendant he had sold to a museum.

"This is Forerunner, and it is authentic. The only piece I have previously seen was taken from a Rostandian tomb. That was decided by the archaeologists to be very much older than the tomb even. Perhaps it had been found by the Rostandian buried there. Its origin is unknown as yet."

In contrast to the three other offerings the fourth was dull, leaden-gray, ugly metal set with an ill-formed cluster of badly-cut stones. It was only the center stone, one of perhaps four carats, which seemed to have any real life, and that, too, had been unimaginatively treated.

"Kamperel work. The centerpiece is a sol sapphire and would pay recutting. The rest"—I shrugged—"not worth working with. A tourist bauble. If this"—I turned to the two men, who had not spoken—"is the best you have to show me, then indeed, rumor has greatly over-rated the take of Waystar."

One of them came around the table to restow the four pieces under the web. I was wondering if I were now to be returned to my cell when the monotonous click of the Veep's voice sounded from some concealed com.

"As you think, this was test. You will see other things. The sal—can you recut?"

Inwardly I sighed with relief. My father had not had that training, I need not be forced to claim it.

"I am an appraiser, not a cutter. It will take skill to

make the most out of that stone after it has been mis-
handled the way it has. I would suggest that it be offered
as is"—I thought furiously—"to such a firm as Phatka
and Njila." Again I pulled names from my memory, but
this time from Vondar's warning about borderline dealers
whose inventories of stones were kept in two or three
different accountings, those they could sell openly, those
to be sold privately. That they had Guild affiliations was
suspected but unproved. But my ability to name them
would be more proof that I had dealt on the border line
of the law.

There was a period of silence. The man who had re-
wrapped the treasures in the web now sealed them into
one of the wall cubbies. No one commented, nor did the
com speak again. I shifted from one foot to the other,
wondering what would happen now.

"Bring here—" the com finally clicked.

So I was taken back to the room where the Orbsleon
Veep wallowed in his fluid-filled seat. Swung out over
the surface of that was a lap table and on it lay a single
small piece of metal.

It had no gem and it was an odd size. But the shape I
had seen before and knew very well indeed. A ring—
meant to fit, not a bare finger, but over the bulky glove
of a space suit. Only this had no zero stone, dull and lifeless, in its empty prongs. That it was, or had been, twin
to the ring which had caused my father's death, I was sure.
Yet the most important part was missing. I knew instantly
that this was another test, not of my knowledge as an
appraiser, but of how much I might know on another
subject. My story must hold enough truth to convince
them.

"There is a snooper ray on." Eet had picked up my
thought.

"What this?" The Veep wasted no time in coming to the test.

"May I examine it?" I asked.

"Take, look, then say," I was ordered.

I picked up the ring. Without its stone it was even more like a piece of battered junk. How much dared I say? They must know a great deal about my father's "death"—So I would give them all my father had known.

"I have seen one of these before—but that had a stone." I began with the truth. "A dim stone. It had been subjected to some process which rendered it lifeless, of no value at all. The ring was found on the space glove of a dead alien—probably a Forerunner—and brought to me for hock-lock."

"No value," clicked the voice of the Veep. "Yet you bought."

"It was alien, Forerunner. Each bit we learn about such things is knowledge, which makes some men richer. A hint here, a hint there, and one can be led to a find. This in itself has no value, but its age and why it was worn over a space glove—that makes it worth payment."

"Why worn on glove?"

"I do not know. How much do we know of the Forerunners? They were not even all of one civilization, species, or time. The Zacathans list at least four different star empires before they themselves developed a civilization, and claim there are more. Cities can crumble, suns burn out, sometimes artifacts remain—given proper circumstances. Space itself preserves, as you know well. All we can learn of those Forerunners comes in bits and pieces, which makes any bit of value."

"He asks," Eet told me, "but the questions are now from another."

"Who?"

"One more important than this half-fish." For the first time Eet used a derogatory expression, allowed an aura of contempt to pervade his mind-touch. "That is all I know. The other wears a protective antiesper, antisnoop device."

"This was a ring," I repeated aloud and laid the plundered circlet back on the lap table. "It held a stone now gone, and it resembles the one I held for a time which had been found on a Forerunner."

"You held—now where?"

"Ask that," I returned sharply, "of those who left me for dead when they plundered my shop." False now, but would any snooper detect that? I waited, almost expecting some loud contradiction of my lie. If any had been made perhaps those in the room were not aware of it yet. And if my last statement was accepted as truth, perhaps there might be awkward questions asked inside the ranks of the Guild, the which would do me no harm at all.

"Enough," the voicer clicked. "You go—sales place—watch."

My escort moved for the door. He did not snap to attention as a Patrolman, but he wore a tangler at his belt and I did not dispute his right to see me to where the Veep ordered my attendance.

We passed along one of the balcony corridors which rimmed the open center. It was necessary to shuffle, not lifting the feet much, keeping a handhold on the wall rail, or the low gravity became a hazard. When our way led down on a curled rod with handholds instead of stairsteps, we managed almost as if we were in a grav lift, coming to the third level below that where the Veep had his quarters.

This possessed some of the bustle of a market place. There was a coming and going of many races and species,

Terrans, Terran-mutants, humanoids, and nonhumanoid aliens.

Most of them wore ship uniforms, though unmarked by any official badges. And all of them wore stunners, though I saw no lasers. And I thought perhaps there might be some rule against more lethal weapons here.

The booth into which I was ushered lacked the elaborate detection equipment of the lab. Another Orbsleon (plainly of inferior caste, since he still had the crab legs long ago removed from the Veeps) squatted in a bowl with just enough liquid washing in it to keep him on the edge of comfort. It was plain he was in charge and must have expected me. He clicked nothing on his talker, but gestured with one tentacle to a stool back against the wall, where I obediently sat down, Eet hunkering at my feet. There were two others there, and seeing them, I realized, with a shudder I hoped I successfully suppressed, just how far outside the bounds of law I was.

There has always been slavery within the galaxy, sometimes planet-orientated, sometimes spread through a solar system, or systems. But there are some kinds of slavery which make men's stomachs turn more readily than the war-captive, farm-labor type most widely known. And these—these—*things*—were the result of selective breeding in a slavery the Patrol had worked for years to eliminate from any star lane.

The Orbsleon's servants were humanoid—to a point. But there had been both surgical and genetic modifications, so that they were not truly "men" as the Lankorox scale defines men in an alien–Terran-mutant society. They were rather living machines, each programed for a special type of service, knowing nothing else. One sat now with his hands resting limply on the table, his whole puffy body slack, as if even the energy which brought him pseudo life had drained away. The other worked with precise and delicate speed at a piece of jewelry, a gem-studded collar such as is worn at a feast of state by a Warlockian Wyvern. He pried each gem from its setting, sorting them with unerring skill, and at the same time graded them, placing the gems in a row of small boxes before him. The many-lensed orbs in his misshapen, too large, too round head were not turned upon what he did but rather stared straight ahead out of the booth, though they were not focussed on anything beyond.

"He is a detect—" Eet told me. "He sees all, reports without defining what he sees. The other is a relay."

"Esper!" I was suddenly afraid, afraid that that loosely sprawling hulk of flesh before us might tune in on Eet, know that we two together were far more than we seemed.

"No, he is on a lower band," Eet returned. "Only if his master wishes—"

He lapsed into silence and I knew he, too, knew the danger.

Why I had been sent here I did not know. Time passed. I watched those go to and from outside. The detect slave continued his work until the collar was entirely denuded of its jewels and then the metal went into a larger box. Now the busy fingers brought out a filigree tiara. Selections were made from the boxes of gems, and with almost the same speed with which they had been pried forth from their first settings they were put into the tiara. Though all the jewels were not used, I could see that the result of the work would be a piece which would easily bring a thousand certified credits in any inner planet shop. But all the time he worked, the slave never looked at what he wrought.

What were to be my duties, if any, I was not told. And

while the activities of the detect slave interested me for awhile, it was not enough to hold my attention too long. I found the inactivity wearing and I was restless. But surely anyone in my situation would want employment after awhile and no one would be suspicious if I showed my boredom.

I was shifting on what became an increasingly hard stool the longer I sat on it when a man stepped inside the booth. He wore the tunic of a space captain without any company insignia and he appeared to be familiar with the establishment, as he bypassed the table where the slaves sat and came directly to the Orbsleon.

He had been pressing his left hand against his middle —reminding me of my own frequent check on my gem belt. Now he unsealed his tunic and fumbled under its edge. The alien pushed forward a swing table much like the one his Veep had used to display the ring.

The spacer produced a wad of ull web, picked it apart to show a very familiar spot of color—a zoran. The Orbsleon's tentacle curled about the stone and without warning threw it to me. Only instinct gave me the reflex to catch the flying stone out of the air.

"What!" With a sharp exclamation the captain swung around to eye me, his hand on the butt of his stunner. I was turning the stone around, examining it.

"First grade," I announced. Which it was—about the best I had seen for some time. Also it was not a raw stone but had been carefully cut and mounted in a delicate claw setting, hooked to hang as a pendant.

"Thank you." There was sarcasm in the captain's voice. "And who may you be?" He lost now some of his aggressive suspicion.

"Hywel Jern, appraiser," I answered. "You wish to sell?"

"I wouldn't come here just for you to tell me it's first grade," he retorted. "Since when has Vonu added an appraiser?"

"Since this day." I held the stone between me and the light to look at it again. "A fleck of clouding," I commented.

"Where?" He was across the booth in two strides, snatched the jewel out of my hand. "Any clouding came from your breathing on it. This is a top stone." He swung around to the Orbsleon. "Four trade—"

"Zorans are not four trade," the talker clicked. "Not even top grade."

The captain frowned, half turned, as if to march out of the booth. "Three then."

"One—"

"No! Tadorc will give me more. Three!"

"Go Tadorc. Two only."

"Two and a half—"

I had no idea what they bid, since they did not use the conventional credits. Perhaps Waystar had its own scale of value.

The Orbsleon seemed to have reached a firm decision. "Two only. Go Tadorc—"

"All right, two." The captain dropped the zoran on the lap table and the alien's other tentacle stretched to a board of small buttons. When that mobile tip punched out a series on it there was no vocal reply. But he used the talker again.

"Two trade—at four wharf—take supplies as needed."

"Two!" The captain made an explosive oath of that word as he left with a force which might have been a stamp in a place of higher gravity.

The alien again threw the zoran, this time to be caught by the detect, who tucked it away in one of his boxes.

And it was then that my earlier guide-guard came to the front of the booth.

"You"—he gestured to me—"come along."

Glad for the moment to be released from the boredom of the booth, I went.

13

"Top Veep," Eet's warning came, to match my own guess as to where we were being taken. We again climbed through the levels to the higher ways of the station, this time passing the one where the Orbsleon had his quarters. Now the time-roughened walls about us showed dim traces of what had once been ornamentation. Perhaps for whatever creatures had built this station this had been officer territory.

I was motioned through a roll door, my guards remaining outside. They made a half-hearted attempt to stop Eet, but he suddenly developed an agility he had not shown before and pushed past them. I thought it odd they did not follow. Then, a moment later, I discovered why the inhabitant of these particular quarters did not need their attendance, for with another step I struck rather painfully against a force wall.

Also, inside this room the light gravity to which I had partially adjusted not only had become full for my race, but had an added pull, so it was an effort to take a step.

Beyond that invisible barrier the room was furnished as might be one in a luxury caravansary on some inner planet. Yet the furniture did not harmonize but was jammed together, showing even differences in scale size, as if some pieces had been made for bodies smaller or larger than my own. The one thing these had in common was their richness, which in some cases was gaudy and blatantly flamboyant.

Stretched in an easirest was the Veep. He was of Terran descent, but with certain subtle differences, modifications of feature, which suggested mutation. Probably he came from a race which had been among the early colonists. His hair had been cut so that it stood above his partially shaven skull in a stiffened roach, making him resemble one of the mercenaries of old times, and I wondered how he got a space helmet over that crest, if he ever did. His skin was brown, not just space-tanned, and there were two scars, too regular to be anything but inflicted on purpose for a patterning, running from corner of eye to chin on either side of his mouth.

Like the gaudy room, his clothing was a colorful mixture of planetary styles from several worlds. His long legs, stretched out in the rest, which fitted itself to give him greatest comfort, were encased in tight-fitting breech-legging-boots of a pliable, white-furred hide, the fur patterned with a watered rippling. Above his waist he wore the brilliant black-and-silver combination of a Patrol admiral's dress tunic complete with begemmed stars and ribbons of decorations. But the sleeves of that had been cut out, leaving his arms bare to the shoulders. Below his elbows he wore on both arms very wide bracelets or armlets of irridium, one mounted with what could only be Terran rubies of the first *water*, the other with sol sapphires and lokerals running in alternate rows, the vivid greens and blues in harmonious contrast. Both armlets were barbaric in taste.

184

In addition, his stiffened top ridge of hair was encircled by a band of mesh metal, green-gold—from which hung, flat against his forehead, a pendant bearing a single koro —about ten carats and very fine. The whole effect was that of what he must be, a pirate chief on display.

Whether he wore that mixture of splendor and bad taste by choice or for the effect such a bold showing of wealth might have on his underlings, I did not know. The Guild men in the upper echelons were usually inclined to be conservative in dress rather than ostentatious. But perhaps as master, or one of the masters, of Waystar, he was not Guild.

He watched me reflectively. Meeting his dark eyes, I had the impression that his clothing was a mask of sorts, meant to bedazzle and mislead those with whom he dealt. He was holding a small plate of white translucent jade in one hand, from time to time raising it to his mouth to touch tongue tip in a small licking movement to the gob of blue paste it held.

"They tell me"—he spoke Basic with no definable accent—"that you know Forerunner material."

"To some extent, Gentle Homo. I have seen, have been able to examine perhaps ten different art forms."

"Over there—" He pointed, not with his empty hand, but with his chin, to my left. "Take a look at what lies there and tell me—is it truly Forerunner?"

A round-topped table of Salodian marble supported what he wanted appraised. There was a long string of interwoven metal threads dotted here and there with tiny brilliant rose-pink gems; it could have been intended as either a necklace or a belt. Next to it was a crown or tiara, save that no human could have worn it in comfort, for it was oval instead of round. There was a bowl or basin, etched with lines and studded here and there with gems, as if they had been scattered by chance or whim rather than in any obvious pattern. And last of all, there was a weapon, still in a sheath or holster—its hilt or butt of several different metals, each of a different color but inlaid and mingled with the others in a way I knew we had no means of duplicating.

But what was more, I knew we had found what we had entered this kolsa's den to seek. This was the larger part of the treasure the Zacathans had found in the tomb; I had been too well briefed by Zilwrich to mistake it. There were four or five other pieces, but the best and most important lay here.

It was the bowl which drew my attention, though I knew if the Veep had not already caught the significance of those seemingly random lines and gems he must not be given a hint, by any action of mine, that it was a star map.

I walked toward the table, coming up against the barrier again before I reached it—a circumstance which gave me a chance to assert myself as I was sure Hywel Jern would have done.

"You cannot expect an appraisal, Gentle Homo, if I cannot inspect closely."

He tapped a stud on the chair arm and I could advance, but I noted that he tapped it again, twice, when I reached the table, and I did not doubt I was now sealed in.

I picked up the woven cord and ran it through my fingers. In the past I had seen many Forerunner artifacts, some in my father's collection, some through the aid of Vondar Ustle. Many others I had studied via tri-dee representation. But this stolen treasure was the richest it had ever been my good fortune to inspect. That the pieces were Forerunner would of course have been apparent even if I had not known their recent past history. But as everyone knew, there were several Forerunner civilizations and this workmanship was new to me. Perhaps the Zacathan expedition had stumbled upon the remains of yet another of those forgotten stellar empires.

"It is Forerunner. But, I believe, a new type," I told the Veep, who still licked at his confection and watched me with an unwavering stare. "As such it is worth much more than its intrinsic value. In fact, I cannot set a price on it. You could offer it to the Vydyke Commission, but you might even go beyond what *they* could afford—"

"The gems, the metal, if broken up?"

At that moment his question was enough to spark revulsion and then anger in me. To talk of destroying these for the worth of their metal and gems alone was a kind of blasphemy which sickened anyone who knew what they were.

But he had asked me a direct question and I dared not display my reaction. I picked up each piece in turn, longing to linger in my examination of the bowl map, yet not daring to, lest I arouse his suspicion.

"None of the jewels is large," I reported. "Their cutting is not of the modern fashion, which reduces their value, for you would lose even more by attempting to recut. The metal—no. It is the workmanship and history which makes them treasure."

"As I thought." The Veep gave a last lick to his plate and put it aside empty. "Yet a market for such is difficult to find."

"There are collectors, Gentle Homo, who are perhaps not as freehanded as the Vydyke, but who would raise much on all their available resources to have a single piece of what lies here. They would know it for a black deal and so keep what they obtained hidden. Such men are known to the Guild."

He did not answer me at once, but continued to stare,

as if he were reading my mind more than concentrating on my words. But I was familiar enough with mind-touch to know he was not trying that. I judged rather that he was considering carefully what I had just said.

But I was now aware of something else which first alarmed and then excited me. There was warmth at my middle, spreading from the pocket which held the zero stone. And that could only mean, since I was not putting it to service, that somewhere near was another of those mysterious gems. I looked to the most obvious setting, that of the crown, but I saw no telltale glow there. Then Eet's thought reached me.

"The bowl!"

I put out my hand, as if to reinspect that piece. And I saw that on the surface nearest me, luckily turned away from the Veep, there was a bright spark of light. One of those seemingly random jewels I had thought were meant to mark stars had come to life!

Picking up the bowl, I turned it idly around, holding my palm to cover the zero stone, and felt both at my middle and from the bowl the heat of life.

"Which do you think of greatest importance?" the Veep asked.

I put down the bowl, the live gem again turned away from him, looking over the whole array as if to make up my mind.

"This perhaps." I touched the strange weapon.

"Why?"

Again I sensed a test, but this time I had failed.

"He knows!" Eet's warning came even as the Veep's hand moved toward the buttons on the chair arm.

I threw the weapon I held. And by some superlative fortune I did not have any right to expect, it crashed against his forehead just beneath that dangling koro stone, as if the force field no longer protected him, or else I was inside it. He did not even cry out, but his eyes closed and he slumped deeper into the hold of the easirest. I whirled to face the door, sure he had alerted his guards. The force field might protect me, but it would also hold me prisoner.

I saw the door open, the guards there. One of them cried out and fired a laser beam. The force field held, deflected that ray enough to send a wave of flame back, and the man farthest into the room staggered, dropped his weapon, and fell against the one behind him.

"There is a way." Eet was by the easirest. He reached up and grabbed at the strange weapon now lying in the Veep's lap. I swept up the other treasures, holding them between my body and arm as I followed Eet to the wall, where he fingered a stud and so opened a hidden door. As that fell into place behind us, he mind-touched again.

"That will not hold them for long, and there are alarms and safeguards all through this wall way. I snouted them out when I explored. They need only throw those into action and we are trapped."

I leaned against the wall, unsealing my tunic and making its front into a bag to hold what I had snatched up. It was so awkward a bundle that I had difficulty in closing the tough fabric over it.

"Did your exploring see a way out?" I asked now. Our escape from that room had been largely a matter of unthinking reflex action. Now I was not sure we had not trapped ourselves.

"These are old repair ways. There are suits in a locker. They still have to patch and repatch the outside. It depends now upon how fast we can reach the suit locker."

The gravity here was practically nonexistent, and we

made our way through the dark, which was near absolute, by swimming through the air. Luckily there were hand-holds at intervals along the outer wall, proving that this method of progression had been used here before. But my mind worried at what lay ahead. Supposing fortune did favor us enough to let us reach the suits, get into them, and out on the outer shell of the station. We still had a long strip of space to cross to the ring of wreckage, and then to find our LB. This time the odds were clearly too high against us. I believed that the whole of Waystar would be alerted to track us down, they to hunt over familiar ground, we lost in their territory.

"Wait—" Eet's warning brought me up with a bump against him. "Trap ahead."

"What do we do—?"

"You do nothing, except not distract me!" he snapped.

I half expected him to make some move forward, for I thought his intention was to disarm what waited us. But he did not. Though no mind-touch was aimed at me, I felt what could only be waves of mental energy striking some distance ahead—and the zero stone in my belt grew uncomfortably warm against my body.

"Well enough," Eet reported. "The energy is now burned out. We have a clear path for a space."

We encountered two more of what Eet declared to be pitfalls, but which I never saw, before we came out of a sliding panel in the wall into a blister compartment on the outer skin of the hull. There we found the suits, just as Eet had foretold. Since I could not stuff myself plus the loot I carried into the one nearest my size, I had to pass the bowl and the tiara on to Eet, who was in the smallest, still much too large for him.

But how we would reach the outer shell of wreckage and the LB, I had not the least idea. The suits were both equipped, it was true, with blast beams, intended to give any worker who was jolted off into open space a chance of returning to the surface of the station. But if we used those, their power might not be enough to take us all the way to the wreckage, and in addition, we would be in plain sight of any watcher or radar screen. However, we did have the treasure and—

"That mistake I made—does the Veep know the importance of the bowl?" I demanded now.

"Part of it. He knows it is a map."

"Which they would not destroy willingly." I hoped that was true.

"You argue from hope, not knowledge," the mutant returned. "But it is all the hope we may have."

I signaled exit from the bubble, and crawled out, the magnetic plates on my boots anchoring me to the surface of the station. Once before Eet and I had so gone into space and I was touched now with the terrible fear which had gripped me then when I had lost my footing on the skin of the Free Trader ship and my contact with security, and floated into empty space.

But here there was a limit to emptiness. The cargo ship which we had followed into this port was gone, but the needle-nosed raider and the yacht were still in orbit, and above, all around, was the mass of wreckage—though I could sight no landmarks there and wondered how we were ever going to discover the narrow inlet in the jagged, tangled mass which hid the LB.

I could see no reason to wait. Either we would coast across to the wreckage or our power would fail. But to wait here any longer was to risk being captured before we had even tried. However, we did take the precaution of linking together by one of the hooked lines meant to anchor a worker to the surface of the station. So united, we took off between the two ships hanging ominously above.

"I cannot reach the controls of my jet—" Eet delivered what might be a final blow, dooming us to capture. Would the power in my own shoulder-borne rocket be enough to take us both over?

I triggered the controls, felt the push thrust which sent me and the suit containing Eet away from the station. My aim was the nearest rim of wreckage. I might be able to work my way along that in search of the passage if I could get to it. But every moment I expected to be caught by tangle beams, somehow sure that the Veep would not risk an annihilating weapon which would destroy his treasure.

The spurt of thrust behind me continued, in spite of the drag Eet caused as he spun slowly about at the end of the line, and there did not come any pursuit or pressure beam. I did not feel any triumph, only a foreboding which wore on my nerves. It is always worse to wait for an attack. I was certain that we had been sighted and that any moment we would be caught in a net.

The thrust failed while we were still well away from the wreckage. And though I got one more small burst by frantic fingering of the controls, it did little more than set me spinning across a small portion of that gap. Eet had been carried ahead of me by some chance of my own efforts, and now I saw his suit roll from side to side, as if, within it, he fought to reach his controls and so activate his own power.

What he did I could not tell, but suddenly there was a lunge forward of his spinning suit, and he towed me with him. The power of his progress intensified, for he no longer rolled. Now he was as straight as a dart flung at some target, and he dragged me easily behind as he headed for the wreckage. Still I could not guess why we had not been followed.

The splintered and dangerous mass of that wall of derelict ships grew more distinct. I trusted Eet could control his power, so that we would not be hurled straight into it. The merest scrape of some projection could tear suits and kill us in an instant.

Eet was rolling again, fighting against the full force of the power. Though I could do little to control my own passage, I rolled, too, hoping to meet feet first a piece of ship's side which would afford a reasonably smooth landing among the debris.

We whirled on at a faster pace than my own pack had sent us. And I guessed suddenly that Eet was making use of the zero stone on the map to trigger the energy of his rocket.

"Off!" I thought that as an order. "We'll be cut to ribbons if you do not."

Whether he could not control the force now, I did not know, but my feet slammed with bone-shaking impact against the smooth bit I had aimed for. I reached out, trying to grip Eet's suit. He had managed to turn, to coast alongside of the debris, just far enough away not to be entangled in it, yet. The magnetic plates in my boots kept me anchored, but not for long. Though I stopped Eet's advance with a sharp jerk, I was immediately thereafter torn loose by the power which dragged him on.

We nudged along beside the wreckage, twisting and turning as best we could to avoid any contact. Even if we might not be picked up by sight scanners against the camouflaging irregularities of that mass of metal, any heat identification ray could pick us up. And I did not doubt in the least that such equipment was in use at Waystar.

Was it that they dared not attack for fear of losing the

treasure? Had they sent ahead of us some command to activate the outer defenses, to keep us bottled up until they could collect us at their leisure? Perhaps when loss of air had rendered us perfectly harmless?

"I think they want you alive." Eet's answer came in response to my last dark speculation. "They guess that you know the value of the map. They want to know why. And perhaps they know that Hywel Jern did not really rise from the dead. I may read minds, but in that nest back there I could not sort out all thoughts."

I was not interested in the motives of the enemy. I was absorbed now in escape, if that was at all possible. Given time, we might work our way completely around the wall of debris to find the entrance. But such time our air supply would not offer.

"Ahead—the ship with the broken hatch," Eet said suddenly. "That I have seen before!"

I could make out the broken hatch. It took the shape of a half-opened mouth. And in me, too, memory stirred. I had set gloved hand to the edge of that very same hatch just before the pressure beam had made us captive. We could not be far now from the entrance, though I could hardly believe in such fortune.

Eet put on an extra burst of speed, drawing out a space from the wreckage, and certainly this energy could not all come from the suit rocket. The spurt was enough to bring us inside the ship passage. And we worked our way back from one handgrip to another, or rather I did so, pulling Eet's suit along. Only the fact that we were both relatively weightless made it possible. And even then, I was weak, shaking with fatigue, not certain I could make the full journey.

Every handhold I won to and from was a struggle. I did not direct my attention to the whole passage yet ahead, but limited it to the next hold only, and then to the next. I even lost my fear of what might lie behind, my concentration was so great on just swinging to the next hold—

We gained, I was not quite sure how, the crevice in which we had left the LB and crawled to its hatch. But once I slammed that door shut behind us I lost my last ounce of energy, and slid down, unable to move, watching Eet, in the clumsy suit, lift one arm with visible effort to reach the inner controls, fail, and then with grim patience try again.

Eventually he succeeded. Air hissed in around me and the inner hatch opened. The suit holding Eet squirmed and wriggled, and then the mutant emerged, kicked the suit away in an almost vindictive gesture, and scrambled over to me to fumble with the sealings which held me in the protective covering.

The ship air revived me to the extent that I was able to shed that shell and crawl on into the cabin. Eet had preceded me, and now squatted in the pilot's web, fingering the buttons to ease us out and away.

I dragged myself to the hammock, lay weakly back in it. I did not believe at that moment that we had the least chance of breaking through the outer defenses of Waystar. We and our ship *must* meet some force field which would hold us, intact, as our captors wanted. But some reckless desire to go down fighting made me take the zero stone out in my shaking hands. I broke the disguise it had given me, or hoped I did. Having no mirror I could not be sure.

Now—there was something I could do which would at least confuse them if they slapped a spy ray on us.

"Such comes now," Eet reported and then closed his mind tightly, intent only on getting us out of the tunnel.

How much time did I have? The stone burned my hands but I held on. I had no mirror to mark the course of my transformation, but I willed it with all the energy and resource I had left. Then I lay back weakly, unable even to put away the precious source of my pain.

I looked blearily down what I could see of my prone body. There were, surely I could not be mistaken, the furred breeches, and above them the brilliance of a space admiral's tunic. I turned my head a fraction from side to side. My arms were bare, below the elbow wearing the gemmed armlets. I was, I hoped, by the power of the zero stone, a complete copy of the Veep. If they now snooped us with a seeing ray, the change might give us a small advantage, a few moments of confusion among our enemies.

Eet did not turn to look at me but his thought rang in my head.

"Very well done. And—here comes their snoop ray!"

Not having his senses, I must take his word for that. I levered myself up in the hammock with what energy I could summon, which was only enough to keep me braced with some small semblance of alertness. Eet suddenly slapped a furred fist on the board and the answering leap of the LB pinned me against the hammock. My head spun, I was sick—then I was swept into darkness.

14

When I roused groggily I lay staring at the rounded expanse above me, not able at once to remember where I was, or perhaps even *who* I was. With what seemed painful and halting slowness, memory of the immediate past returned. At least we were still in existence; we had not been snuffed out by some defense weapon of the pirate stronghold. But were we free? Or held captive by a force beam? I tried to lever myself up and the LB hammock swayed.

But I had had a look at my own body and I was not now wearing the semblance of the Veep—though a furry dwarf still hunched at the controls of the small craft. My hand went to the bulge in my belt. The sooner I was sure I was myself again, the better. I had a strange feeling that I could not think or plan until I was Murdoc Jern outwardly as well as inwardly, as if the outer disguise could change me from myself into a weak copy of the man my father had been. Eet had been a cat, but I had willed that on him without his desire. This I had taken upon myself by my own wish, meant to be outer, not complete. What *did* make sense any more?

"You are yourself," came Eet's thought.

But there was something else. My hand rested upon a pocket wherein all those days, months, I had carried the zero stone. And there was no reassuring hard lump to be felt. It was flat—empty!

"The stone!" I cried that aloud. I drew myself up, though my body was weak and drained of energy. "The stone—"

Then Eet turned to me. His alien face was a mask as far as I was concerned. I could read no expression there.

"The stone is safe," he thought-flashed.

"But where—?"

"It is safe," he repeated. "And you are Murdoc Jean outwardly again. We are through their defenses. The snooper ray caught you in the Veep's seeming and was deceived long enough for the stone to boost us out of range."

"So that is the way you used it. I will take it now." I held myself upright, though I must still clutch at the hammock to keep that position. Eet had used the zero stone even as we had once used it to boost the power of a Patrol scout ship and so escape capture. I was angry with myself for having overlooked that one weapon in our armament. "I will take it now," I repeated when Eet made no move to show me where it was. Though I had worked on the LB under Ryzk's direction I could not be sure where Eet had put it for the greatest effect in adding to our present drive.

"It is safe," he told me for the third time. Now the evasiveness of that reply made an impression on me.

"It is mine—"

"Ours." He was firm. "Or, rather, it was yours by sufferance."

Now I was thinking clearly again. "The—the time I

turned you into a cat. . . . You are afraid of that—"

"Once warned, I cannot be caught so again. But the stone is danger if used in an irresponsible fashion."

"And you"—I controlled my rising anger with all the strength I had learned—"are going to see that it is not!"

"Just so. The stone is safe. And what is more to the purpose—look here." He pointed with one of his fingers to something which, for the want of other safekeeping, lay in the second hammock.

I loosed one hand to pull that webbing a little toward me. There lay the bowl with the map incised on its outer surface. A moment later I held it close to my eyes.

With the bowl turned over, the bottom was a half sphere on which the small jewels which must be stars winked in the light. And I saw, now that I had the time and chance to view it searchingly, that those varied. My own species rate stars on our charts by color—red, blue, white, yellow, dwarfs and giants. And here it would seem that the unknown maker of this chart had done the same. Save in one place alone, where next to a yellow gem which might denote a sun was a zero stone!

Quickly I spun the bowl around, studying the loose pattern. Yes, there were other planets indicated about those colored suns, but they were done in tiny, almost invisible dots. Only the one was a gem.

"Why, think you?" Eet's question reached me.

"Because it was the source!" I could hardly believe that we might hold the answer to our quest. I think my unbelief was born in the subconscious thought that it would be one of those quests, such as fill the ancient ballads and sagas, wherein the end is never quite in the grasp of mortals.

But it is one thing to hold a star map and another to find on it some already known point. I was no astro-navigator and unless some point of reference marked on this metal matched our known charts, we could spend a lifetime looking, unable even to locate the territory it pictured.

"We know where it was found," Eet suggested.

"Yes, but it may be another case of a relic of an earlier civilization treasured by its finder long after and buried with one who never even knew the life form that fashioned it, let alone the planets it lists."

"The Zacathan may furnish our key, together with Ryzk, who does know these star lanes. The stars this shows may be largely uncharted now. But still, those two together might give us one point from which we can work."

"You will tell them?" That surprised me somewhat, for Eet had never before suggested hinting to anyone that the caches we had disclosed to the Patrol were not the sum total of the stones now in existence. In fact, our quest had been his plan from its inception.

"What is needful. That this is the clue to another treasure. The Zacathan will be drawn by his love of knowledge, Ryzk because it will be a chance for gain."

"But Zilwrich is to be returned with the treasure to the nearest port. Of course—" I began to see that perhaps Eet was not so reckless as he seemed in suggesting that we plunge into the unknown with a map which might be older than my species itself as our only guide. "Of course, we did not say *when* we would return him."

There was in the back of my mind the thought that the Zacathan might even willingly agree to our plan to go exploring along the bowl route, the thirst for knowledge being as keen as it was among his kind.

But though I held that star map in my hand, my attention returned to the more important point for now.

"The stone, Eet."

"It is safe." He did not enlarge upon that.

There was, of course, this other stone, which, compared to the one we had used, was a mere pin point of substance, now so dull as to be overlooked by anyone not aware of its unusual properties. Did the amount of energy booster depend upon the size of the stone? I remembered how Eet had produced that burst of power which had brought us along the barrier of the wreckage. Had all that come from this dull bit which I could well cover with only a fraction of the tip of my little finger? It must be that we had learned only a small portion of what the stones could do.

I was most eager to get back to the ship, away from Waystar. And as the LB was on course, I began to wonder at the length of our trip. Surely we had not been this far from where we had set down on the dead moon.

"The homer—" I moved to see that dial. Its indicator showed set to bring us back on automatics to the *Wendwind*. Suddenly I doubted its efficiency. Most of the alterations in the controls of the LB had been rigged by Ryzk, were meant to be only temporary, and had been made with difficulty—though it was true that a Free Trader had training in repairs and extempore rigging which the average spacer never learned.

Suppose the linkage with the parent ship was faulty? We could be lost in space. Yet it was true we were holding to a course.

"Certainly," Eet broke into my ominous chain of thought. "But not, I believe, to the moon. And if they go into hyper—"

"You mean—they have taken off? Not waiting for us?" Perhaps that fear, too, had ever lain in the depths of my mind. Our visit to Waystar had been so rash an undertaking that Ryzk and the Zacathan could well have written us off almost as soon as we left for the pirate station. Or Zilwrich might have begun to fail and the pilot, realizing the Zacathan was too far spent to object, and wanting to get him to some aid— There were many reasons I could count for myself for the *Wendwind* to have taken off. But we were still on course for something—a course which would hold only until the ship went into hyper for a system jump. If that happened, our guide line would snap and we would be adrift—with only a return to Waystar or a landing on one of the dead worlds for our future.

"If they left for out-system they would hyper—"

"If they do not know the system they must reach its outermost planet before they do," Eet reminded me.

"The stone—if we use that to step up energy to join them—"

"Such a journey must be made with great care. To maneuver the LB and the ship together during flight—" But it was apparent that Eet was thinking for himself as well as for my enlightenment. He studied the control board and now he shook his head. "It is a matter of great risk. These are not true controls, only improvised, and so might not serve us at a moment of pressing need."

"A choice between two evils," I pointed out. "We stay here and die, or we take the chance of meeting with the ship. As long as we remain on course we are linked with her. Why doesn't"—I was suddenly struck by a new thought—"Ryzk know we are following? The fact that we are should have registered—"

"The indicator in the ship may have failed. Or perhaps he does not choose to wait."

If the pilot did not want to wait—he had the *Wendwind,* he had the Zacathan, and he had an excellent excuse for our disappearance. He might return to the near-est port with the rescued archaeologist, the co-ordinates of Waystar to deliver to the Patrol, a ship he could claim for back wages. All in all, the master stars lay in his hand in this game and we had no comets to cut across the playing board to bring him down—except the zero stone.

"Into the hammock," Eet warned now. "I shall cut in the stone power. And hope that the ship does not hyper before we can catch up."

I lay down again. But Eet remained by the controls. Could the alien body he had wished upon himself stand the strain of not using such protection as the LB afforded? If Eet blacked out, I could not take his place, and we could well strike the *Wendwind* with projectile speed.

In the past I had been through the strain of take-offs in ships built for speed. But the LB was not such. I could only remember that the original purpose of the craft was to flee a stricken ship, and that it must thus be fit to take the strain of a leap away from danger. To sustain such energy, however, was another matter. Now I lay in the hammock and endured, though I did not quite black out. It seemed as if the very material of the walls about us protested against the force. And the bowl, which I still held, had a fiery spot of light on its surface where the infinitely smaller stone answered the burst of power from the larger, which Eet had concealed.

I endured and I watched through a haze the furred body of Eet, his arms flung out, his fingers crooked to hold in position at the controls. Then I heard the loud rasp of painful breathing which was not mine alone. And every second I expected a break in the link tying us to the ship, the signal that the *Wendwind* has gone into hyper, vanished out of the space we knew.

Either my sight was affected by the strain or else Eet

was so pinned by our speed that he could not function
well, but I saw mistily his one hand creep at a painfully
slow rate to thumb a single lever. Then we were free of
that punishing pressure. I clawed my way out of the
hammock, swung across to elbow Eet aside, and took his
place, facing the small battery of winking lights and
warnings I did understand and which Ryzk had patiently
drilled me to respond to.

We had reached match distance of the *Wendwind* and
must now join her. Automatics had been set up to deal
with much of this, but there were certain alarms I must
be ready to answer if they were triggered. And if Ryzk
had ignored our following signal, he could not, short of
winking instantly into hyper, avoid our present homing.

I sweated out those endless seconds at the board, my
fingers poised and ready to make any correction, watching the dials whose reading could mean life or death not
only to us but to the ship we fought to join. Then we
were at our goal. The visa-screen winked on to show the
gap of the bay for the LB and we bumped into it. The
screen went dark again as the leaves of the bay closed
about us. I was weak with relief. But Eet arose from
where he had crouched, hanging to one end of the other
hammock.

"There is trouble—"

He did not complete that thought. I cannot tell now—
there are no words known to my species to describe what
happened then—for we were not bedded down, prepared
for the transition as was needful. We were not even
warned. Seconds only had brought us in before the ship
went into hyper.

There was the taste of blood in my mouth. I drooled
it forth to flow stickily down my chin. When I opened my

eyes I was in the dark, a dark which brought the terror of blindness with it. My whole body was one great ache which, when I tried to move, became sheer agony. But somehow I got my hand to my head, wiped it without knowing across the stickiness of blood. I could not *see!*

"Eet!" I think I screamed that. The sound echoed in my ears, adding to the pain in my head.

There was no answer. The dark continued. I tried to feel about me and my hand struck against solid substance as memory stirred. I was in the LB, we had returned to the ship just an instant before it had gone into hyper.

How badly I was hurt I did not know. As the LBs had originally been fashioned to take care of injured survivors of some space catastrophe, I needed only get back to the hammock and the craft would be activated into treating me.

I felt about me, seeking the touch of webbing. But though my one arm obeyed me, I could not move the other at all. And I touched nothing but wall. I tried to inch my body along, sliding my fingers against that wall, seeking some break, some change in its surface. The quarters of the LB were so confined that surely I could soon find one of the hammocks. I flung my arm up and out, rotating it through the thick darkness. It encountered nothing.

But I *was* in the LB and it was too small for me not to have found the hammock by now. The thought of the hammock, that it was ready to soothe my pain, to apply restoratives and healing, so filled me that I forced myself to greater efforts to find it. But my agonizing movements, so slow and limited, told me that there was no hammock. And whatever space in which I now lay was not in the LB. My hand fell to the floor and touched a small, inert body. Eet! Not as I had seen him last, my exploring fingers reported. But Eet, the mutant, as he had been from birth.

I drew my fingers down his furred side and thought I detected a very faint fluttering there, as if his heart still beat. Then I tried to discover by touch alone whether he bore any noticeable wounds. The darkness—I would not allow myself to accept the thought that I was *blind*—took on a heavy, smothering quality. I was gasping as if the lack of light was also a lack of air. Then I feared that it was, and that we had been sealed in somewhere to suffocate.

Eet did not answer my thoughts, which I tried to make coherent. I felt on, beyond him, and sometime later gave up the hope we were in the LB. Instead we lay in a confined space with a door which would not yield to the small force I could exert against it. We must be on board the *Wendwind*—and I believed we were now imprisoned in one of those stripped lower cabins which had been altered for cargo transport. This could only mean that Ryzk had taken command. What he might have told the Zacathan I did not know. Our actions had been strange enough to give credence to some story that we operated outside the law, and Ryzk could testify truly that we had brought him on board without his knowledge. The Zacathans were esper—telepaths. Ryzk could tell the exact truth and Zilwrich would have to believe him. We could well be on our way now to being delivered to the Patrol as kidnapers and shady dealers with the pirates of Waystar. Yes, as I painfully marshaled the facts as another would see them I realized that Ryzk could make an excellent case, and Zilwrich would back him up.

That we brought back part of the treasure meant nothing. We could have done that and still planned to keep it, and the Zacathan, for ransom. Such deals were far from unknown.

If Ryzk had been black-listed, bringing us in might return him to the rolls. And if we underwent, or I underwent, deep interrogation—the whole affair of the zero stone would be known. It would be clear that we were guilty of what the Patrol might deem double-dealing. Ryzk had only to play a completely honest man at the nearest port and we would have lost our big gamble.

It seemed so hopeless when I thought it all out that I could see no possible counter on our part. Had we one of the zero stones we might—so much had I come to accept the unusual powers of those strange gems—have a fighting chance. Eet—if he were not dead—or dying— might just—

I felt my way back to that small body, gathered it carefully up so that Eet's head rested against me, and put my good arm protectingly around it. I thought now that I no longer felt that small stirring of a heartbeat. There was no answer to my mind-call. So there was good reason to believe that Eet was dead. And in that moment I forgot all my annoyance at his interference in my life, the way he had taken over the ordering of my days. Perhaps I was one who needed such dependence upon a stronger will. There had been my father, then Vondar Ustle, then Eet—

Only I would not accept that this was the end. If Eet was dead, then Ryzk would pay for that death. I had thought of the aid of the stone, and the aid of Eet, and both of them were gone. What remained was myself, and I was not ready to say I was finished.

I had always believed that I was no esper. Certainly no

such talent was apparent in me before I met Eet. He had touched my mind for communication and I had learned that use from him. He had at one uncomfortable time given me mental contact with another human in order to prove our innocence to a Patrol officer. Then he had taught me to use the hallucinatory change and I had been the one to discover that the zero stone could bring about an almost total change.

But Eet—he was either dead or very close to it. I had neither Eet nor the stone. I was hurt, how badly I could not tell, and I was a prisoner. There was only one small— very small—spark of hope left—the Zacathan.

He was normally esper, as was Eet. Could I possibly reach him now? Make some appeal?

I stared into a dark which I hoped would not be my portion all the rest of my life, but in my mind I pictured the face of Zilwrich as I had seen it last. And I strove to hold that face in mind, not now for the purpose of making it mine, but rather as a homing point for my thought-seek. And I aimed, not a coherent thought, but a signal for attention, a cry for help.

Then—I touched! It was as if I had put tip of finger to a falder leaf which had instantly coiled away from contact with my flesh. Then—it returned.

But I was racked with disappointment. With Eet mind-touch had been clear, as it had been with the Zacathan when the mutant was present. This was a jumble of a language I did not know, poured at me in a wealth of impressions too fast for me to sort and understand, forming a sickening, chaotic whirl, so that I must retreat, drop touch.

Eet was the connecting link I must have. Otherwise I could only try until that whirl of alien thought drove my brain into mindlessness. I considered the chances. I could stay prisoner here for whatever purpose Ryzk had in mind. Or I could try the Zacathan again. And it was not in me to accept the helplessness of that first choice.

So, warily, as a man might seek a path across a quaking bog ready to swallow him up in a thousand hungry mud mouths, I sent out once more the mind-seek. But this time I thought my message—slowly, impression by impression, and doggedly held to what I had to convey as the stream of the alien mind lapped over it. I did not try to tell Zilwrich anything, as I would have "talked" to Eet. I merely thought out over and over again what I would have him know, letting it lie for him to pick up as he could. Though I feared my slow channel was as unintelligible to him as his frighteningly swift flow was to me.

Once, twice, three times, a fourth, I thought through what I made as my plea. Then I could hold no longer. The pain of my body was as nothing compared to the pain now filling my mind. And I lost contact as well as consciousness, just as I had when we had snapped into hyper.

It was as if I were being pricked over and over again by the sharp point of a needle. I stirred under that torment, which was small and far away at first, and then became so much the greater, more insistent. And I fought to remain in the safety of nothingness. Prick—the summons to what I did not want continued.

"Eet?" But it was not Eet—no—

"Wait—"

Wait for what, who? I did not care. Eet? No, Eet was dead. And I would be dead. Death was not caring, not needing to care, or feel, or think— And I wanted just that—no more stirring of life, which hurt both mind and body. Eet was dead, and I was dead, or would be if the pricking would only stop and leave me in peace.

"Awake—"

Awake? I thought it was "wait." Not that it mattered. Nothing mattered—

"Awake!"

A shouting in my head. I hurt and that hurting came from outside. I turned my head from side to side, as if to shake out the voice in my mind.

"Keep awake!" screamed that order and the pain it caused me aroused me further from my stupor. I was moaning a little, whimpering through the dark a plea to be let alone, left to the death which was rest.

"Keep awake!"

Hammering inside my skull. Now I could hear my own whimpering plaint and was unable to stop. But also with the pain came an awareness which was a barrier against my slipping back into the nothingness.

"Awake—hold—"

Hold what? My rolling head? There was nothing to hold.

Then I sensed, not words echoing through my bruised mind, but something else—a stiffening, a support against which my feeble thoughts could find root and sustenance. And this continued until I stared wide-eyed into the dark, as much another person inwardly as I had been outwardly with the hallucinations born of the zero stone. For only a limited time, somehow I knew, would that support me. And during that time I must make any attempt I could to help myself.

15

Somehow I got to my feet, still holding Eet against me with my good arm, my other hanging uselessly by my side. I was ready to move, but where, against what—or whom? Realizing I was still helplessly caught in this pocket of dark, I was ready to slump again into a stupor.

"Wait—be ready—" There was a sense of strain in that message, as if he who sent it were making a vast effort.

Well, I was waiting and ready, but for how long? And in this dark time seemed forever and ever, not measured by any standard I had known.

Then came sound, a small grating, and I knew a leap of heart—I was not blind after all! There was a line of light to my right. I lurched in that direction as that line grew from a slit into an opening I could squeeze through —though I was blinking against the discomfort of light.

I brought out and up against the wall of the well which was the core of the ship, too spent for a moment to turn and see who had freed me. But leaning one shoulder against the wall, I was able to face about.

Zilwrich, whom I had last seen lying on the pallet, supported himself with his two arms rigid against the floor, clearly at the end of the flutter of strength which had made him crawl to the door of my cell. He lifted his head with manifest effort.

"You—are—free— To you—the rest—"

Free but weaponless, and as near the end of my resources as the Zacathan, though not yet finished. Somehow I was able to lay Eet on the floor, get my good arm about Zilwrich, and half drag the Zacathan back to the bed he had crawled from. Then I stumbled out, picked up the mutant, and brought him back, nursed against me, though no tending would return life to that small body.

"Tell me." I used the Basic speech, glad to be able to relinquish touch with that bewildering alien mind. "What happened?"

"Ryzk"—Zilwrich spoke slowly as if each word came hard—"would go to Lylestane—return me—the treasure—"

"And turn us in," I ended, "probably as accomplices in Guild plotting."

"He—wishes—reinstatement. I did not know you had returned alive—until your mind-seek. He said—you died —when we went into hyper."

I glanced down at the limp body pressed to mine. "One of us did."

I might be free inside the ship, but that I could do anything to change the course of events I doubted. Ryzk would return us to Lylestane and we—I—would find the balance of justice heavily weighted against me. Not only were circumstances largely in the pilot's favor, but under a scanner they would have out of me all that the zero stone meant. And—the zero stone!

Eet had concealed it somewhere in the LB. As far as I knew Ryzk did not suspect it. If I could get hand on it again— I was not sure how I could use it as a weapon. But that it had possibilities of this sort there was no doubt. The LB—but Eet had hidden the stone and Eet was dead.

The bowl—if I had that I could trace the zero stone by the fire of the one inlaid in it.

"The treasure—where is it?"

"In the lock safe." Zilwrich's eyes were on me with piercing keenness, but he was ready enough with that information.

The lock safe— If Ryzk had sealed that with his own thumb, I had no chance of getting the bowl. The compartment would remain closed until he chose to release it.

"No." It would seem that like Eet the Zacathan could readily read my mind, but that did not matter. "No—it is sealed to me."

"He allowed that?"

"He had to. What is this thing you must have—that the bowl will bring you nearer to—a weapon?"

"I do not know if it can be a weapon. But it is a source of power beyond our reckoning. Eet hid it in the LB; the bowl will find it for me."

"Help me—to the lock safe."

It was a case of the lame leading the crippled. We made a hard journey of a short space. But I was able to steady the alien while he activated the thumb lock and I scooped out the bowl. He held it tightly to him as I guided and supported him back to his bed.

Before he released the bowl to me he turned it around in his hands, examining it closely. Finally one of his finger talons tapped the tiny zero stone.

"This you seek."

"We have long sought it, Eet and I." There was no use in concealing the truth any longer. We might not make the voyage we had planned, going out among the un-charted stars in search of an ancient world which was the source of the stones, but it was the here and now which mattered most—the finding of the one Eet had hidden.

"It is a map, and you hunt the treasure you believe lies at its end?"

"More than such treasure as you found in the tomb." And, as tersely as I could, I told him the story of the zero stones—the one in my father's ring, those of the caches on the unknown planet, that which Eet had secreted, and how we had used it since.

"I see. Take this then." Zilwrich held out the bowl. "Find your hidden stone. It would seem that we were on the edge of a vast discovery when we uncovered this—but one which would unleash perils such as a man thinks twice about loosing."

I held the bowl to me as I had held Eet, using my shoulder against the wall to keep erect, shambling from Zilwrich's cabin to the ladder, down which I fell rather than climbed, to reach the LB's berth. The last steps of that journey were such a drain that I could hardly take them.

Then I was back in the craft which had served us so well. I fought to keep moving, holding the bowl a little away from me now, watching the zero stone. It glimmered and then broke into vivid life. But it was hard to see how I could use it as a guide, since there seemed no variation in that light. However, I must try.

I moved jerkily, first to the tail, without any change I could detect in the degree of emanation from the bowl stone. But as I came up the right side of the small ship on return the bowl moved in my grasp, fought my hold. I released it. As the zero stone, on its first awakening, had pulled me across space to the derelict ship where others of its kind lay, so did the bowl cross, to hang suspended against a part of the casing. I jerked and tore at the rim of the casing, hoping Eet had not been able to seal in the stone too tightly. As my nails broke and my fingers were lacerated by the sharp edging I began to despair. One-handed there was little I could to force it.

But I continued to fight, and at last I must have touched what lock was there, for a whole section of panel fell down and I saw the brilliant blaze of the large stone within. The bowl snapped to meet it until stone touched stone, and I did not try to part them. With the bowl I began to retrace my way.

When I subsided beside Zilwrich, the bowl on the floor between us, he looked at the gems but seemed as content as I at that moment to do no more. Not only was I too weak to prod my body to more effort, but my thoughts were dulled, slow. Now that I had found the second stone, I could not see any way to make use of it against Ryzk. It seemed that, having achieved this one small success, I was finished.

Eet lay on the edge of the Zacathan's pallet and one of the alien's scaled hands rested on the mutant's head.

"This one is not dead—"

I was startled out of my lethargy. "But—"

"There is still the spark of life, very low, very dim, but there."

I was no medico, and even if I had been I would have had no knowledge to deduce the mutant's hurts. My own helplessness was an added burden. Eet would die and there was nothing I could do—

Or was there?

For a little beyond Eet's head was the bowl, the stones close-welded together. The zero stone was power. It had the power to turn us into the seeming of others and hold that seeming. And I had been able to turn Eet into a cat because I had sprung that change on him when he did not expect it. Could I will, not change, but will life itself into the mutant's body?

As long as there was a faint spark left, I must try.

I took the left hand on my limp and useless arm with my right, moved the numb palm to rest on the stones, not caring if I would be burned. At least I would not feel it. The right I put on Eet's head. I set my mind to the task, summoning, not some strange disguise for my companion, but rather the sight of him as he was alive. So did I fight my battle—with mind, with a hand which will always bear the scars, with my determination, against death itself, or what Eet's kind knew as the end of existence. And I strove with the power passing through me to find that spark Zilwrich said existed, to fan it into flame.

The stones made a fire to fill one's sight, shutting out the cabin, the Zacathan, even Eet, but I continued to hold the image of the live Eet in my mind. My eyes which had been useless in the dark of the cell were now blinded again, by light. But I held fast in spite of that in me which cringed, and cried, and tried to flee.

Nor was I truly conscious of why I fought that battle, save that it was one which I must face to the end. I was at last done, my seared hand lying palm up on my knee, the bowl and stone hidden from me by a fold of cloth. Eet no longer lay limp, with the semblance of death, but sat on his haunches, his paw-hands folded over his middle, his stance one of alert life, of complete restoration.

I caught communication, or the edge of it, between the Zacathan and my companion. But so difficult was it now for me to hold to any thought that it was more like hearing a murmur or whisper from across a room.

Eet moved with all his old agility, bringing out the aid

kit, seeing to my hand, giving me also a shot to counteract the hurt in my arm. But to me this had little or no meaning. I watched the Zacathan agree to something Eet suggested and the mutant carry the bowl out of the room—into hiding again, I supposed. But all I wanted was sleep.

Hunger awoke me. I was still in the Zacathan's cabin. If Ryzk had paid him a visit during the time I slept he had not seen fit to return me to custody. But that I had slept worried me vaguely. There was much to be done and I had failed to do it.

Eet whisked in, almost as if my waking had sent him some signal. He carried in his mouth as he came two of those tubes of E-rations. And seeing them, for a second or two I forgot all else. But when I had squeezed one into my mouth and savored the first few swallows (though normally I would not have considered them appetizing) I had a question:

"Ryzk?"

"We can do nothing while in hyper," Eet reported. "And he has found his own amusement. It seems that this ship was not too thoroughly searched when it was taken in as a smuggler. Somehow Ryzk uncovered a supply of vorx and is now having sweet dreams in his cabin."

Vorx was potent enough to give anyone dreams—though whether they were sweet was another question. It was not only an intoxicating drink, but so acted on Terran bodies that it was also hallucinatory. That Ryzk had been searching the ship did not surprise me either. The boredom of space travel would set any man immured within these walls during hyper passage to do such to relieve his tedium. And Ryzk might have known this was a smuggler sold after confiscation.

"He had help—" Eet commented. There was such a bubbling renewal of well-being in him as made me envious, perhaps tired of being on the edge wash of such energy.

"From you?"

"From our distinguished colleague." Eet nodded to the Zacathan.

"It would seem that Ryzk's weakness is drink," Zilwrich agreed. "While it is wrong of anyone to play upon another's weakness, there are times when such a fall from Full Grace is necessary. I deemed that I might take on error-load for once in this way. We need Ryzk's room rather than his company."

"If we come out of hyper in the Lylestane system we shall be in Patrol territory," I replied a little sourly.

"It is possible to come out and go in again before a challenge of boarding can be delivered," Zilwrich returned. "I have a duty to report the raid on our camp, that is true. But I have also a duty to those who sent my party there. This map is such a find as we come upon perhaps once in a thousand years. If we can find a clue to the location of the planet it marks, then a scouting trip thither at this time means more than arousing the law as to what has happened in one raid."

"But Ryzk is pilot. He will not agree to go off known charts. And if he's made up his mind to turn us in—"

"Off the charts," repeated the Zacathan thoughtfully. "Of that we cannot be sure as yet. Look—"

He produced a tri-dee projector which I knew to be part of the equipment of the control cabin. At a push of his finger there flashed on the wall a blowup of a star chart. Being no astro-navigator, I could not read it to any real purpose, save that I could make out the position of stars and sight the coded co-ordinates for hyper jumps under each.

"This is on the edge of the dead strip," Zilwrich informed me. "To your left and third from the corner is the blasted system of Waystar. It must have been scouted three centuries ago, by your time, from the dates on this chart. This is one of the old Blue maps. Now, look upon the bowl, imagine that the dead sun of that system is a red dwarf, turn the bowl two degrees left—"

I held up the bowl and rotated it slowly, looking from it to the tri-dee chart on the wall. Though I was not taught to read such maps I could see he was right! Not only did the blasted system we had just fled appear on the bowl as one about a red-dwarf star—a dying sun—but there was a course to be traced from that to the zero stone.

"No co-ordinates for hyper," I pointed out. "It would be the most reckless kind of guesswork. And even a scout trained for exploring jumps would take chances of two comets to a star of coming out safe."

"Look at the bowl through this." It would seem that Eet must have been gathering aids from all over the ship, for what the Zacathan handed me now was my own jeweler's lens.

As I inspected the constellation engraved on the metal through the magnification of the lens I saw there were minute indentations there, though I could not translate any.

"*Their* hyper code perhaps," the Zacathan continued. "Still no good to us."

"Of that I am not sure. We have those of the dead system—from that—"

"You can work?" Of course, he was an archaeologist and such puzzles were common to him. I lost something of my mood of depression. Perhaps because my hunger had been satisfied and I could now use my arm and hand to better advantage, I was regaining confidence not only in myself but in the knowledge and ingenuity of my companions.

When I put the bowl on the floor, open side down so that its star-specked dome was revealed, Eet squatted by it. He had taken up the lens, holding it in his paw-hands, his head bent over it as if his nose were smelling out the pictured solar systems.

"It can be done." His thought was not only clear; it was as confident as if there had been no obstructions at all between us and success. "We return to the dead system by reversing Ryzk's tape—"

"And so straight into what may be a vla-wasp nest," I commented. "But continue. Perhaps you have an answer for that also. Then what do we do, unless the Honorable Elder"—I gave Zilwrich the proper title of formal address—"can read these co-ordinates."

Eet did not close his mind as he had upon occasion, but I read a side flash of what might be indecision. I had never read fear in Eet's communications—awareness of danger, but not fear. But this had an aura of just that emotion.

And inspiration hit me in that same instant. "*You* can read these!" I had not perhaps meant it as an accusation, but it came forth that way.

His head turned on his too-long neck so that he could look at me.

"Old habits, memories, die hard," he answered obliquely, as he sometimes did. He turned the lens about, giving me the impression of uneasiness, of one wanting to escape coming to a decision.

I caught a flicker of alien mind-flow, and for a moment resented that communication I could not share. It was my guess that the alien and the mutant might be in argument about just the knowledge I accused Eet of having.

"Just so." Eet resumed touch with me. "No, I cannot read these. But they are enough like another form of record for me to guess to more purpose than the rest of you." And such was the finality of that answer that I knew better than to try to pry at how he could be familiar with any record approximating that of a Forerunner race living millenniums ago. The old problem of who—or *what*—Eet was crossed my mind again.

Though he made no more comment, the impression remained that any guessing he would do would be against his inclination and that he had a personal reason for disliking the situation fortune had forced upon him.

It seemed that now I was to serve as his hands. And back in the control cabin I made ready to follow his instructions to reverse the course Ryzk had set and return us, as soon as we emerged near Lylestane, to the vicinity of Waystar.

Ryzk did not appear. Apparently the smugglers' drink was of great potency. What would have happened when we came out of hyper and he was not at the controls, I do not know. Perhaps we would have aimlessly cruised the Lylestane system as a traffic hazard until some Patrol ship linked beam and dragged us in as a derelict.

I punched out the figures Eet fed me and we were wrenched back on a return course once again from Lylestane. Once more in hyper, we had plenty of time to meditate on the numerous dangers our appearance near Waystar would range against us. Certainly our successful escape with the treasure had alerted all the defenses of the pirate stronghold. They would be expecting a visit from the Patrol on one hand, now that strangers knew the co-ordinates of their hide-out, and trouble from others, perhaps even the Guild, demanding an account of how or why loot could be so summarily removed from what was believed to be an impregnable safe place.

The only answer would be that we dared not linger long enough in the dead system to be detected. Our unarmed ship had no defense against what the Jacks could easily muster. Therefore, we must follow exactly the same procedure we had on emerging near Lylestane: We must have the other course ready to punch in and spend as little time in normal space as we could.

Success in that maneuver would depend entirely on what Zilwrich and Eet could produce in the way of a new course. And since I was no help to them, the ship and Ryzk were my concern.

My most practical answer to Ryzk was to apply a force lock on his cabin. He sobered up when we were back in hyper and his struggle with the door lock led me to state through the intercom that we had taken over. More than that I did not explain, and I turned off the com thereafter, so his demands went unheard. E-rations and water went to him through the regular supply vent and I left him to consider, soberly I hoped, the folly of the immediate past in relationship to the *Wendwind* and her owners.

For the rest I tinkered in the small repair shop. The crossbows Ryzk had earlier produced I refined, making more zoran heads for their bolts. I had no mind to go exploring on an unknown planet unarmed, as I had once done in the past.

If by some miracle of fortune we did reach the world indicated by the zero stone, we would not know what we might face there. It could be a planet on which those of our kind could not live without suits; it could be inhabited by beings infinitely superior to us in every way, who would be as hostile to strangers as the Veeps of Waystar. Though the civilization the bowl represented must have ended eons past, others could have arisen from the degenerate dregs of that, and we might face such challengers as we could not even imagine. When I got to that point in my speculations, I handled my crossbows with very bleak attention to all their manifest defects.

Our first test would come when we left hyper in the dead system. As that moment approached I was tense and nervy. I saw practically nothing of Eet and Zilwrich except when I supplied them with food and drink. And I was almost tempted to let Ryzk out of his cabin in order to have someone to match fears with.

But when the alarm shattered the too-great silence of the ship, Eet was on hand in the control cabin. He curled into my lap as I settled in the pilot's seat—though he kept his mind closed, as if it were full of some precious knowledge and sharing that too soon might spill what could not be regained.

We came out of hyper and I punched the proper buttons for a reading of our present site. At least fortune had favored us to the point that we had emerged very close to that place where we had entered on our first trip, at the outer edge of the dead system.

But we were given very little time to congratulate ourselves on besting what was perhaps the smallest portion of the ordeal facing us. For there was an alarm ringing wildly through the cabin. We had been caught by a snooper and now we could expect a traction beam. My hands rested on the edge of the control board. I was ready to punch out the course Eet supplied. But would he feed me one, and could I set it quickly enough to avoid the linkage which would hold us for taking by the enemy?

16

Eet was ready for me, though the co-ordinates he flashed into my mind had no meaning for me. I was merely the means of putting finger tip to controls to punch them in. Only, it seemed those fingers did not move fast enough. I could feel the force of the locking beam catch at our ship.

We passed into hyper. But once the dizzy spin in my head cleared and I knew we had made the transition, I was aware that we had brought our enemy with us. Instead of snapping the lock beam in our return to hyper, we had, through some balance of force against force, dragged the source of that beam with us! We had danger locked to the ship, ready to attack as soon as we moved into normal space again.

There is no maneuvering in hyper. To do so would be to nullify the co-ordinates. And one would emerge utterly lost in space, if one were lucky, or perhaps in the very heart of a blazing sun. We were both prisoners here until we finished the voyage the Zacathan and Eet had set us. But there was this much: The enemy was as helpless as we—until we went out. And not being prepared for hyper transfer, they might be badly shaken, though they would have the length of our trip in which to pull themselves together.

"Jern!" Ryzk bawled through the ship's com. "Jern, what are you trying to do?"

It sounded very much as if the pilot not only had recovered from his drinking bout but was genuinely alarmed. Alarmed enough, I speculated, to be willing to work with us? Not that I trusted him now.

I picked up the mike. "We are in hyper—with a companion."

"We're linked!" he roared back.

"I said we had a companion. But he cannot move any better than we. We are both in hyper."

"Going where?"

"You name it!" Our momentary escape was acting on me like a shot of exult. Not that I had ever tried the stuff, but I had heard enough to judge that this must be akin to the heady feeling those addicts gained. When we snapped out of hyper we might be in grave danger, but we had now a respite and time to plan.

But his question echoed in my mind. Going where? To a planet which might or might not still exist. And if it did—what would it be like?

At that moment I felt as if I would more than anything like to be a believer in the gods of the planet-rooted. This was the time when one would prefer to kneel in some fane as did, say, the Alfandi, thrusting a god-call deep into ground already pitted with holes left by other's rods, pulling hard upon the cord which would set its top quivering to give off the faint sound meant to reach the ear—if one might grant a spiritual being an ear—of that

High One, and thus alerting the Over-Intelligence to listen to one's plea. I had met with the worshippers of many gods and many demons on many worlds. And complete belief gave a man security which was denied to the onlooker. That there was a purpose behind the Galaxy I would be the first to agree. But I could not bow my head to a planet-based god.

There was one belief I had read in the old tapes, that brain and mind are not the same. That the brain is allied to the body and serves it, while the mind is able to function in more than one dimension—hence esper talents, born of the mind and not the brain.

Now when I came from the control cabin I found Zilwrich seated on his pallet, and it seemed that he tried to prove the truth of this old theory, for he held between his two hands the bowl. His eyes were closed and he was breathing in small, shallow gasps. Eet, who had preceded me at his usual speed, had taken a position which mimicked that of the Zacathan, his small hand-paws resting on the rim of the bowl, his eyes also closed. And there was an aura of esper power which even I could feel.

What they were trying to do I did not know. But I felt that my presence was an intrusion there. I backed away, closing the door behind me. But at the same time my triumph ebbed. And the fact that we had a companion locked to us began to assume the shadow of menace. If Ryzk could only be trusted! Perhaps he could as long as his own skin was in danger. The co-ordinates which had brought us here—I reclimbed the way to the control cabin. We had used a return of Ryzk's setting to take us back to the dead system. Suppose I now erased those co-ordinates from the tape. Then no move of Ryzk's could return us, only what lay in Eet's and the Zacathan's memories. Loosed in the unknown, the pilot would be no great danger, and we needed badly any knowledge he might have to help us to deal with the enemy once we returned to normal space.

I set the erase on the tape before allowing myself to have second thoughts. Then I went to unseal the pilot's cabin. He lay on his bunk but turned his head to stare at me as I stood in the doorway. I had not brought one of the crossbows. After all, I was trained in a variety of weaponless fighting methods, and I did not think we were less than evenly matched, since he had nothing save similar skills to use against me.

"What are we doing?" He had lost the anger tinged with alarm which had colored his first demand through the com.

"Heading for a point on a Forerunner chart."

"Who's linked with us?"

"Someone out of Waystar is our best guess."

"They followed us!" He was genuinely astonished.

I shook my head. "We came back to the Waystar system. It was the only recognizable point of reference on the chart."

He turned his head away, now looking to the ceiling. "So—what happens when we come out of hyper?"

"With luck we are in a system not on the charts. But— can we break linkage when we come out of hyper?"

He did not answer at once. There was a sharp frown line between his brows. And then he replied to my question with another.

"What are you after, Jern?"

"Perhaps a whole world of Forerunner artifacts. What is that worth?"

"Why ask me? Anyone knows that is not to be reckoned

in credits. Is Zilwrich behind this? Or is it your gamble?"

"Both. Zilwrich and Eet together set up the co-ordinates."

He grimmaced. "So we sweat out a landing, maybe to be sun-cooked or worse when we come out—"

"And if we are not, but take the others with us?" I brought him back to the one matter over which we might have some control.

He sat up. The sickly-sweet smell of the drink was strong. But to my eyes he appeared sober. Now he put his elbows on his knees and bent over to rest his head on his hands. I could no longer see his face. He sighed.

"All right. In hyper we can't switch course. So we can't try to shake them loose. We *can* set the emerge on high velocity. It will mean blacking out, maybe taking a beating. But it is the only way I know of to break the link. We will have to rig special webbing or we won't survive at all."

"And if we do break the link?"

"If we pulled them in with us, the course is only set on our ship. The break will take us out, not them. They would have to gamble on an emerge. It might land them in the same system, or somewhere else. How do I know? I say it is barely possible. I am not planning on more than one thin chance in ten thousand." And his voice said that was very optimistic odds.

"You can do it?"

"It looks as if we have no choice. Yes, I can rig it, given time enough. What are the odds if we come out still linked?"

"We are unarmed, and they can take us over. They have no use for us, only what we carry."

He sighed again. "About what I thought. You're all fools and I have to go along."

But perhaps he was not wholly convinced until we entered the control cabin and he pushed past me to read the dial above the journey setting.

"Erased!" He whirled to face me, his lips twisted into a snarl.

"No turning back." I braced myself, tensed against attack. Then I saw his eyes change and knew that if he meant me harm in the future, he was willing to wait for such a reckoning. The main interest now must be the ship and our possible manner of escape from our unseen companion.

Just as Eet and Zilwrich in their mysterious occupation with the bowl had given me no explanations, so did Ryzk keep his own counsel about the alterations he made in some wiring. But he did keep me with him as a very ignorant assistant, to hand tools, to hold this or that while he made delicate adjustments.

"This will have to be redone," he said, "before we make a return. It is only temporary. I cannot even swear it will work. We'll need heavy webs—"

We set about providing those, too. The two shock-prepared seats in the control cabin were reinforced with what we could strip off the bunks in our two cubbys. Then we descended to the section where Eet and the Zacathan were in session to provide Zilwrich with such safeguards as we could rig. Eet, I supposed, would share my seat as usual.

I tapped lightly on the door behind which I had left the two enwrapt, with the bowl between them.

"Enter," called Zilwrich.

He lay now, his whole body expressive of a vast exhaustion. I could not see the bowl. Eet, too, lay there, but his head came up and he watched us almost warily.

I explained what we would do.

"This thing *is* possible?"

Again Ryzk shrugged. "I cannot swear to it on my name, if that is what you mean. It remains theoretical until we prove it one way or another. But if what you say is true, we have little choice."

"Very well," the Zacathan agreed. I waited for some comment, pro or con, from Eet. But such did not come. And that made me uneasy. But I would not press him, lest he confirm my worst doubts. It is better not to be met by pessimism when the situation already looks dark.

But Zilwrich had suggestions as to the rigging we must provide to counteract the strain on his body. And we carried out his instructions with all the skill we could summon. When we fastened the last of the improvised webbing Ryzk arose and stretched.

"I'll take cabin watch," he said as if there was no disputing that. But I did not miss the sudden flicker of eye Zilwrich made in my direction, as though he expected me to protest. However, we did not have Ryzk's experience and training in the pilot's seat. And with the erase on I did not see how he could do any harm.

He could have no reason to wish to surrender to a Waystar force. And they would give him, I was certain, no time to parlay if he tried it. He left and I said to Eet via thought-send: "The tape is on erase. He cannot send us back."

"An elementary precaution," Eet returned crushingly. "If he does not kill us all at emerge, and his theory works, we may have a small chance."

"You do not sound too sure of that." My inner uneasiness increased.

"Machines are machines and cannot be made to function too far from their norm, or they will cease to function at all. However, doubtless this is the only answer.

And we shall have other matters to consider after the emerge."

"Such as what?" I was not prepared to accept vagueness now. Forewarned is always forearmed.

"We have tried psychometry," the Zacathan broke in. "I am not greatly talented in that direction, but the two of us working so—"

The term he used meant nothing to me and he must have read my ignorance, for he explained, and I was glad that it was he and not the mutant, for he did not condescend.

"One concentrates upon some object and he who has the talent can so gather information concerning its past owners. There is, of course, the belief that any object connected with high emotion in usage, say a sword used in battle, will carry the most vivid impressions to be picked up by the sensitive."

"And the bowl?"

"Unfortunately it has been a center point for the emotions of more than one individual, of more than one species even. And some of those owners must have been far removed from the norm we accept today. Thus we received a mass of emotional residue, some violent. Many impressions are overlaid, one upon another. It is as if one took a tattered skin, put over it a second, also rent but in other places, and over that a third such, then tried to see what lay beneath those unmatched rents.

"Our supposition that the bowl might be much older than the tomb in which it was found, belonging to a people different from those with whom it was buried, is right. For we have deduced, though it is very hard to define any one well, at least four overlays left by former possessors."

"And the zero stone?"

"That perhaps is the source of some of the difficulty we encountered. The force which animates it might well govern the unfortunate mixture of impressions. But this we can tell you—the map was of prime importance to those who first wrought it, though the bowl itself meant more to later possessors."

"Suppose we do find the source of the stones," I said. "What then? We cannot hope to control the traffic in them. Any man who has a monopoly on a treasure sets himself up as a target for the rest."

"A logical deduction," Zilwrich agreed. "We are four. And a secret such as this cannot remain a secret long, because of the nature of what we must exploit. Like it or not, you—we—shall have to deal with the authorities, or else live hunted men."

"We can choose the authorities with whom we deal," I replied, an idea forming in my mind.

"Logical and perhaps the best." Eet cut across my thought, picking it up in its half-formed state, following it straight to a decisive conclusion.

"And if those authorities are Zacathan—" I said it aloud.

Zilwrich eyed me. "You pay us much honor."

"By right." It gave me a small quirk of shame to have to answer so, to admit that it was the alien whom I might trust above those of my own species. Yet that was so. And I would hand to any one of their Council the secret of what we found here (if we found anything worth the title of secret) more willingly than I would to any of my own leaders. The Zacathans have never been empire builders, never sought colonies among the stars. They are observers, historians, teachers at times. But they are never swayed by the passions, desires, fanaticism which has from the first made both great heroes and villains among my own kind.

"And if this secret might well be one not to be shared?" Zilwrich asked.

"That, too, I could accept," I said promptly. But I knew that I did not speak for Eet, or for Ryzk, who must now be included as one of our number.

"We shall see," Eet answered, his reservations plain. Not for the first time I wondered whether Eet's dogged insistence that the quest of the stone's source be our main goal did not have some reason he had never shared with me. And then, could I, myself, completely surrender the stones, knowing what I could do with them, knowing that perhaps there was more, much more, we might learn from them? Supposing the Zacathans advised us to hide, destroy, blot out all we know of the gems. Could I agree to that with no regret?

Later I lay in my cabin thinking. Eet, lying beside me, did not touch those thoughts. But at last, to escape a dilemma I could not resolve until we had passed many ifs and buts in the future, I asked the mutant:

"This reading of the past of the bowl, what *did* you learn of its past?"

"As Zilwrich said, there were several pasts and they were overlaid, mixed with one another until what we gained was so disjointed it was difficult to read any part of it and be sure we were correct. It was not made by those who fashioned the tomb. They came, I believe, long after, finding it themselves as a treasure-trove, leaving it with some ruler to whom they wished to pay funeral honor.

"The source of the stone—" he hesitated and the thought I picked up was one of puzzlement—"was not clear. Save that we do go now, if we have read the co-ordinates right, to that source. And the stone was set in the chart as a guide to those to whom it was very important. But that its native planet was their world of origin—that I do not think is the truth either. However, the reading was enough to set one's mind upside down, and the less I rethink on it the better!" With that he snapped mind-touch and curled into a ball to sleep. A state I followed.

The warning that we were at the end to our journey in hyper came some time later. As the Zacathan had assured us when we rigged his protection that he could manage it by himself, I made speed to the control cabin, Eet with me. Soon I was well wrapped in my webbing, watching Ryzk, in a like cocoon at the controls, trying to relax when the final test of our drastic emerge came.

It was bad, as bad or perhaps a fraction worse than that which had hit when we had joined the ship in the LB before the other jump. Only this time we had all the protection Ryzk's experience had been able to devise, and we came out in better shape.

As soon as I was fully conscious I looked to the radar. There were points registering on it, but they marked planets, not the ship locked to us through hyper.

"We did it!" Ryzk almost shouted. At the same time Eet scrambled along my still nearly immobilized body. I saw then what he held in a forepaw against his upper belly—the zero stone.

It was blazing with a brilliance I had not seen before except when we had put it to action. Yet now it was not adding to any power of ours. The glare grew, hurting the eyes. Eet gave an exclamation of pain and dropped it. He tried to pick it up again, but it was clear he could not use his paw-hand near that spot of fire. Now I could not even look directly at it.

I wondered if it was about to eat its way through the deck by the heat it was engendering.

"Blanket it!" Eet's cry was a warning. "Think dark—black!"

The power of his own thought swept mine along with it. I bent what mental energy I could summon to thinking dark. That we were able to control the surge of energy in the stone by such means astounded me. That awful brilliance faded. However, the stone did not return to its original dull lifelessness; it continued to contain a core of light which set it above any gem I had ever known and it lay in a small hollow which its power had melted out of the substance of the deck.

"Pliers—" I did not know whether they would help, for the heat of the stone might melt any metal touching it. But we could not pick it up in bare fingers and we dared not leave it lie, maybe to eat straight through the fabric of the ship level by level.

Ryzk stared at it, unable to understand just what had happened. But I had pulled out of the cocoon of webbing and managed to reach the box of tools he had used earlier. With pliers in hand I knelt to pick up the gem, fearing I might find it welded to the floor.

But it came away, though I could still feel heat and see that a hole in the deck beneath it was nearly melted through. Once on land, once in space, once on the edge of the wreckage we had used the zero stone as a guide. Could this small gem now bring us to the final goal of its home world?

We did not need it, since the bowl chart had already located the planet for us, fourth out from the sun. And oddly enough, once placed within the bowl, the furious blaze of the loose stone subsided into a fraction of its glow, as if the bowl governed the energy.

Though we kept a watch on the radar, there was no sign that the enemy had followed us into this system. And Ryzk set course for the fourth planet.

I half expected that time would have wrought a change in the sun, that it might have gone nova, imploded into a red dwarf, even burned out. But this was not so. It tested in the same class as was indicated on the ancient chart.

We went into scan orbit, our testers questing to inform us it was truly Arth type, though we were suspicious enough to keep all indicators on alert.

What we picked up on our viewers was amazing. I knew that Terra, from which my species had come into an immeasurably ancient galaxy, had been monstrously overcrowded in the last days before general emigration to the stars began—that cities had soared skyward, tunneled into depths, eaten their way across most of the continental land masses, even swung out into the seas. I knew that, but I had never seen it. Terran by descent I am, but Terra is across the galaxy now and more than half legend. Oh, we see the old tri-dees and listen to archaic tapes which are copied over and over again. But much of what we see is meaningless and there are long arguments as to what really did or did not exist in the days before Terrans roamed the star lanes.

Now I looked upon something like the jostling, crowded—terribly crowded—erections those tri-dees had shown. This was a planet where no empty earth, no sign of vegetation showed. It was covered, on the land masses by buildings, and even across the seas by strings of large platforms which were too regular in outline to be islands.

The whole gave one a terrible sensation of claustrophobia, of choking pressure, of erection against erection, or against the earth of its foundations.

We passed from day to night in our orbit. But on the dark side no light showed. If there was life below—

But how could there be? They would be smothered, pushed, wedged out of existence! I could not conceive of life here.

"There is a landing port," Ryzk said suddenly, but he had a keener eye than I, or else we had swung over and past what he had seen. To me there was no break in that infernal mass of structures.

"Can you land?" I asked, knowing that treasure or no treasure, stone or no stone, I must force myself to set foot down there.

"On deters," Ryzk said. "Orbit twice for a bearing. There are no guide beams. Probably deserted." But he looked far from happy, and I thought perhaps he might share some of my feeling about what lay below.

He began to set a course. Then we lay back in our seats, our eyes on the visa-screen, watching the dead city-world reach up—for that was what it seemed to be doing—as if its towers were ready to drag us down to the world they had completely devoured.

237

17

It was a tribute to Ryzk's skill that our landing was three-point, exactly on fins. He rode the ship down her tail rockets as only a master pilot could do. And not for the first time I was led to wonder what had exiled him from his kind—drink alone? Then we lay in our webbing watching the visa-screen as our snooper made a complete circuit of what lay about us, reporting it within.

With that report I came to respect Ryzk's skill even more. It was as if we had been threaded into a slit between walls of towers whose assault against the sky was such that one could not immediately adjust one's thoughts to what one's eyes reported. Only now that we were in that forest of man-made giants could we see the hurts time had dealt them.

For the most part they were either gray-brown or a blue-green in color, and there was no sign of seam or join as one might sight with stone blocks or the like. But there were cracks in their once smooth sides, rents in their fabric, which were not windows or doors. We could see no indication of those.

Ryzk turned to check the atmosphere dials. "Arth type, livable," he said. But he made no move to leave his webbing, nor did I.

There was something about those crowding lines of buildings which dwarfed, threatened us, not actively, but by their being. We were as insects, unable to raise ourselves from the dust in which we crawled, confronted by men who were giants with clouds gathering about their barely seen heads. And about it all there hung a feeling that this was a place of old death. Not a decent tomb in which honor had been paid to the one who slept there through the centuries, but rather a place in which decay had reduced to a common anonymity all that had meant aught—men, learning, belief—

Nothing moved out there. No flying thing flitted among the towers. There was no sign of vegetation. It was truly a forest of bones long removed from life. We could see nothing to fear, save that feeling which grew in us, or in me (though Ryzk's actions led me to believe he must share my uneasiness), that life had no place here now.

"Let us move!" That was Eet. There was a tenseness in his small body, a feral eagerness in the way his head darted from side to side, as if he tried to focus more intently on the visa-screen—though as that continued its slow sweep I saw no change in the monotony of the towered vista.

I left the webbing, Ryzk also. The bowl with the zero stone was on the deck, with Eet crouched over it as if he were on guard above its contents. And the stone blazed, though perhaps with not the same intensity as earlier.

We climbed down to join Zilwrich. The Zacathan was on his feet, leaning against the wall. He looked to Eet and I guessed some message passed between them. I lent my shoulder to the Zacathan's support and, together with Ryzk, aided him out of the hatch, down the ramp, to the apron of the space port.

There arose a hollow moaning and the pilot slewed around in a half crouch, looking down one of the narrow passages between the towers. Save for the open pocket of the port, there was gloom unbroken in those ways, such dusk as I had seen in forests of other worlds. The moaning shrilled and then our startlement vanished as we realized it was caused by the wind. Perhaps that acted upon the rents in the buildings to produce such sounds.

But outside the *Wendwind* the vast desolation was worse even than it had seemed on the screen. And I had not the slightest desire to go exploring. In fact, I was gripped by the feeling that to venture away from the port was to enter such a maze as one could never issue from again. As to where to search— Seen from the air, this planet-wide city covered all the ground, part of the sea. We might be half, three quarters, or the world away from what we sought, and it would take days, months of searching—

"I think not!" Eet had brought the bowl with him. Now he held it out and we saw the double blaze of the point on its surface and of the jewel within. He turned his head sharply to the right. "That way!"

But whatever lay "that way" might still be leagues from the port. And Zilwrich could certainly not tramp any distance on his unsteady feet, nor would I leave any of our party with the ship this time. We had the flitter—if we could crowd two of us into its cargo space, then we could quest some distance above the surface.

We settled Zilwrich with Eet at the end of the ramp and returned to the ship. What supplies we had room for and the crossbows went into the flitter. Three of us, plus Eet, would make such a heavy load we could not gain much altitude, but it was the best we could do. The LB had been so modified it might take days to alter it again, and we had no time to waste.

Judging by the sun, it was late afternoon when we were ready. I suggested waiting until the morning, but to my surprise the Zacathan and Eet overruled me. They had been in a huddle over the bowl and seemed very sure of what must be done.

As a matter of course Eet took command after we packed ourselves into the small craft, using my hands to his service. We hovered perhaps twice my height from the ground, then headed off sharply to the right, crossing the edge of the port, turning down a dusky channel between the towers.

The dark closed about us more and more as the buildings cut out the sun. Again I wondered how men could have lived here. Away from the port there appeared aerial runways connecting the buildings at different levels, crisscrossing into a net which finally grew so thick as to shut off most of the light from the level at which we traveled. Some of the ways were broken, and the debris of their disintegration weighted those below, or had landed in a heap of remains on the surface of the break below.

We had the beamer on, and I cut the speed to hardly more than a hover lest we crash into one of those piles. Yet Eet seemed entirely sure of our direction, sending me out of one half-filled lower way into another.

Dusk became full night. I had a growing fear we would be utterly lost, forever unable to find our way back to the comparative open of the port. There was a sameness to this level, just here and there the remains of a bridge fallen from the heights, the smooth bases of the buildings totally unbroken by any sign of an entrance.

Then the beamer picked up a flash of movement. It had been so quick that I thought my imagination had betrayed me into thinking I had seen it—until our beam trapped the thing against one of the walls. So cornered, it turned to face us, slavering defiance, or perhaps fear.

I have seen many strange beings on many worlds, so that weird defections from what is the norm to my species were not unknown to me. Yet there was something about this thing in the dark and forgotten ruins which brought an instant reaction of loathing in me. Had I been in the open, a laser in my hand, I think I would have slain it without thought or compassion.

Only for a moment did we see it so, backed against the unyielding buttress, pinned by the light. Then it was gone, with such speed as left me astounded. It had gone on two legs, then dropped to four. And the worst thing was that it looked like a man. Or what might have been a man eons ago, before time had burned out all which makes my kind more than an unthinking creature set upon survival alone.

"So it would seem that the city still has its inhabitants," Zilwrich commented.

"That thing—what was it?" The disgust in Ryzk's voice matched my own emotion. "Where did it go?"

"Turn to the left." Eet appeared unaffected by what we had seen. "In there—"

"There" was the first opening I had seen on the ground level of any building. It was too regular to be another rent. The gap was large enough to accommodate the flitter. But I had a very unpleasant suspicion that it was also where the scuttling creature had disappeared. To search further would mean leaving the craft, and to be trapped by that "thing" or others of its kind—

Yet I obeyed Eet's direction, bringing the flitter to a

standing hover within the shell of chamber beyond that doorway. We were in a circular space. If there had been any furnishings, those were long since gone. But the floor was heaped with gritty, flaky stuff which perhaps had once been fittings. This was pathed, beaten solid in some places. And the paths—there were two of them— led directly to another dark opening in the floor, a well.

I moved the flitter cautiously until we nosed the lip of that descent. We could indeed lower into it in the machine. But to do this, unaware of what might lie below, was a peril I was not ready to face. If I had such fears, Eet was not concerned with them. He hung over the bowl in which the gem blazed.

"Down!" he urged. "Now down!"

I would have refused, but the Zacathan spoke.

"It is true. There is a very strong force below us. And if we go with caution—"

I certainly would not descend outside the flitter, but to go in it would give us a small measure of protection. Yet I thought it foolhardy to try at all. I fully expected a protest from Ryzk. Only when I glanced to him I saw he was as bemused by the gem in the bowl as Eet.

Moving out over the well I eased the flitter onto settle-hover, thankful that we were using a craft meant for exploration. And I kept a wary eye on the walls as we began the descent at as slow a speed as I could hold us to.

What had been the original use of this opening we could not know. Perhaps it had the same function as our grav lifts. But that it was also a passage for later users was apparent. Into the once smooth walls had been pounded or wedged a series of projections meant to serve as hand- and footholds, a very crude ladder. And the bits and pieces so used were rough, some of them surely ripped from more complex fittings. The work was very bad, its

243

quality far beneath that of the city constructions, as if it had been done by a race who was at a primitive level.

We were descending by floors, passing dark openings in the walls of the shaft, as if that were a hub of a series of wheels whose spokes were evenly spaced passages. I counted six such levels, yet the circumference of the well did not dwindle in size as I feared it might. And though the crude ladder led to several of the cross-corridor openings, it also continued on down and down, as if it served a vast warren of burrows.

I watched the mouths of any opening the ladder served, but there was no sign of life, and our beamer could not penetrate them very far. Down and down, six levels, ten, a dozen, twenty—the wall grew no smaller. But it was a growing strain to hold the flitter on settle-hover at this slow speed. And always that ladder kept pace with us. Fifty—

"Soon, very soon now!" Eet's thought was excited, more filled with emotion than any I had ever received before. I looked to the dials. We were some miles below the surface. I cut our speed to the lowest and waited. There was a bump, and we had landed. Only a single tunnel mouth faced us now, a little to the right. And it was too small for the flitter. Any further exploration must be on foot, and I had no desire to leave the confines of the small safety offered by that craft.

My prudence was justified. There was movement at the mouth of that tunnel, though I remembered that crude ladder had ended four levels above our present position. Only what came into our beam was a machine, unlike any I had seen before. But there was enough resemblance to things I knew to suggest that the tube rising to aim at us was about to discharge something meaning no good to invaders.

When I put a finger to the rise button, both Eet and the Zacathan spoke, Eet by thought, the alien in Basic.

"Do not!"

Do not? They were crazed. We had to get out of the range of that thing, if we could, before it fired!

"Look—" That was Zilwrich. Eet was still staring at the stone in the bowl.

Look I did, expecting death to come at me from that sinister tube. What I did see was—nothing at all!

"Where—?"

"Esper impressions," Zilwrich answered. "It is known that certain things, trees, water, stones—and perhaps other objects—can hold visual impressions for many years, release them to one in the proper frame of mind for reception. The builders here may have known and used that principle. Or what we have seen may be only a report of its use at some time in the past, action which impelled such heightened emotions in those viewing it that the impression remained to be activated by us."

"We go—there—" Eet brushed aside the need for any explanation. Instead he was pushing the bowl ahead, using it as an indicator that our way led down that dark passage.

In the end he had his way. Otherwise he and the Zacathan would have set off alone. And my pride, such as it was, would not let me hold back. Because we were now a party united against the unseen perils of the unknown, I gave Ryzk one of the crossbows. So armed, we started out, Eet riding on my shoulder, where his weight was something of a problem, Zilwrich and Ryzk on my heels.

I had taken a smaller beamer from our supplies, but we did not need its ray long. Soon the gem in the bowl gave us light. And what it showed ahead for a goodly space was smooth, unbroken walling, as if we were advancing along a great tube.

Distance in the dark underground was relative. I thought we might find lack of air a danger. But apparently whatever system supplied this depths with a breathable atmosphere was still operative.

At last we came to the end of the passage and out. Not into a mine burrowing, as I had come more and more to expect, but into a room crammed with apparatus, equipment, some firmly based on the floor, the rest on tables or long counters. In the middle of this expanse was a blaze of light toward which Eet wanted to go.

A cone-shaped object perhaps as tall as I sat on a table by itself. And in it a transparent porthole allowed one to view an inner rack on which rested a dozen of the zero stones, vibrant with glowing life as we brought the two we carried closer to their container.

Resting beside the cone, on the table, was a second rack to which were clamped a further dozen rough, uncut stones. They were as black as lumps of carbon, yet they did not have the burned-out look of the exhausted zero stones we had found in the derelict space ship on our first trial of the power of the gems.

Eet sprang from my shoulder to the top of the table, put down the bowl, and set about prying at the porthole in the cone, trying to get at the jewels within. But something about that whole array triggered my memory.

There are many ways of cheating known to the experienced gem buyer. Stones may be so treated as to change their color, even hide flaws. Heat will transform amethyst to golden topaz. A combination of heat and chemicals skillfully used can make a near undetectable royal rovan of the best crimson hue from a pale-pink one. Heat can do—

I loosened one of the black lumps from the rack and brought out my jeweler's lens. I had no way of testing the thing I held, yet there grew in me the belief that this was the matrix, the true zero stone. They might not be natural gems at all, but manufactured—which could logically give them the power to step up energy.

The thing I held was certainly odd. Its surface was velvety to the eye, but not the touch. If it had been shaped like a seed pod—I drew a deep breath. Memory was playing a strange trick on me. Surely it had to be a trick.

Once before I had found stones, or what appeared to be stones, tumbled in a stream. To the eye, though not to the touch, they had had a velvety, almost furred surface. One of those stones had been appropriated by the ship's cat, who had licked it, swallowed it, to give birth to—Eet! These were hunks of mineral, not rounded, podlike. But their surfaces—

I looked to Eet as I weighed that lump in my hand. He had discovered the secret of the latch on the porthole, jerked it open, and was taking out the rack with the finished gems. Then, to my amazement, as the weight of the tray was lifted from the latches which held it, I saw the cone come to life, a light flash on in its interior. Without thinking (further than wanting) past my desire to prove the truth of my suspicion, I inserted the second rack, saving out only the lump I had taken from it. My fingers were almost trapped as the porthole snapped shut of its own accord. And blazing light, blinding to any direct gaze, gathered behind the view-plate.

I had my answer. "Made stones."

Zilwrich picked up one from the other rack, took from me the black lump to compare.

"Yes, I believe you are correct. And I do not think

that this"—he indicated the black lump—"is true ore or matrix either." He turned his bandaged head from right to left to view the room. The light was breaking in fierce waves from the cone, giving us a far radiance. "This was, I am certain, a laboratory."

"Which means," Ryzk commented, "that these are the last stones we may ever see. Unless they left records of how—"

There was sudden horrible shrilling, hurting one's ears, reaching into the brain. I gave one glance at the cone and grabbed for Eet, shouldered Zilwrich back, and cried out a warning. Then fire broke through the top of the oven, fountained up. Somehow I hit the floor, Eet fighting in my hold, the Zacathan's body half under mine.

Then—the light went out!

The following dark was so thick it smothered one. I groped for the beamer at my belt, for the second time unable to be sure whether my eyes or the light itself had failed. But a ray answered my press of button.

I aimed at the table, or where the table had stood. Now there was nothing at all! Nothing but a fan of clear space, as if the power had eaten a path for itself—but away, not toward us. Only one thing still lay there, seemingly unharmed, as if it was armored for all time against destruction—the map bowl. Eet uttered a sound, one of the few he had ever made. He broke from my hold and ran for it. But before he reached it he stopped short and I cried out even louder, moved by emotion in which fear and awe were mingled.

For in the beam of the torch Eet's furred body shimmered. He reared on his hind legs as might an animal caught by a throat collar and tight leash as it reached the end of the slack allowed it.

His hand-paws flailed at the air, and from his jaws

came a wail of agony. But no mind-touch. It was as if then he was only animal.

With his back stiff, high-reared on his hind legs, he began to move jerkily, in a kind of weird, manifestly painful dance, round in a circle, the center of which was the bowl. Froth gathered on his muzzle, his eyes rolled wildly, and his body continued to shimmer until he was only a misty column.

That column grew taller, larger. It might be that the atoms which had formed the substance of Eet's half-feline body were being dispersed, that he was literally being shaken into nothingness. Yet, instead of spreading out then into whisps, the mist began to coalesce again. Still the solidifying column was not as small as Eet, nor was it gathering into the same shape.

I could not move, nor did Zilwrich, nor Ryzk. The beamer had fallen from my hand, but lay so that its ray, if only by chance, held full on Eet, or what had been Eet, and the bowl.

Darker, thicker, and more solid grew the column of that shuddering thing. Eet had been as large as his foster mother, the ship's cat. This was almost as tall as I. At last it stopped growing, and its frenzied circling about the bowl became slower and slower, then finally halted.

I was still held in frozen astonishment.

I had seen Eet take three shapes by hallucinatory disguise: the pookha, the reptilian thing at Lylestane, and the hairy subhuman who had entered Waystar with me. But that he had willed this last chance I was certain was not true.

He was humanoid and—

A slender body, yet curved, with long shapely legs, a small waist, and above that—

He—no—SHE—stood very still, staring at her outstretched hands, their skin soft, with a pearly sheen to their golden hue. She bent her head as if to view that body, ran her hands up and down it, perhaps to reassure herself that this *was* what she now saw.

While from Zilwrich broke a single word: "Luar!"

Eet's head turned, she looked at us with large eyes, a deeper and richer golden than her skin, drew her long dark-red hair about her as a cloak. Then she stooped and picked up the bowl. Balancing it on the palm of one hand, she walked to us along the beam of the torch, as if to impress upon us her altered appearance.

"Luar?" Her lips shaped the word. "No—Thalan!"

She hesitated, her eyes not on us for a moment but looking beyond us, as if they saw what we never could. "Luar we knew, yes, and dwelt there for a space, Honorable One, so that we left traces of our passage there. But it was not our home. We are the Searchers, the Born-again ones. Thalan, yes. And before that, others, many others."

She held out the bowl, reversed it so we could see the map. But the wink of the zero stone on it was dead, and that other stone it had held had vanished. "The treasure we sought here—it is now gone. Unless your wise ones, Honorable Elder, can read very forgotten riddles."

"Thanks to you, Jern!"

I staggered as a sudden blow against my arm threw me hard against one of the pieces of equipment based on the floor. I clung to it so as not to go down.

Eet, in one of those lightning movements which had been his—hers—as a feline mutant, snatched up the beamer from the floor. She swung the full light on Ryzk as the pilot was setting another bolt to his crossbow. And from her lips came a clear whistle.

Ryzk twisted as if his body had been caught in the shriveling discharge of a laser. His mouth opened on a scream which remained soundless. And from his now powerless hands dropped his weapon.

"Enough!" Zilwrich, moving with the dignity of his race, picked up the bow. The whistle stopped in mid-note and Ryzk stood, turning his head from side to side, as if he fought against some mind daze and tried thus to shake it away.

Gingerly I investigated my hurt by touch, since what light there was Eet had focused on Ryzk, now weaving back and forth as if his will alone kept him on his feet. I could find no cut, but the flesh was very tender, and I guessed it had been so close a miss that the shaft of the bolt had bruised me sorely.

"Enough!" the Zacathan repeated. He dropped his hand on the pilot's shoulder, steadied him as if they had been comrades-in-arms. "The treasure—the best treasure—still lies about us. Or"—he looked to Eet measuringly—"is now a part of us. You have what you have long wished, One Out of Time. Do not begrudge lesser prizes to others."

She spun the bowl on her hand and her lips curved in a smile. "Of a surety, Honorable Elder, at this hour I wish no hurt to any, having, as you have pointed out, achieved a certain purpose of my own. And knowledge is treasure—"

"No more stones," I said aloud, not really knowing why. "No more trouble. We are luckier without them—"

Ryzk raised his head, blinking in the light. He looked to where I leaned against my support but I think he did not really see me.

"Well enough!" Eet said almost brisky then. "The

Honorable Elder is right. We have found a treasure world, which he and his kind are best fitted to exploit. Is this not so?"

"Yes." I had no doubts of that.

Ryzk shook his head once more, but not in denial. It was rather to try and clear his mind.

"The stones—" he said hoarsely.

"Were bait for too many traps," I answered. "Do you want the Guild, those of Waystar, the Patrol, always at your heels?"

He raised his hand, wiped it back and forth across his face. Then he looked to Zilwrich, keeping his eyes carefully from Eet, as if from the Zacathan alone he might expect an answer he could accept as the truth.

"Still treasure?" There was something curiously childlike in that question, as if Eet's strange attack had wiped from the pilot years of suspicion and wariness.

"More than can be reckoned." Zilwrich spoke soothingly.

But treasure no longer interested me. I watched rather Eet. As mutant and trader we had been companions. But what would follow now?

Mind-touch instead of words, amusement in part but delicately so, came swiftly in answer to my chaotic thoughts. "I told you once, Murdoc Jern, we each have in us that which must depend upon the other. I needed your body in the beginning, you needed certain attributes which I possessed in the woefully limited one I acquired. We are not now independent of each other—unless you wish it, just because I have found a body better for my purposes. In fact, one which, as I remember, served my race very well thousands of years ago. But I do not declare our partnership at an end because of that. Do you?"

She came forward then, tossing from her the bowl, the

torch, as if both were no longer of service to her. Then her touch was on my body, light, soothing above my bruised hurt.

I had chaffed against Eet's superiority many times, sought to break his—her (I still could not quite accept the change) hold on me, that tie which fate, or Eet, had somehow spun between us since he—she—had been born on my bunk in the Free Trader.

It seemed that her touch now drew away the pain in my arm and side. And I knew that for better or worse, for ill times and good, there was no casting away of what that fate had given me. When I accepted that, all else fell into place.

"Do you—?" Her mind-touch was the faintest of whispers.

"No!" My reply was strong, clear, and I meant it with all of me.